McNab

A NOVEL

DAVID MULHOLLAND

Published by

GENERAL STORE
GSPH **PUBLISHING HOUSE**

499 O'Brien Rd., Box 415,
Renfrew, Ontario, Canada K7V 4A6
Telephone (613) 432-7697 or 1-800-465-6072
www.gsph.com

ISBN 1-897113-46-3
Printed and bound in Canada
Copyright © 2006 David Mulholland

Cover design, formatting and printing by
Custom Printers of Renfrew Ltd.

The McNab clan crest is based on a sketch by Commander Stanley
Archibald Nettle, Chief Archibald McNab's great-grandson.

Library and Archives Canada Cataloguing in Publication Data

Mulholland, Dave
      McNab / Dave Mulholland.

Includes bibliographical references.
ISBN 1-897113-46-3

      1. McNab, Archibald, 1781?-1860. 2. McNab (Ont. :
Township)—History. I. Title

FC3095.M33M84 2006   971.3'81   C2006-903865-1

AUTHOR'S NOTE

WHAT YOU ARE about to read is fiction. Although the historical record is the basis for some events, I imagined how they may have occurred. Other events I completely made up. Also, some characters *might* resemble real persons, but they, too, are a product of my imagination. I'm simply attempting to give you "a good read." I emphasize: this is a novel; it is *not* history.

It isn't practical to list all the books I read in researching this story. I do, however, wish to acknowledge the ones that were most helpful. The two at the top of that list are Peter Hessel's *McNab—The Township* and Dugald C. McNab's (no relation to the Laird, but was his secretary for a short time) *The Last Laird of McNab*, which served as a guide for part of my plot.

I am also indebted to Francis Collinson's *The Bagpipe— the history of a musical instrument*; Frank Adam's *The Clans Septs and Regiments of the Scottish Highlands*, revised by Sir Thomas Innes; I.F. Grant's *Highland Folk Ways*; T.C. Smout's *A History of the Scottish People: 1560–1830*; Wallace Nolestein's *The Scot in History*; David Craig's *On the Crofters' Trail—In Search of the Clearance Highlanders*; John Prebble's *The Highland Clearances*; Jessie Buchanan's *The Pioneer Pastor*; Calvin Glenn Lucas's *Presbyterianism in Carleton County to 1867*; Gerald M. Craig's *Upper Canada —The Formative Years—1784–1841*; Thomas H. Raddall's *The Path of Destiny—Canada from the British Conquest to Home Rule*; Marianne McLean's *The People of Glengarry— Highlanders in Transition, 1745–1820*; Edwin C. Guillet's *Early Life in Upper Canada*; Dave McIntosh's *When the Work's All Done this Fall*; Canniff Haight's *Country Life in Canada*; Isabel Skelton's *The Backwoodswoman*; John W. Hughson and Courtney C.J. Bond's *Hurling Down the Pine*; Arthur B. Gregg's *Old Hellebergh*; Daniel F. Brunton's *Nature* and *Natural Areas in Canada's Capital:*

An Introductory Guide for the Ottawa-Hull Area, and *Provincial Justice: Upper Canadian Legal Portraits from the Dictionary of Canadian Biography*, edited by Robert L. Fraser.

I also drew information from numerous websites, the most helpful being www.rampantscotland.com.

I received information and inspiration from several individuals. Among them: Larry Eshelman, Nick Neley, Roddy Henderson, Susan Lewthwaite, Wendy MacIntyre, Nancy Payne, Ann McPhail, Susan McNicol, Sandra Garland, David Braeley, and, foremost, two individuals who gave generously of their time and expertise—Rory "Gus" Sinclair, piper, who, among other things, explained that you can't play the pipes while sitting on a horse; and Peter Hessel, writer, historian, and part-time archivist at the Arnprior & District Archives, who promptly and patiently answered my many questions regarding the history of Clan McNab and the founding of the township. And to the Archives itself for the photo of Chief McNab from which the cover image was taken. I am also indebted to editor Susan Code McDougall for her detailed evaluation of my manuscript; my publisher, Tim Gordon, for his belief in the story; and my editors, John Stevens and Jane Karchmar, for their patience and expertise in guiding me through the editing. To all, I extend a sincere "thank you." I take responsibility for any errors.

To the memory of my father,
from whom I inherited my creative talent;
and to the memory of my mother,
from whom I inherited the discipline
to make use of that talent.

"History is the version of past events that people have decided to agree upon."

N<small>APOLEON</small> B<small>ONAPARTE</small>

PART ONE

Report of a Committee of the Honourable Executive Council on the Application of the Laird of McNab for a grant of Land.

Executive Council Chamber, at York }
Wednesday, 5ᵗʰ November, 1823}

Present: The Hon. James Baby, Presiding Councillor; the Hon. Samuel Smith, the Hon. And Rev. Dr. John Strachan.

To His Excellency, Sir Peregrine Maitland, K.C.B., Lieut.-Governor of the Province of Upper Canada, and Major-General Commanding His Majesty's Forces therein, &c., &c.

May It Please Your Excellency:
The Committee, of the Executive Council to which Your Excellency has been pleased to refer the letter of the Laird of McNab, dated York, 15ᵗʰ Oct., 1823, proposing upon certain conditions to settle a township of land with his clansmen and others from the Highlands of Scotland, most respectfully report, That a township of the usual dimensions be set apart on the Ottawa River, next to the township of Fitzroy, for the purpose of being placed under the direction and superintendence of the Laird of McNab for settlement. That the said township remain under his sole direction for and during the space of eighteen months, when the progress of the experiment will enable the Government to judge of the propriety of extending the period. That patents may issue to any of the settlers of said township, on certificate from the Laird of McNab stating that the settling duties are well and duly

performed, and his claims on the settlers arranged and adjusted; or patents may issue to Petitioner in Trust, for any number of settlers, certified by him as aforesaid; the fee on each patent to be One Pound Five Shillings and Fourpence, sterling. That the conditions entered upon by the Laird of McNab and each settler be fully explained in detail, and that it be distinctly stated that such have no further claim upon the Government for Grants of Land; and that a duplicate of the agreement entered into between the Leader and the settlers shall be lodged in the office of the Government. That the Laird of McNab be permitted to assign not less than One Hundred Acres to each family or Male of Twenty-one years of age, on taking the oath of allegiance …

That the old settlers pay the interest on the money laid out for their use by the Laird of McNab, either in money or produce, at the option of the settler; and that the settler shall have the liberty to pay up the principal and interest at any time during the first seven years.

All of which is respectfully submitted.

James Baby
Presiding Councillor

I AM MALCOLM Kenneth MacGregor, Piper to the Laird of McNab, 13th Chief of Clan McNab.

It grieves me to tell ye, grieves me to even think . . . the Laird's domain in the Highlands of Scotland once stretched from Tyndrum west into Argyll and east down Glendochart to Killin where the stately McNab Castle stood with majestic pride on the island of Eilean Ran on the north bank of the River Lochay.

Alas, the glory of those days is no more. Aye! tis true! Sir Henry Raeburn's portrait of Francis immortalized my Chief's predecessor, a striking figure attired as a Colonel of the Breadalbane Volunteers. Ah, but tis also true, Francis, rogue that he be, fathered many a lad and lassie, but never took a wife. And he had a grand liking for the bottle! His unconscionable neglect left our clan a debt of some thirty-five thousand pounds, our estate lands so hopelessly encumbered, his nephew, my Laird, could not save them. His legal position tenuous, at best, the McNab had no choice but to abandon his beloved estates and flee the country.

I tell ye, twas most humiliating—*most* humiliating indeed! Twas a trying time for my Chief, the McNab already grieving from the departure of Margaret and the children. Why the marriage failed, I canna say. The Laird, spontaneous and uplifting in spirit, is a private man in matters of the heart. There was talk of his frequenting the brothels in Paris, but . . . nay, I canna say.

Ah, but I *can* attest to the Laird's resolve! He be a man of tenacious character and much innovation. On our voyage to this new land, he spoke often of his plans to build a settlement of his clansmen. He told me with great relish how he intends to accumulate adequate wealth to pay his debt and return home in triumph. His first order of business: reclaim his estates from the Earl of Breadalbane, that shameless rascal who seized McNab lands upon the Court of Session issuing a *writ* of foreclosure.

I am grateful to the Almighty that on our voyage across the Atlantic—although tiring and in accommodations considerably less pristine than that to which we are accustomed—the forty-nine days went by without incident. In our leisure, we reminisced, expounding for hours on the long and noble tradition of the Scottish clans, a topic of which I never tire. Tis an uncertain and erratic chronicle, but the earliest known use of "clan" appears in the *Book of Deer* in the twelfth century. And we know from the Irish *Book of Ballimote* . . . twas issued in 1383 . . . and the *Book of Lecan* in 1407, the nomenclature of at least twenty-six Highland clans. Ah, but their pedigrees are questionable. Perhaps fictitious! The Gael, a crafty people, created many pedigrees to justify the power of families. How else could some eighteen clans claim descent from the Dalriadic tribe of Loarne? Tis known that the Picts annihilated the tribe in 736. Aye, a family could boast the eminence of a clan name, the Lord Lyon bestowing upon it a charter, but twas a hollow title unless the men had a fighting spirit and arms sufficient to hold it.

Tis nae something of which I am proud, but my own ancestors may have had a hand in the annihilation of the people of Loarne. We MacGregors trace our heritage back to the Picts, so named by the Romans when they witnessed the tribe painting and tattooing their skin with the yellow-flowered woad plant. But twas the Picts who drove the Romans out of Scotland. Twas, at the time, known as Pictland and then Alba before King Kenneth MacAlpin united the Picts and the Celts in 849. If the record be true—tis always uncertain—when Kenneth passed on, his younger brother, Gregor, became king. Tis the eponym for our clan. We are "Mac"—sons of Gregor—descendants of the MacAlpin kings. Our motto in the Gaelic: *'S Rioghail Mo Dhream*—So Royal My Race. Aye, a proud clan, but a scattered clan; dispossessed of our lands by the Campbells

when Robert the Bruce rewarded Sir Neil with the Barony of
Loch Awe for helping the Bruce attain the throne in 1306. I tell
ye, there be no love lost between MacGregors and Campbells.
Many clansmen were forced to live as outlaws. And the most
unbearable insult of all: in 1604—twas more Campbell
shenanigans—James the 6th issued an edict prohibiting use of
our very *name*! That outrage forced my ancestors to roam the
Highlands nameless, or take a name twas nae their own. This
sad state inspired our renowned writer, Sir Walter Scott, to call
we MacGregors "Children of the Mist." For years we were
confined to the lands of Glenstrae, our honourable surname
not fully restored until 1774.

Time vanished as the McNab and I harkened back to
ages past. When the harbour at Quebec came into view, ye
could hear a collective sigh of relief. Aye, a riotous
cacophony ensued as passengers scurried about preparing to
disembark. While descending the gangplank, we witnessed a
scuffle between a Canadian and a Highlander. The former, a
porter, was attempting to be of assistance by loading the
latter's trunk on to a little cart. Ah, but the Highlander,
apparently thinking the man was attempting to rob him,
swore at him in Gaelic. Although ignorant of the language,
the Canadian could not mistake the tone and replied with a
volley of curses in French. The incident attracted a small
crowd who chuckled at the spectacle. After a brief tug-of-
war, the Highlander wrestled his trunk from the hands of the
caddie and, with the assistance of his three sons, carted it off.

The McNab and I had no time to dally. We immediately
boarded a steamer for the journey up the St. Lawrence to
Montreal. There, none other than the Governor General of
the Canadas, Lord Dalhousie himself, was on hand to greet
us with a delegation of prominent city officials. To me, twas
a surprise. But the Laird thought it quite appropriate this
esteemed Scot would travel from Quebec to welcome him.
Aye, but tis quite possible his presence in Montreal had

more to do with representing His Majesty in the laying of the first stone for a new cathedral. The Earl introduced us to a Mr. Jacques Viger, a Montreal historian and retired soldier who fought the rebellious colonials in 1812. He told us he had placed in the stone a gold sovereign bearing the likeness of George the 4th, and a medal from the Monarch's coronation. I suggested to the McNab that perhaps *that* was the *real* reason for the Governor General's attendance in this beautiful, vibrant city. But the Chief dismissed my comment and assured me twas because the city was being honoured with the presence of a Scottish Highland Chief. The McNab told me Lord Dalhousie intends to take leave and return home early next year. Twas a great honour to meet this revered gentleman. Sir Walter Scott, his high school classmate in Edinburgh, says his friend has served his country in every quarter of the world, and will be forever a steady, honest and true-hearted gentleman.

Twas regrettable that duty hastened the Governor General's return to Quebec. He was not in attendance when city officials favoured the Laird with the ceremonial homage one would expect for the Chief of an illustrious Highland clan. Aye, twas a proud moment when I led the McNab into the great dining hall, celebrating his arrival with the "ground" from his rousing *piobaireachd*, "McNab's Salute."

We did not linger in Montreal, but proceeded to Glengarry County by calash. Following our long sea voyage in quarters clammy and confined, twas most exhilarating to bathe in the sun, breathe in the pure, vibrant air and gaze at wave upon wave of cultivated fields awaiting the fall harvest. Our expedition over bumpy roads, jolting to one's constitution, was interrupted at the village of La Chine, where the rapids required us to board a *batteau*, a large, flat-bottomed boat with five rowers and a sixth man who steers with a paddle. On the opposite shore, we entered an impoverished but clean boarding house where the jovial proprietor served a hearty meal. The McNab and I be robust fellows, but by now the long passage . . . aye, we were exhausted and so retired to our rooms for a sound night's sleep. The following morning, we partook of a nourishing breakfast before engaging a second calash and continuing our journey.

At Glengarry, we received a spirited welcome and took great pleasure in the generous hospitality of that august prelate, Bishop Alexander Macdonell. Now there be a man of the finest character, his angelic countenance radiant with the grace of his Saviour. Myself, I dinna believe in the officious, patronizing rules of religion, but, still, tis gratifying to find a venerable Christian spreading the message of the gospels to all who thirst for the Word, be they Protestant or Catholic. And twas the good Bishop who informed the McNab that land for settlement was to be had along the Ottawa.

As ye would surmise from its name, Glengarry boasts a growing community of Highlanders; many from the districts of Inverness-shire and a few acquaintances from Killin and Kenmore in Perthshire. But most come from the old Glengarry estate: some near the end of the last century; some as recently as eight years ago; all encouraged by the founders of the settlement who fled the rebellious colonies and have remained loyal to the mother country. There be no denying the peasantry of Glengarry are uncultivated in manners. Ah, but they welcomed us with much kindness into their humble but comfortable homes. Scottish hospitality! There be none like it! Aye, we swapped tales at many a *ceilidh*! Twas a jolly good time indeed. In my heart . . . I truly believe our stay in Glengarry bodes well for a promising future.

After a fortnight, fully rested, we bid a kind farewell to our generous hosts and continued our journey by coach to the provincial capital of York. There I again witnessed the McNab's commanding personality. Wielding the subtle skill of the diplomat, he cultivated a bond with the honourable members of the Assembly, particular deference being shown to those on the Executive Council. A letter of introduction from Bishop Macdonell facilitated an audience with Sir Peregrine Maitland, Lieutenant-Governor of the Province of Upper Canada. I must confess, while this esteemed gentleman was courteous and hospitable, I found him rather cold and aloof. His manner, however, did not dampen the Laird's enthusiasm. Over a private dinner at Government House, the Laird respectfully presented Sir Peregrine with his plan to settle a township. And although I was honoured to salute my Chief at his reception in Montreal, and to entertain His Excellency, the Bishop, in Glengarry, I felt a special pride in taking up my pipes for His Majesty's representative in Upper Canada. I performed—because I knew twould be most appropriate—"I Got a Kiss of the King's Hand," composed in 1651 by the great Patrick Mor MacCrimmon to honour Charles the 2nd on his visit to Stirling. With the munificent applause of Sir Peregrine, Lady Sarah, and the McNab ringing in my ears, I took my place at the imperial dining table. Twas a splendid repast. Attendants adorned in elegant liveries served a scrumptious meal of pheasant, wild rice and sweet yams. The McNab took much delight in the charms of Lady Sarah, Sir Peregrine's gracious spouse and the daughter of the late and much revered 4th Duke of Richmond. But our dinner conversation was . . . how should I say . . . guarded. While the McNab was his usual gregarious self, I again thought our host rather stiff and unduly formal. Throughout the evening, he expressed only cautious optimism for the Laird's scheme. The McNab, however, is not one to be discouraged. He pressed the issue, explaining to the Lieutenant-Governor that he feared his clansmen would abandon the Empire and emigrate to the new union of the rebellious colonies. The Laird also gave assurances he would bring the settlers out at his own expense. Twas no surprise to me that the Laird's arguments were persuasive. As we were taking leave, twas obvious Sir Peregrine had a change of heart. He told us his Surveyor-General had just ordered surveyed a large tract of land on the banks of the Ottawa. And then His Majesty's representative said—I thought I detected a reservation in his tone—but he said he would forward the Laird's request to London and Lord Bathurst's attention at the earliest opportunity. He added that if the Minister for the Colonies ruled in his favour, the Laird could name the settlement after himself. Of course Chief McNab was elated. Twas only a matter of weeks when Sir Peregrine informed the Laird that the Home Office *had* approved his application—but then, a delay of several months while we awaited completion of the survey.

We were comfortably housed at the residence of my Chief's cousin, Mr. David McNab, who is Sergeant-at-Arms in the House of Assembly. His spacious, two-storey home sits atop a knoll that affords a magnificent view of the surrounding woods near the valley of the Don. Each day, if the weather be fair, Mr. McNab and my Chief strolled . . . aye, marched! . . . the entire length of King Street. Up and back! Tis a good mile-and-a-half! I declined their invitation to join them. Tis more exercise than my constitution will bear. Despite the generous hospitality of our host, we were most anxious to proceed. For myself, the delay was frustrating. But the McNab is not one to dawdle: he finds opportunity in all circumstances. The Laird drew upon his cousin's influence and arranged for a *soiree* at the British Coffee House. Tis the capital's leading hotel, a two-storey brick structure erected at the corner of King and York. Since twas the appropriate piece, I led my Chief into the establishment's large conference room piping once again the "ground" from "McNab's Salute."

"I am McNab of McNab, 13th Chief of Clan McNab," the Laird's sonorous baritone announced to those assembled before him. The eyes of York's most influential men turned towards the Laird. Eminent men of the highest rank in Upper Canada. Men such as our Attorney-General, John Beverly Robinson, our Solicitor-General, Henry John Boulton, and the distinguished member for Kingston, the Honourable Christopher Alexander Hagerman. Arriving a short time later was the Reverend John Strachan, who is not only on the Executive Council, but is Rector of the Church of England and Headmaster at York's grammar school. And there were others. I must tell ye, I felt much awe in their presence.

On such illustrious occasions, my Chief holds court attired in full Highland regalia. He had clothed his stalwart figure from head to foot in the red and black tartan of Clan McNab; his sporran of grey horsehair lay against the brilliant sett of his kilt; the generous plaid crossed his capacious breast and was thrown over his left shoulder; he topped his solemn features with a blue Balmoral bonnet sporting three eagle feathers. Shod in black patent brogues, his tartan hose gartered under the knee, the Laird held himself erect; his walking stick—the blackthorn with the silver plate on the end of the handle—grasped firmly in hand. He was, as he always is, a commanding presence.

Aye, the Chief entertained! 'Twas lavish and I thought at times extravagant, but the McNab was determined to secure a bond with these and other men of authority in the provincial capital. He said 'twould ensure succour when needed.

The survey was completed, finally, in early summer; the Laird notified by an official from the Surveyor-General's office. He informed us that the eighty-thousand acres contained seventeen concessions: thirteen full and four broken. And so, having accomplished our mission, we left York and proceeded to the new township that would soon bear the name "McNab."

Kinnell Lodge,
On the Banks of the Ottawa,
10th Aug., 1824.

My Dear Leney, —From my last letter you
will have gleaned what my intentions are,
and of the progress I have made. Now I am
happy to inform you that all my
arrangements for settlement are complete.
The township of McNab has to-day been
handed over to me by Sir Peregrine, and it
contains 80,000 acres of fine, wooded,
arable land - and upwards. You will send
out to me, according to your offer, twenty
families at first. Give them three months'
provisions, and make each head of a family,
before you give him a passage ticket, sign
the enclosed bond, which has been specially
prepared by the Attorney-General. I will meet
the settlers in Montreal, and see each one on
the land located to them, and will provide
for their transport to their lands. They
should embark early in April, and I should
feel obliged if you would personally
superintend their embarkation at Greenock.
Now I am in a fine way to redeem the estate
at home, and in a few years will return after
having established a name in Canada, and
founded a translantic colony of the clan.
The preparations can be all made this
winter for their emigration, and I shall be
fully prepared to receive them. I have a
large log house erected close to the banks of
the Ottawa, which, as you will see by the
heading of this letter, I have called after my
estate on Lock Tay, &c., &c.

McNab

HIS DAY'S WORK done, Donald Cameron stood outside the door of his stone cottage and thrust his shovel into the damp earth. Before him lay the barren, rock-infested patch that had yielded the fall's meagre potato crop. He tugged at his trimmed whiskers. Not for the first time, worry seized his mind. He was wondering how his family could survive another winter when the bleating of sheep intruded upon his thoughts. Beyond the hedge of choppy boulders that partitioned his miserable holdings, he could see the black faces of Lintons and the thick, knotted coats of Cheviot ewes. They were grazing on hilly pasture—pasture he had once farmed.

"Donald, supper," Elizabeth Cameron called to her husband through the open window.

"Aye." From inside he could hear the voices of his two young children as they sat down for the evening meal. What of their future? His father's Laird had followed the practice of generations of Highland chiefs and allowed his tenants to hand down a portion of their small crofts adequate enough to raise a few cattle and plant a few crops. Then came the Clearances. Now the Camerons drew sustenance from whatever Elizabeth's imagination could do with salted herring and greying potatoes garnished with aqueous butter from their one bony milch cow.

When the Laird dismissed his tacksman—a nephew who rented land from his uncle and sublet to the crofters— the man uprooted his family and emigrated to America. Several of Cameron's neighbours followed and encouraged him to do the same. But Donald thought it inconceivable to abandon his family's steadfast allegiance to a history that dated back several centuries, gaining prominence in the fifteenth when his namesake united the branches of three families under the banner of Clan Cameron. Staunch Royalists, his kith and kin sacrificed their lives alongside those of other clans in ill-fated battles to keep Scotland free from English rule. The Jacobite Rising of 1745 took its toll on the Camerons. While fighting for the Stuarts—the Young Pretender, Prince Charles Edward—many of Donald's ancestors were massacred by the English at Culloden. The victorious Hanoverians burned the Cameron homes, seized their lands and forced the clan to disperse. Now, descendants of the Lairds the Camerons served were pushing him and his fellow crofters off the land. Wealthy border sheep-masters coveted the sweet hill grass of the shielings—and greedy Highland chiefs coveted the exorbitant rents.

Companionship was often the only solace for a crofter. He rose each day before the sun and, somehow, drew from a reservoir of optimism: practical optimism to be sure, but optimism nonetheless. He had never been his own master— and never would be. Oppression bound him to others, also oppressed, and through that companionship he refilled his emotional reservoir to be drawn from again the next day and the day after that. To occupy a portion of the land had been an inherent right of every clansman. Now sheep were more valuable than people—and land was just another commodity.

Each year, the Clearances were pushing Cameron and his neighbours towards the edge of their pastures; forcing them onto land whose yield could barely support their families. And so in the scorching heat of last summer, he and eleven other crofters travelled to Wester Ross in Skye to gather a tawny seaweed that grew along the ocean's rocky shores: kelp, rich in alkali, could be made into fertilizer and was much in demand for bleaching linen and manufacturing glass and soap.

"What were she like, Donald?" his neighbour, Iain Storie, asked on his return.

"She was hell, Iain, pure hell."

"How so? I hear tis wet work an—"

"Wet! Aye, tis wet for sure! But that's jus the half of it! Soon as tide's out we tramp down to the shore, tear the weed off the rocks an spread it on the machair to dry. I swear I never lifted anythin so heavy in all my . . . And cold! The sea is bitter cold, Iain; it gets in your bones. Just thinkin about it, I still feel the ache . . . While the weed's dryin we dig trenches, long an narrow, to burn—"

"A kiln."

"Aye, a kiln. Have ye ever seen a kelp iron?"

"Nay, dinna believe I has."

"I don't ever want to see one again. It's . . . it's long, like a thin pole; I'd say nine, maybe ten foot; with an iron rod, oh, maybe three foot, on one end and the tip is bent into a hook—"

"Tis what ye gather the kelp with?"

"Aye, and stir it in the kiln. The peat has to burn the kelp even, so it needs a steady heat; it turns into a brittle slag—"

"Donald." Elizabeth's call broke into his reverie. The memory of his conversation with Iain Storie returned often, a memory that seemed to portend his future. But Cameron's struggle was not only with fidelity to the surviving vestige of his ancestors; the thirty-four-year-old crofter was also ensnared by his practical nature: since returning from Wester Ross, he found he could no longer dismiss the possibility of emigrating. His conscience forced him to give it serious consideration—if not for his sake, then for the sake of Elizabeth and the children.

"Aye, I'm coming." As he turned towards the cottage door, the bleating of sheep drew his attention once more to the rolling hills beyond. The landlord's shepherd was leading more ewes into pasture. A wave of nausea rolled through his body. His narrow, angular jaw tightened and he tugged at his brown beard. The Perthshire Emigration Society was meeting that night at Leney House in Callander, the home of the society's chairman, Dr. Hamilton Buchanan. Many of Cameron's neighbours said they would attend. He pushed open the heavy wooden door, bowed his lanky frame and entered.

"MEN, YOUR ATTENTION, please!" Dr. Buchanan's robust baritone broke through the din of conversations among the thirty-one men bunched together in the spacious living room of his baronial mansion. He peered over rimless glasses perched on the tip of his bulbous nose. When all eyes were focused on his austere presence, he waved a piece of paper above his head. "I have in my hand a letter from Chief Archibald McNab. I have very good news. The Executive Council of Upper Canada has granted Chief McNab a township with some eighty thousand acres of fine, wooded, arable land. The McNab has gained much influence since his arrival in the colony. He is on the best of terms with Sir Peregrine Maitland; the Lieutenant-Governor has become a good and true friend. Sir Peregrine and the colonial government have seen fit—quite rightly I must say—they have seen fit to honour Chief McNab with this newly surveyed township. It now bears his name. All we need—"

"Where be this land?" The throaty voice was that of Walter Ross, a crofter whose landlord had squeezed him to the very edge of the pasture.

"Tis on the banks of the Ottawa River in Upper Canada. Tis yours for the settling if—"

"And is our passage to this new land to be free?" This was Duncan McDonald. "Are we so hated, the English will pay us to leave Scotland?" Disgruntled voices rolled through the gathering.

"Lads! Lads! Please! America is a new land, a land in need of settlement, a land where hard-working men can prosper, a lan— "

"Aye, but will potatoes and peat pay our passage?" Duncan McDonald again, swaying slightly, as if tipsy; his comment provoking snickers among the crofters.

"Ye want us to leave our luxurious estates!" Lorn McCaul said, inciting a round of derisive laughter.

"Hah, Lorn," McDonald said. "Now wouldn't ye make a fine nobleman!"

"Gentlemen, please, tis a serious matter. Will ye nae allow me to explain?" Buchanan peered over his glasses and waited until the banter died down. "Ye know your passage is not free. Your neighbours' passage was not free. Nay, Chief McNab has enclosed a bond prepared by the Attorney-General. With the help of the society, the McNab will pay your passage and you will repay him when you are settled on your new land. He asks for twenty families, with more to follow. Tis an opportunity to start a new life, an opportunity to . . ."

As Buchanan droned on, Donald Cameron scrutinized the faces of the men standing around him. These were loyal neighbours, as their kin had been loyal neighbours to his father and grandfather before him. Generation after generation had endured hardship and struggled together as a community. He noticed the doctor had the rapt attention of Robert Miller and Angus McLaren. He wondered how his family's life would change if these two men emigrated. Each spring, the Millers, the McLarens and his own brood gathered peats along the river bank; one man wielding the peat iron, the other two lifting the soft, oblong cubes to dry land where the women and children spread them carefully in the sun. It was gruelling work. But for the better part of May and June, the families pulled together, tired muscles tempered by the laughter of their grimy children frolicking along the shore. Their labour was finished, finally, when they'd gathered enough peats to ensure adequate fuel for their families.

"There be no rest for the weary" was his grandfather's expression. With the peats dried, stacked and wheeled home

on barrows, they turned to harvesting the spring hay.
Cameron could hear the scythes slicing through the dusty
air while the women and older children sickled every strand
from under the bushes. He could see the bent bodies of
Helen Miller, Cathrine McLaren and Elizabeth as they
bundled the precious straw and piled it in the field for the
children to tramp into stacks.

Next came harvesting the turnip crop; not to feed their
families, but their precious cattle, for without turnips the
cattle would not survive the coming—

The sudden shifting of the room interrupted Cameron's
reverie. The men moved towards a long, mahogany table
against the side wall. Each man took a single sheet of paper
from a stack. Some crofters asked the meaning of the word
"bond"; some asked a neighbour what the paper said; others
stared blankly at the words.

Cameron was surprised to see Dennis McNee approach the
table; surprised to see him at the meeting. A reclusive individual,
Donald knew the Clearances had not yet affected him. McNee
was fortunate that so far his small croft had not been enclosed
with the large tracts of pasture needed for grazing sheep.

"Does everyone have a copy?" Buchanan glanced
around the room. "Good. I regret . . . as you can see, tis
written in the abominable language of lawyers. But allow me
to explain; my own affairs require me to decipher their long-
winded prose. The bond says you promise to pay the Laird
thirty-six pounds, thirty for your wives and sixteen for each
of your children. In return . . . aye, tis most generous, the
Laird will settle you on one hundred acres of his land. When
you meet the settlement duties—"

"Aha!" Duncan McDonald again. "Settlement duties!
I's heard uh them! But what might they be?"

"I was coming to that, Mr. McDonald. I believe tis a
most generous offer. Tis only natural you would be required
to cultivate your land. Tis required by the Crown of all

grantees. But for the first three years you pay no rent. Tis rent free! Beginning the fourth year you pay to the Laird and his heirs one bushel of wheat or like grain for every cleared acre granted ye by the—"

"Only one bushel!" Lorn McCaul said, not believing so little rent possible. "Why, tis nothing!"

"Aye, Lorn, tis nothin, a bushel an acre, but the cost of our passage; we has to pay the cost of our passage," Duncan McDonald said. "And what might that be, Dr. Buchanan?"

"I was coming to that, Mr. McDonald, if ye would allow me." The doctor shuffled through his papers. "That would be thirty-five pounds for each man, twenty-five for your wives and older children and fifteen for the young lads and lassies."

Voices, uncertain and anxious, rumbled through the room as the men tried to calculate the cost of their passage. There were many occasions when Cameron was thankful his departed mother insisted he learn to read and write and do simple sums. He added the figures in his head to ninety pounds for himself and his family.

"Ah, but lads, I have more good news!" Again Buchanan waited until all eyes turned towards him. "Here you are indebted to your landlord and your children and your children's children are indebted. But the Laird, being a generous soul, in his generosity he has added a provision that will entitle ye to your land forever free of encumbrance. Pay the debt on your bond . . . tis a moderate interest of five per cent per annum; pay your debt to the Laird within seven years and ye will hold free and clear title to your land!" Buchanan removed his glasses; his smug countenance gazed at the men who erupted into animated conversations.

"Is it what the paper says?" John Drummond asked.

"Aye, tis, I believe!" Hugh Alexander said. "Canna ye no believe it, John? If me father—God rest his soul—if he had lived to see the day . . . me own land!"

"So you're going, Hugh?" Drummond said.

"Well, me an Kate, we'll talk about it, but . . . we already
. . . nay, we canna go on like this; the crop, the land . . . well,
ye knows yourself—"

"Aye, deed I do, deed I do." Drummond removed his
woollen hat and ran weather-beaten fingers through the
strands on his balding head. "And there's the reason!" he
shouted, thrusting his hat in his neighbour's face.

"Are ye going, Donald?" Hugh Alexander asked Cameron.

"I don't know, Hugh."

"Your own land, Donald! Only seven years!" Lorn
McCaul said. "Think of it! Your own land!"

DONALD CAMERON DID think about it. Circumstances
forced him to think about it during the long, dark winter
that set in a few weeks after the society meeting. He thought
about it when nine-year-old Janet came down with the
croup. Her feeble body tossed and moaned with the
sickness. Her father gazed upon the child's sunken, sallow
face and the ache in his gut turned to anger. But there was
nowhere to vent that anger: his Laird had left Perthshire for
the winter; his new tacksman was little better off than
himself. Elizabeth nourished the girl as best she could, but
Donald believed it was her mother's love that finally
brought down his daughter's fever and restored the colour
to her cheeks. Cameron thought about it when he noticed
the deep creases under Elizabeth's blue eyes, a painful
reminder of the constant struggle aging her beyond her
thirty years. He thought about it at a *ceilidh*, when talk of
emigration replaced the merriment of singing and story
telling. And he thought about it every time he heard the
resonant bleating of sheep on the winter pasture.

Then, in late February, Angus McLaren knocked on his
door.

"What brings ye out in this weather, Angus?" A
blizzard had struck the night before. McLaren had tramped

through mounds of snow swept into eddies by a bitter wind. The crofter, his right leg slightly shorter than his left, limped into the cottage. Cameron and his visitor squatted on low stools next to the hearth in the middle of the clay floor. McLaren tipped his hat to Elizabeth, who welcomed their guest as she spun crimson yarn on a spindle in the corner. The Cameron children, bundled in blankets, sat on the floor at her feet and took turns holding the distaff, which was feeding yarn to their mother. Donald banked the smouldering peats against the hearth's flat stone. A cloud of smoke hovered just under the thatched roof. McLaren clutched his woollen bonnet and stared into the glowing embers. "What is it, Angus?" The crofter lifted his head.

"We've been given notice." Cameron shifted on his stool.

"When?"

"Yesterday."

"Nay, I mean when do ye have to be out?"

"Three months."

"More sheep?"

McLaren nodded and returned his gaze to the fire.

"What are ye gonna to do?"

McLaren's shoulders heaved and his body released a deep sigh. "Go to America. The Canadas. Tis nothin left for us here. Cathrine and the children . . . my grandfather . . . God rest his soul . . . he died fighting for this land; the land itself took me father. There's nothin left, Donald. We'd be scallags. Aye, we'd be better off as scallags. At least we'd pay no rent."

Scallags, the lowest of the low, could be seen prowling along the shore, prying limpets off rocks, carrying them to their makeshift huts of sods and branches. Some were crofters who had lost their farms to debt or were driven off by their landlord; others were born to landless cottars. On a scrap of land at the edge of a moor, they raised paltry crops of kale, barley and potatoes. Boiled to a pulp, with limpets and fish, it was their only food.

Cameron stared at his neighbour; the heavy hollow in his gut crushed, finally, any hope he'd been nourishing. He looked over at the smiling faces of his children, spellbound by their mother as she skilfully drew the yarn off the distaff and twisted and lengthened it on to the spindle. He had seen the gaunt children of scallags; he would not let that happen to his children.

IN THE TRANSLUCENT light of dawn, the Camerons packed their clothing and few transportable possessions into hemp bags and a trunk. Donald began loading the horse-drawn wagon supplied by the Emigration Society.

"Tis a big ship?" eleven-year-old John asked his father, who heaved a bag onto the wagon and noted the anticipation of adventure in his son's voice.

"I don't know, son; aye, twill be big enough, I'm sure. Go on now, like a good lad, an help your mother." The youngster scampered towards the cottage. As Cameron hoisted the trunk into place, the sun broke over the horizon, dissolving the suspended haze. His calloused hands gripped the wagon's rough side-board. He took in the sunrise, his last sunrise on Scottish soil. In the few weeks leading up to their departure, he had worked the land as he did every spring, ploughing melting patches of snow into the ground and tilling the soil with the *cas chrom* in preparation for spring planting. Only once did Elizabeth open the cottage door and ask why he bothered. He looked at her in disbelief and continued to plough. His grip on the side-board tightened. He inhaled deeply and cast clouded eyes over the land. Head bent, he stiffened momentarily before heaving sobs shook his body. He felt a touch on his arm, turned, and fell into his wife's embrace.

ON APRIL 22, 1825, the *Niagara*, a 276-ton brig built in Quebec the year before, set sail from Greenock with 115 Highlanders destined for McNab Township on the banks of the Ottawa River in Upper Canada.

PART TWO

THE *NIAGARA* DOCKED at Quebec to discharge some
passengers and cargo before continuing up the St. Lawrence
to Montreal where the Highlanders were met by the Laird
and his piper. Preparations were then made for the arduous
journey by steamer, *batteau,* and on foot. Twenty-eight days
later, the exhausted immigrants arrived in the township.

It was an overcast afternoon in late summer when the
neophyte settlers crowded into the living room of Kinnell
Lodge—Chief McNab's roomy, two-storey, log home
overlooking the Ottawa River. Families clustered together:
women and older men flopped down on the few wooden
chairs; mothers cradled babies in their arms; the younger
men and adolescents stood along the walls. The room was
abuzz with the banter of eager anticipation until the shrill of
the bagpipes brought conversations to a halt. The piper
marched into the living room followed smartly by the Laird
carrying bundled papers in one hand and his crooked, blackthorn walking stick in the other. They stopped in front of a
long table of polished oak. The men who were seated rose
quickly and doffed their woollen bonnets. The piper
brought his short piece to an end and stood to the side.
Chief McNab's regal presence commanded the full attention
of the Highland peasants. With his blunt chin raised, he
peered over the settlers and addressed them in a manner
befitting a solemn occasion.

"Greetings, my fellow clansmen. Tis a great honour to
welcome you to Kinnell. Ye have had a long and tiresome
journey, but, at last, tis over. Let us give thanks to the
Almighty for your safe arrival." The Laird bowed his head
and kept it bowed for close to a minute, the immigrants
likewise. "Twas a pleasure to greet many of you at dockside.
We will have many opportunities to become better
acquainted." McNab turned sideways and glanced at the
surveyor's map of the township spread across the table. "I
believe Dr. Buchanan informed you that the government of

the Province of Upper Canada has granted me this township. I am pleased . . . most pleased the honourable members have shown me the respect due a Highland Chief. And ye know they have named the township McNab! Tis a great honour. I have promised our esteemed Lieutenant-Governor I will settle it with a body of sober, industrious Scots. I will inform the government of your safe arrival, and thank Sir Peregrine for this opportunity to be of service to my clansmen. I know ye'll be deserving liegemen." McNab paused again; he cast his eyes over the settlers as if sizing them up. "I believe my dear cousin has chosen well; I trust ye'll be loyal clansmen—and of steady habits. I trust ye'll honour your bond—as I will honour my responsibility to you." The expatriate Scots remained quiet and still while McNab seated himself in a high-backed, leather chair behind the table. "We have much work ahead of us before the first snows of winter. Winter can be quite severe in this province, so we shan't delay. I will assign you your lots."

When the Laird called his name, the settler approached the table, hat in hand. He put his mark on his location ticket, grasped it firmly, thanked McNab and, allowing himself the hint of a smile, returned to his family. Donald Cameron had been one of the first called. He stood with Elizabeth and the children at the back of the room. While the Laird apportioned the remainder of the lots, Cameron read his ticket. What he read troubled him.

I, Archibald McNab of McNab, do hereby locate you, Donald Cameron, upon the rear half of the 19th lot of the 8th concession of McNab, upon the following terms and conditions. That is to say: I hereby bind myself, my heirs and successors, to give you the said land free of any quit-rent for three years from this date, and also to procure you

*a patent for the same at your expense, upon
your having done the settlement duties and
your granting me a mortgage on said
lands, that you will yearly thereafter pay to
me, my heirs and successors forever, one
bushel of wheat or Indian corn, or oats of
like value, for every cleared acre upon the
said lot of land in name of quit-rent for the
same, in the month of January in each year.
Your subscribing to these conditions being
binding upon you to fulfil the terms thereof.
Signed and sealed by us at Kinnell
Lodge, this 24th day of August, 1825.*

Signed: *Archibald McNab*
Signed: *Donald Cameron*

"Has everyone their ticket?" McNab glanced around at the assembly. Heads nodded and there was a muttering of response. "Very well, I trust ye'll find your lots satisfactory. We will build a strong community of industrious Scots; a community that will make—"

"Excuse me, Chief," Cameron said. He noticed a twitch in McNab's bushy, black eyebrows.

"'Tis Mr. Cameron, I believe." The Chief's sonorous baritone resonated with annoyance.

"Aye, tis."

"What is it, Mr. Cameron?"

"Dr. Buchanan said if our debt be paid within seven years the land be ours. That is what it says on our bond."

"Aye, if your debt to me be paid within seven years, I will procure for ye a patent at your expense and ye will hold clear title to your land. That is what it says on your ticket."

"Aye, but it also says that after three years we owe ye quit-rent. To you and your heirs forever." Cameron paused. "Quit-rent . . . tis a feudal rent, like at home. But if the land be ours, then why do we owe ye quit-rent after the seventh year?" McNab pushed himself to his feet.

"Mr. Cameron, are ye questioning the word of your Chief?" the Laird shouted. His plaid slipped off his shoulder, he tossed it back. "Tis my land, but I will grant ye a mortgage. We have responsibilities. I will honour mine. I trust ye will honour yours." A low snort escaped from McNab's nostrils. He stared at the crofter over the heads of the settlers. All stood perfectly still, as if holding a collective breath. Cameron opened his mouth as if to reply. He didn't, because even though he had not yet seen his land, quit-rent of one bushel per cleared acre should be of no real consequence. McNab raised his chin and glared at the gathering. "Very well. I am pleased to have ye in my township. I know ye will make me proud to be your Chief." The Laird wheeled on his brogues and, without waiting for his piper to lead the way, marched out of the room, the stocky piper scampering close behind.

DONALD CAMERON WOUND his way through the dense forest of grey bark: centuries-old white pine with the military bearing of unyielding sentinels. He gulped the still, sweet air, his breath catching in his throat. He craned his neck to peer up at branches so far away they permitted only glimpses of filtered, blue sky. When he reached the surveyor's markings that told him this was his lot, he thrust a shovel into sandy soil and contemplated the location assigned to him. The land was so unlike the straths and glens of his Highland home. Despite the scampering of squirrels, the chirp and cry of sparrows and jays, the place seemed so at rest, so peaceful: it was as if the planet had stopped moving.

He could not recall when he'd last swung a broadaxe. He was swinging one now—from sunrise to sunset. Dr. Buchanan had promised one hundred acres of arable land that could be cleared and planted within a few weeks. Cameron winced at the memory of those words. He *did* have one hundred acres, more land than he'd ever had—even before the Clearances. He sighed and leaned on his shovel; a muffled thud told him he'd struck another submerged boulder.

Seemingly insurmountable challenges were nothing new to hardy Scots. The cooperative spirit that had enabled the crofters to endure hardship in the Highlands was serving them well in the daunting task of carving out a home in the wilderness. McNab was allowing them to camp on the grounds at Kinnell until they built their shanties. While wives and older children sewed and knitted winter clothing, the men bundled axes and bushwhacks and trekked to their land over muddy trails, skirting around the glut of tree stumps. The division of lots was not always clear: the surveyor's blazing of trees did not always correspond to the crude map the Laird had spread over the table at Kinnell. Many of the families, however, had been neighbours in Perthshire; had worked their land as cooperatives: precise boundaries were of no great concern. Working in "bees" throughout the remainder of the summer and into the fall, they slashed the tangled underbrush, chopped down the smaller trees, piled both into heaps and burned them.

"Let's rest, men," Cameron said to Hugh Alexander and Angus McLaren on an afternoon when the sun was exceptionally hot for the end of September. They had been working since sunrise. Now they eased tired bodies onto the ground, leaned aching backs against tree stumps and drank from jars of black tea. They reclined in silence, keeping company with perplexing thoughts on the challenges of this new life. Then Angus McLaren asked what had been on his mind for some time—what was on the minds of most, if not all, of the settlers.

"Have ye heard anythin more, Donald?" he said. "About there bein no end to the quit-rent?"

"Nay, I haven't."

"D'ye think he'll hold it agin ya?"

"Hold what?"

"Ya know, questionin his right to—"

"I don't know, I can't say." More than a month had passed since the incident at Kinnell. While the settlers talked about it in hushed tones, rarely did anyone express openly the growing undercurrent of unease among them. Although their lives in Perthshire were lives of destitution, they had abandoned their homes, their ancestry, to take a leap of faith across an ocean. They expected to face difficult challenges; they simply had to persevere. "Have ye heard something, Angus?"

"Nay, nothin. I've heard nothin." McLaren drained his jar of tea. "We canna fault the Chief. He's been generous lettin the wives an young uns camp on his land; and he takes many into his home, as many as room permits. He be a most generous man. Nay, we canna—"

"Tis true," Alexander said, "but people is resentful. The land is not what Dr. Buchanan promised, and our provisions is almost gone. Ye remember, Dr. Buchanan said McNab was to give us a year's—"

"There is nae provisions," McLaren said. "I meant to tell ye; Lorn says the Laird told him Dr. Buchanan misunderstood; he only promised provisions at Greenock; only nough to get us to his township."

"A bushel per acre . . . twill be nothing if the land is fertile," Cameron said. "We won't know till planting, but . . . the soil seems awful sandy."

"There's better soil to the north," Alexander said. "Walter told me he spake to . . . I dinna know him, but he told Walter twas rich loam. But the soil on my lot . . . tis all the same in this concession." Alexander removed his hat and wiped perspiration from his forehead. The men lit their pipes and retreated again into the silence of the surrounding forest. Their contemplation was broken when a grey squirrel scampered part way up and back down a nearby pine.

"Tis a shame to cut down that bushy-tailed fella's home," McLaren said, "but if we don't, we won't have homes."

"Ah, Angus, don't fret it, lad," Cameron said. "If we felled trees for nigh on a hundred years, there'd still be plenty for the squirrels. Let's get at er!"

PROVIDING SHELTER FOR their families was foremost in the minds of the settlers, overshadowing any misgivings in their relationship with the Laird of McNab. As the chill of fall nights descended upon the community, the need for permanent lodgings took on greater urgency. Once the smaller trees and underbrush were demolished, Cameron's land was readied to build a shanty. The crofter selected a flat area next to the Madawaska River, near where someone had named its rushing waters, "Flat Rapids." First came the dangerous task of felling the larger pine: each tree had to fall through the remaining trees. The men were fortunate: only one tree caught in the branches of another. During the night, it crashed to the ground. The men stripped the trees of their branches, chopped the trees into manageable logs, selected the best for building, piled the remainder high, and burned them.

On a clear, cold morning in mid-October, while Elizabeth and the children looked on, John Drummond, who had always been more adept at carpentry than crofting, organized twenty-four men into a "raising bee." The frosty nip in the air caused the men to shiver—until Duncan McDonald arrived with a bottle of home-made *usquebaugh*, one of several he had stowed in his trunk before leaving Perthshire.

"Ah, Duncan, you're a good laddie!" Hugh Alexander said as he rummaged in his gunny sack for a tin cup.

"We knew we could count on ya, Duncan," Lorn McCaul said. "He'll make a good grog-boss. Won't he lads?" The men bellowed their agreement and lined up for McDonald to fill their cups.

"Easy on the whisky, lads," Drummond said. "We has a long day's work ahead. We dinna want Donald's shanty to tilt." The crofters laughed as they sipped the potent brew.

"C'mon, lads, let's get at er!" Iain Storie said. He had not imbibed. The men cut the sturdiest timber into twelve-foot lengths to form the base of the shanty. When the logs were in place, Drummond showed them how to mortise the ends and anchor the base with boulders—of which there were plenty. With six men on each side, they raised the walls by stacking log upon log and fitting the notched ends together.

"Aye, that's it men, she's taken shape," Drummond said. "Your adze, Donald. Use your adze to square those timbers for the rafters." The frame secured with rafters, they roofed in the shanty with overlapping layers of cedar and elm bark, binding them with thick withes to slanted pine poles.

"Tis gonna to be terrible breezy in there," Cameron said, as he peered through cracks between the logs.

"Patience, Donald, patience me lad," Drummond said. He took his short-handled ship's axe and chopped soft ash into wedge-shaped pieces. "Shove these into the cracks." The others followed his example. "That's it. Now, like at home, we chink the cracks with moss an mud . . ."

THAT NIGHT, THE pale white beam of the full moon caught an undulating ribbon of smoke as it rose from the chimney of the log shanty and dissolved into the clear black sky. Inside their new home, the Cameron children, exhausted from the day's adventure, were bundled in blankets and sleeping soundly off to the side of the stone fireplace. Their parents were also weary, but it was the fatigue of productive labour: the heady scent of fresh-cut pine had revived their spirits. They settled down on cushioned, wooden chairs in front of the hearth. Held by the hypnotic dance of the flames, they sat in silence: Donald smoked his favourite bone pipe; Elizabeth threaded a needle and skilfully mended a tear in the sleeve of a blouse.

"Tis cosy," Elizabeth said, finally breaking the silence.

"Aye, tis that." Donald took in the serenity of the woman he had married twelve years ago. He was smitten the first time he saw her. She was sixteen, he was twenty. They met at a church social, as did many young people in Perthshire. He courted her for two years before their parents gave their approval and their blessing for the marriage. From the time they were old enough to dig with a potato dibber, Donald and Elizabeth had worked the land and cared for livestock. A crofter's life was all they'd ever known. When the Clearances began pushing them off the pasture, Donald came to appreciate the strength of character in the girl who had become his wife. That fortitude would serve her well—serve them both well—in making a home in this new land. God had blessed them with two healthy children. That blessing was their joy, their motivation to overcome the tribulations of yet another day.

To satisfy her son's curiosity, Donald's mother had given him books on the history of Clan Cameron. He traced the family's genealogy back to the fifteenth century, discovering that his ancestors had lost their direct line of descent around 1569 when anarchy ensued following the murder of Chief Donald Dubh, the clan's first Chief. Although the historical record is dubious, there was speculation his own clansmen murdered their Chief. From that time forward, it appears the Camerons had been crofters, living as tenants under several chiefs. The same was true for Elizabeth's family, the Mor MacLeans.

There were times when Donald was consumed with longing for Perthshire. He knew there would always be an ache, an invisible scar that would never heal. But with the decision made and the journey completed, he was determined to provide a comfortable life for his family. He anticipated a challenge, but from the land, not from the Laird of McNab. He realized the conditions under which they were living were new not only to the settlers, but to McNab as well. Perhaps the Chief was struggling with his own adjustments, his own responsibilities, which were considerable for a man entrusted—and thus burdened—with the settlement of a community. In any case, he would have no time to concern himself with the vagaries of the Laird: his days would be filled with work on the land. Memories of home would always remain, but he would persevere and learn to love this land, this virgin soil. In time, it, too, would become a part of him.

Elizabeth stood up.

"We will have to make do with the quilts for tonight," she said.

"Aye. Tomorrow the men will help me build beds." Elizabeth pulled the quilts from the trunk. Donald shovelled ashes over the embers to ensure the fire smouldered throughout the night. "We'll be snug enough wrapped in the quilts, don't ye think?" His mischievous grin brought a rosy flush to her cheeks.

"Aye, as long as we sleep in our clothes," she said with a smile.

Donald stepped forward and put his arms around his wife. She dropped the quilt and returned her husband's embrace. "Tis a new beginning."

"Aye, my dear, tis that; a new beginning in a new world. Tis not exactly what we expected, but if we work hard . . ." They held each other a few moments, then spread the quilts over the smoothed timbers. Giving in, finally, to the day's labour, they slept soundly in each other's arms.

- - -

KATE ALEXANDER PICKED up a small knife and carefully stripped the fur off three black squirrels. Together with the Indian corn boiling in the iron pot over the hearth, their lean bodies would serve as the evening meal for seven people: Hugh, their five children and herself. Kate was a resourceful woman who had kept her family alive on pottage, potatoes and bannock during the Clearances. Now, in the wilderness of Upper Canada, that resourcefulness was once again being put to the test.

She was not alone. By the first snowfall, all the settlers had erected crude shanties to house their families. But with their provisions exhausted, and none coming from McNab as expected, the next challenge was even more daunting: feeding themselves throughout the long winter.

Kate removed the scent glands from the squirrels' backs and from under their legs. Their dark red bodies and the single band running along the underside of their tails told her these were old animals. She placed the carcasses in a pail of diluted vinegar. Soaking would help tenderize the meat.

"TIS AWFULLY THICK, Donald." Their faces wrapped in scarves against a ripping north wind, Iain Storie and Donald Cameron were once again swinging their broadaxes: not to fell another pine, but to break through the ice of the Madawaska.

"Aye, tis." First, one, then the other, struck the spot they'd chosen some forty yards off shore. Splinters of blue ice flew against their eyelids; instant icicles hung from their eyelashes. "We're almost through." Partially buried in the snow beside the would-be fishing hole was a sack containing pieces of wild pigeon. Under the sack were two slim pine poles, one end of each whittled into sharpened points. Storie had his axe above his shoulder when a gust of wind spun him around.

"Look, Donald!" Cameron turned and looked down the length of the frozen river. Several men were at the same task: crofters determined to become spear fishermen so they could feed their families.

"OUT OF THE depths have I cried unto Thee, O Lord. Lord, hear my voice. Let Thine ears be attentive . . ." The slippery footing caused him to limp more than usual, but his faith kept Angus McLaren trudging through mounds of drifting snow, all the while praying to his God, speaking aloud the 130th Psalm as he wheezed and manoeuvred around exalted pines whose frozen branches bowed and balanced their precarious, pure white burden. The McLarens had been living on squirrels, a porcupine, and ground nuts. Five days ago, Angus set a trap further into the woods. Now, a few yards from it, he stopped. "Honour and praise be given to Thee, O Lord God Almighty, most dear Father . . ." McLaren recited a prayer from the John Knox liturgy. He had reason to be thankful. His home-made trap had snared a large, brown rabbit. Cathrine and the children would not go hungry—at least not tonight.

MARY CARMICHAEL STOOD at the table in her shanty and pounded the bark and buds her husband, Colin, had stripped from hemlock, maple, and basswood trees. Sitting at her feet were four very young children clutching their stomachs and in danger of choking on their hiccupped sobs. Colin had taken his Brown Bess and returned to the woods to shoot a wild pigeon, or a squirrel, or a ground hog— anything edible. "Twon't be long, children," Mary said, her usually strong voice a mere whisper. "Play a game. Ye winna be so hungry if ye dinna think ye's hungry." She tossed the tree chips, some Indian corn and a few nuts stolen from a squirrel's nest into a cauldron of boiling water. The mixture would boil into a kind of soup, but it would take time. The cries of her children grew louder. Mary grimaced at the sound, a sharp ache strangling her heart; her own tears began to flow. From the sack beside the table, she picked up a handful of the raw Indian corn, chewed the yellow grain to soften it and handed some to each of her children. "Give it a good chew before ye swallow."

THAT FIRST WINTER, some men hired out to farms and lumber camps in nearby Pakenham and Fitzroy townships. Others received food on credit. Jobs were scarce, but settlers in neighbouring townships, remembering their own struggle to make a home, were willing to help the newcomers as best they could. Occasionally, a man received a bag of flour as payment; it was immediately shared among neighbours, fresh bread being a luxury. When not working outside the township, or attempting to gather food, the men cleared their acreage—a slow, onerous process that tested their mettle.

But the co-operative "bees" and the struggle to survive that first winter accomplished much more than the clearing of soil in which to plant crops: their daily labour bound the settlers into a supportive community—a kinship of families resolute in their determination to make a productive life in this new land. Voiced at times, silent at others, that initial bond would bolster their resolve for years to come.

"WE NEEDS A *ceilidh*!" Duncan McDonald said to Lorn McCaul one bleak, February afternoon while felling pine on McDonald's lot. They'd been working in silence for nearly three hours, lost in the rhythm of chopping small trees and tossing them into piles. "It jus come to me, a *ceilidh* would lift our spirits, don't ye think, Lorn?" McCaul leaned on the handle of his broadaxe.

"Aye, twould for sure! Some spirits would lift our spirits, too!" Through wiry whiskers he flashed a smile at

McDonald, who never seemed to mind the ribbing he took about his propensity towards the drink.

And so the following Saturday, the Flat Rapids men gathered at McDonald's shanty. Duncan, as *Fear an Tigh*, started the evening with a story about poaching game on the tacksman's property. He had just slain a young deer when he looked behind him and saw the tacksman and his Laird coming over the crest of a distant hill, halberds in hand. McDonald wove a wild tale about how he escaped with his bounty—a tale that became more improbable with his every sip from a tin cup. That set the tone and others followed with far-fetched yarns about poaching and outsmarting their Laird and his tacksman. When it was Donald Cameron's turn, he told again the story about gathering kelp in Skye. Only this time the tawny seaweed came alive and slithered around the workers' ankles, anchoring them in the soft sand where the sun shrivelled their bodies and transformed them into wilted water lilies.

"Ah, Donald, tis a good yarn, lad, but how did *you* escape?" Lorn McCaul asked, challenging the tale with a mischievous grin. Cameron tugged at his whiskers, shifted on his chair and gazed at the floor's rough timbers. The others, sitting in a circle, waited in anticipation.

"My hat, Lorn."

"Your hat! What do ya mean?"

"I scooped up water with my hat and poured it over me till the sun went down. That's when the kelp go to sleep and tis easy to walk out of the water." Cameron's story elicited laughter and applause—and another round of toddies.

"Did I ever tell ye when I was a wee lad about seein the ghost of Coinneach Odhar?" Angus McLaren asked. He drew on his pipe and waited for the others to urge him on with the story, which they did immediately. "Twas in early summer and as the oldest lad twas me job to herd the cattle at night and keep them out of the corn. Now I'd heard the old folk talk of Coinneach and what a great seer he was, but I knew he'd been dead for nigh on a hundred years. Twas a peaceful, clear night with a full moon shining in the high glen when suddenly the cattle becomes restless. I looks round for a fox, but, nay, I see nothin. Then the wind gets up an near blows me off me feet. So I turns me back to the wind and looks up towards the ridge, oh, some seventy yards away, and that's when I seen him." McLaren paused; his pipe had gone out and he took his time relighting it.

"Arrgh, Angus, lad, ye is keepin us in suspense," Iain Storie said. "Git on with it."

"Well, I thinks me eyes is playin tricks on me. I sees this big man—tall—an he's wearin a long robe of many colours, like Joseph's coat in the Bible; cept it has a brown hood an I canna see his face, but there's long, stringy, white hair flowin out underneath. Then he starts walkin towards me. I starts shiverin an . . . I fear me bowels is gonna to move. The wind is stronger and is blowin agin him, but it don't seem to bother him none; he just keeps walkin very slow towards me. Then I hears somethin behind me. I turns just as one of the lambs walks by an it seems . . . well, it seems like it's in a trance. The ghost and the lamb keeps walkin towards one another, but the ghost is walkin faster an soon he be only ten, maybe twelve foot in front of me." McLaren's pipe had gone out again. He replenished the bowl with tobacco from his leather pouch. This time the men waited patiently for him to resume. "Twas then I seen his face in the moonlight. Twas craggy and thin, with a pointed nose and deep, black eyes. I dinna know where I found the courage, but I spoke. I asks who is ye and what does ye want? By now the lamb is beside him. It lays down at his feet. He spoke. Twas a rough, hollow voice. He says his name is Coinneach Odhar. He says jus before he entered the world of the spirits, his tacksman hired him to forecast the abundance of the fall harvest. He says a lamb was to be his payment. He looks down at the lamb. He says he's come for his payment. I did nae know what to say, but I was no longer fearful. The wind had ceased. I remembers the cattle and looks behind me; they is all standin like statues, still as stone. When I looks back, the ghost an the lamb is walkin side by side towards the ridge. The black night air is now very still—like the Almighty is holdin His breath. The only sound is the lamb's hooves on the hard earth. Like I say, he was a big man—more than six foot, I'd say. Nae could I see what he had on his feet, cause of his long robe, but there was nary a sound from his footsteps. When they gets to the top of the ridge, they walks over the side and disappears." McLaren's story was greeted with sustained applause.

"Tis a good yarn," Hugh Alexander said.

"Tis nae a yarn, Hugh. Tis true. At daybreak, I walks up to the ridge expectin to find the lamb. There be no sign of it." The men shifted on their chairs. The awkward silence that followed was broken when McDonald blurted out that "a *ceilidh* wouldn't be a *ceilidh* without a feast!" His comment was greeted with hearty laughs from the inebriated crofters. The food would be less than needed for a feast. They would make do with a rabbit, a beaver tail, two pickerel and a few potatoes and turnips prepared by their wives. But before the food was passed around, Donald Cameron asked Malcolm Kenneth MacGregor, the Laird's piper, to play "All the Blue Bonnets are Over the Border," which got a few of the men dancing a jig. MacGregor followed that with "Devil Amang the Tailors" and another reel, "Mrs. MacLeod of Raasay." When their stomachs began to growl, the men passed around the food, only to interrupt the "feast" now and then with more singing and fanciful tales. But Duncan McDonald was right: reviving memories of home revived the men's spirits. The effects of the *ceilidh* were apparent in the weeks that followed, as the crofters took to clearing their land with renewed vigour.

- - -

BRACED AGAINST A bitterly cold wind, Walter and Ann Ross were clearing brush about forty yards from their shanty when they heard the shouts of their son, Charles. They turned in unison to see the twelve-year-old waving frantically outside their log home. Behind him, flames shot out the chimney and through the side window. Walter plodded through the heavy snow and when he came within some fifteen yards of the burning structure, nine-year-old Mary came scrambling out.

"Lizzy! Where's Lizzy?" Ross shouted, as Mary, sobbing, ran past him and into the embrace of her mother, who was only a few steps behind her husband. Walter looked back towards the shanty just as Charles was going back inside. "Nay, Charles! Nay, lad!" But his son had already disappeared. As Ross pressed through the shanty door, the thick smoke billowed and swirled, blinding and choking the crofter. Having destroyed the wall around the fireplace, the flames darted across the back and side walls. Walter held his handkerchief over his mouth and peered through the blur. His eyes stung and welled with tears. "Charles! Lizzy! Where is ye?" Even though the shanty was only one room—Ann having removed the canvas that partitioned their sleeping quarters—he could see neither his son nor his six-year-old daughter. A sharp crack overhead told him the fire had spread to the cedar laths of the roof. "Charles! Lizzy! Canna ye hear me, children? Where is ye?" A piece of the roof fell directly in front of him. He could hear Ann calling his name. Perhaps, somehow, his son and daughter had escaped. He made his way back out, but only Ann and Mary were there, clinging to one another. Moments later, close neighbours began arriving. They found the partially burned bodies of the children lying together just outside the razed back wall. While the men shovelled snow onto the smouldering structure, the women consoled the traumatized family.

Robert Miller offered his shanty for the wake, his lot being adjacent to the Rosses'. Helen Miller covered mirrors and pictures with white linen, a long-standing custom among Highlanders. The children's bodies were wrapped in cotton and laid in pine boxes sawn and hammered by John Drummond, who also constructed the biers. In the absence of clergy, the elderly Francis MacAulay, a devout member of the Auld Kirk, read from his Bible.

"I will read from Matthew, chapter eighteen." The grieving immigrants crowded around him. "And Jesus called a little child unto Him, and set him in the midst of them, and said, Verily I say unto you, Except ye be converted, and become as little children, ye shall not enter into the kingdom of heaven. Whosoever therefore shall humble himself as these little children, the same is greatest in the kingdom of heaven."

Ann and Mary sat beside the bodies and wept continually during the overnight vigil. Walter kept his head bowed and his pain private. Neighbours took turns visiting the cramped shanty. They prayed for the repose of the children's souls and placed their hands on the charred hands of the dead children, believing the touch protected them against disturbing memories of the deaths. A few older women took to keening beside the coffins. The settlers called upon their staunch, Presbyterian faith; a faith that had sustained their spirit during years of hardship in Perthshire; a faith tested time and again during the Clearances; a faith from which they now drew strength and consolation: the belief that God had called the children to Him, that *He* had more need of them.

At daybreak, the settlers closed the vigil in unison with the prayer they had memorized as children: "Glory be to the Father, and to the Son, and to the Holy Ghost; As it was in the beginning, is now, and ever shall be, world without end. Amen." Walter remarked that the children would be alone; they would not be buried alongside their kin, a time-honoured Highland tradition. His fellow crofters assured him the Lord would understand: there was an ocean between them.

A black flag tied to the bass drone of his pipes, Malcolm MacGregor led the procession to the burial site. McNab would have attended, but he was in York. Men took turns carrying the biers to a far corner of the Rosses' property. The day before they had hacked and dug two deep holes in the partially frozen ground. The grieving family and their male neighbours followed the pallbearers. The women remained behind, except for the elderly Mary MacAulay, a *bean-tuirim* in Perthshire, who cried the *coronach*. When the pallbearers began lowering the boxes into the ground, Walter stepped forward and placed a few rounded pebbles on top of each coffin. The men marked the children's graves with small stone cairns. Then, without further ceremony, they made the mournful journey back to the Rosses' shanty, each grateful it wasn't their children they had buried.

Departing neighbours embraced the family and once more expressed their condolences. A few of the women remained behind. Just after dusk, a stooped, solitary figure could be seen plodding through the heavy snow towards the graves. Walter stood before the cairns, hat in hand. His thoughts turned from his children to his childhood. He couldn't recall his precise age—perhaps five or six—but he could easily recall being in the Presbyterian graveyard near his home, his mother weeping bitterly as pallbearers steadied ropes under a small wooden box; neighbours gathered in a circle, heads bowed, attentive to the minister reading from his psalter; the men holding the ropes taut, gradually lowering the tiny coffin; his father standing beside his mother, hands gripping his bonnet in front of his waist; Walter, standing beside his father, looked up into a countenance of stone, the image forever branded on his heart. And he shed no tears for his baby brother. Now, he stared at the cairns that marked the graves of his children; the tightness in his chest would not release; his tears would not come. If he had had a mirror, he would have seen the face of his father.

***

I AM EXTREMELY pleased with my cottage on modest but fertile acreage adjoining Chief McNab's. As is the custom at home, aye, the custom for untold centuries, by virtue of the Office of Piper, my land is rent free. From ancient times, we Pipers have held a high and honoured position in the clan. As a lad, I heard many stories about the brave Pipers who led our clansmen into battle, the roar of the Great Pipes sending cold shivers through the heart of an enemy. Now ye might think it far-fetched . . . but I tell ye, tis true . . . the English thought the Great Pipes so vital to victory, they declared them an instrument of war! Many a Piper fronting a charge with his clansmen has been felled by the musket and sword. And should he have the misfortune to be captured . . . At the Rising of the '45, captured Pipers who led the charge for Bonnie Prince Charlie were tried by the courts of the Loyalist government. If found guilty, they were hanged in the public square! A Piper's only duty: play well and be loyal to his Chief. Tis all that is asked of him.

I have a fine view of the Ottawa and my pipes resonate with a resounding magnificence over the swirling blue waters. Chief McNab is most gregarious; we have kept fine company these many years. Tis a noble privilege and great honour to fulfil my responsibilities as Piper to the Laird. I play for my Chief each morning while he dons his attire, and always when he sups in the evening.

Another duty that gives me great pleasure is to summon his clansmen when the McNab wishes to address them. Aye, tis true, not all settlers are of Clan McNab, but since all are in the Laird's charge, he says tis his duty to shelter them under the McNab crest. Tis a feudal tradition of shared responsibility that goes back . . . tis impossible to say, but some learned men trace it back to 1058 when Malcolm Ceanmore became King after killing MacBeth. Medieval, aye, but an honourable means of mutual support that has become a proud, Highland tradition: the Chief is protector of his clansmen; they, in turn, show unconditional obedience and allegiance to their Chief. Tis how the clans survived in times of lawlessness.

I remember the first time the McNab ordered a gathering of the clan. At home, as a distinguished member of the Chief's entourage, I had my own *gille* who carried my pipes whenever the Laird had business away. Alas, the settling of this new land does not afford that privilege.

Our horses carried us from Kinnell along a beaten path to the outskirts of the settlement. I dismounted and shouldered my pipes for a rousing rendition of the "ground" from "The McNab Gathering"—a magnificent *piobaireachd* composed by my grandfather, Rory Iain MacGregor. What a prodigious Piper he was! Ah, but he had the most magnificent teacher: the celebrated Patrick Mor MacCrimmon himself! Grandfather never tired of telling what an honour it was to study at the MacCrimmon College of Piping in Boreraig on the Isle of Skye. *Piobaireachd*— Gaelic for "the great music" of the pipes—rousing music invented by the MacCrimmons, legendary Pipers to Clan MacLeod. We owe much to the MacCrimmons. They have bequeathed to Scotland—and now to the Province of Upper Canada—a legacy of the music of the Great Highland Bagpipe.

"The McNab Gathering" reverberated through the woods, echoing off the rocky terrain, commanding his settlers to obey the summons of their Chief and convene at the lodge. When the men presented themselves in Kinnell's spacious living room, the Laird addressed them. That is, he addressed one of them.

"Mr. Drummond, would ye step forward, please," the McNab commanded John Drummond. Although we are boon companions, my Chief does not always confide his intentions, and so I was not privy to his reason for calling this assembly. From the sombre tone of his voice, twas evident he was displeased. A hush pervaded the room, interrupted only by the shuffling of boots as Mr. Drummond shouldered his way towards the front. The McNab, as is his usual custom, was attired in dress appropriate for a Highland Chief. While Mr. Drummond made his way through the settlers, the Laird fidgeted with his richly embossed dirk.

"Mr. Drummond, it has been brought to my attention ye have sold timber off your land. What do ye say for yourself?" John Drummond is a big man. Congenial by nature, he is known to have a temper when aroused. I wonder if he be a descendant of his namesake, the Deputy Forester of the Royal Forest of Glen Artney who hung a band of MacGregors in 1589 when he caught them poaching deer in the royal game preserve. The poachers' accomplices took revenge by cutting off Drummond's head and parading it before his sister, Lady Margaret Stewart of Ardvorlich. Ah, but the McNab tells me it might not have been MacGregors who did the dirty deed. He says one of his ancestors, an Alexander McNab, swore a deposition twas nae MacGregors. The incident brought the wrath of the government upon the heads of we MacGregors: the Privy Council issuing a commission to hunt down certain members of our clan. But then we know the feud was settled. At the Rising of the '45, MacGregors and Drummonds fought side by side at the Battle of Prestonpans under the command of Bonnie Prince Charlie.

Standing in my place next to the Laird, I could see John Drummond's cheeks swell and take on a ruby hue. He stared at his Chief, who returned his steady gaze. "Well, Drummond, what say ye?"

"What of it?"

"What of it?" There was a noticeable twitch to the McNab's thick, black eyebrows. I, too, was surprised and shocked by Drummond's retort.

"At the pleasure of the government, I hold timber rights to the township. Ye have—"

"Nay. I has seen no paper givin ye rights to our timber!" Drummond motioned to the men fidgeting behind him. "Donald says all we owe ye is a bushel uh grain for the acres we plants crops on—and the quit-rent disna begin till the fourth year. Donald says our tickets says nothin bout timber rights." I peered through the gathering in an attempt to locate Mr. Cameron, but he did not appear to be present. I thought that unusual. Tis a serious offence not to heed the summons of your Chief. I could sense the McNab's annoyance at Drummond's challenge, but he held his composure and replied with decisive resolve.

"Mr. Drummond, Mr. Cameron is not Chief of Clan McNab! Have ye forgotten ye owe allegiance to your Chief? Has the fresh air of this new land infused your brain with too much oxygen? I am sorrily disappointed in this questioning of my authority." The Laird took two steps sideways and his face puffed out . . . twas like that of a blowfish. "It should nae be necessary to remind you men of who I am. At home you . . . many of you were loyal tenants. But if I need remind ye: I am McNab of McNab, 13th Chief of a proud clan with an illustrious history. Aye, the McNabs are rooted in the eighth century! Tis true, we are in a new land, but I am still your Chief. All of ye are in my charge. As your liege lord, your obedience is duty bound. We are descendants of a proud clan tradition; a proud, noble tradition that has honoured us these hundreds of years. Tis our duty to instil that tradition in this plebeian colony."

Here the McNab paused, seemingly to compose his temper. The men stood very still. I believe we were all holding our breath. "I am most generous—to a fault some would say—but most generous to those who are loyal. The Government of the Province of Upper Canada has seen fit to entrust me with this township. I have been delegated by our esteemed Lieutenant-Governor to settle this land. Tis truly a great honour Sir Peregrine has bestowed upon me. I must have discipline if . . . tis *imperative* I have the obedience of my clansmen if I am to succeed—and I *will* succeed!"

The Chief returned his attention to John Drummond, who was standing—had stood throughout the reprimand—with arms akimbo. "Mr. Drummond, I will send a man to survey your property and determine the quantity of timber ye have cut and sold illegally. I will then have my solicitor prepare and present ye with a bill, which ye will pay if ye wish to remain on the land I have generously granted you. That is all. Good day, my men."

Drummond appeared to be contemplating a reply, but the Chief turned smartly on his heels, marched around the men and out the door. I, of course, followed. I could hear mumbled conversations behind me, but only the gruff voice of John Drummond was clear. "Aye, we shall see," he said.

❖❖❖

THROUGHOUT THE LONG winter, the whack and thud of the broadaxe resonated across the community as the settlers cleared their land for spring planting. Felled trees crackled in crude, stone fireplaces emitting waves of cosy warmth that eased aching muscles. When the sun melted the lingering patches of grey snow, finally banishing winter's biting spirit, Donald Cameron stood outside the door of his shanty and contemplated his winter's toil: three cleared acres pock-marked with tree stumps. His thoughts were lost on this scene one spring morning when he heard Iain Storie calling his name. Cameron looked across the field to see his neighbour lumbering towards him in knee-high rubber boots. Storie had been his closest neighbour in Perthshire and now, by chance, his closest neighbour in Upper Canada. With their lots adjacent to one another, both men, their wives, and their children, were grateful for small mercies.

"Iain, how goes it, lad?"

"Has ye heard the news?"

"I don't know. What news?"

"Colin says McNab forbids us to leave the township anymore less we has his permission."

"Eh! What's that?"

"As our liege lord . . . them was Colin's words. He says Chief McNab told him he's our liege lord and his settlers is nae to leave the township without his permission. And he told Colin he couldn't leave! What do ya think uh that?" Cameron shook his head.

"Why won't he let him leave?"

"I dinna know; Colin says he dinna know. McNab wouldn't say."

"How does he expect us to feed our families? We won't have a harvest till fall. The land . . . the soil is poor, it may not yield enough to feed us; and what are we to sell at market?"

"Aye, tis true. But he be our Chief! We signed his bond, we must obey. Without him we'd still be scratchin a livin at home. By now we might be scallags!"

"Perhaps, but the land is not what we were promised. What is Colin doing?"

"Well, ye know Colin. The lad's beside himself with worry. He says he's been offered work in Fitzroy. He says he's goin. I told him, nae Colin; I told him McNab be our Chief; tis his township an we must obey. But he says if he canna grow nough crop . . . he's gonna go. He says he has to feed his family."

"It may be McNab's township, but that doesn't give him the right to deny us a living. If I need to work outside the township—I will."

"Ah, Donald, laddie, ye already angered the Laird askin about the quit-rent. But tis your skin; I wouldn't want to be in it if he finds out."

"Perhaps he wouldn't find out."

"Donald, me lad, is ye daft? Course he'd find out! His spies is everywhere! They's loyal to McNab! Course he'd find out!"

As Cameron watched his friend tramp off over the field, an ancient quarrel came to mind: the gladiatorial Battle of the North Inch of Perth in 1396. If the historical account was correct—and that was always in doubt—the Camerons and Macintoshes staged a contest to settle their differences. Twelve men were chosen from each clan to fight with sword and targe before King Robert the 3rd, who acted as judge. The account he read was not clear, but the dispute was likely over land, as were most battles throughout the Highlands. If peace had followed, it might have justified the men's sacrifice. But the men who lost their lives that day lost them in vain. The feud did not end with the day's bloodletting: it continued for another 350 years!

A sudden fatigue sent shivers through Cameron's body. He stroked his beard and wondered if emigrating had been wise after all. But the strong-willed crofter quickly dismissed the thought. He inhaled the spicy, spring air and pulled from deep within a determined resolve: there was no going back to Perthshire; he would make a life here for his family—even if it meant defying the Laird of McNab.

THE TORRID HEAT of summer behind them, those settlers who had cleared sufficient acreage to plant spring crops were now beginning their fall harvest. Those whose soil was too sandy for a bountiful yield continued to work in adjacent townships—if

McNab would give them permission. But many settlers found themselves scratching their heads. For no reason—at least none that was forthcoming—the Chief said "aye" to some and "nay" to others. Despite Colin Carmichael's earlier declaration that he was going to leave, repeated warnings from his neighbours kept the irascible crofter at home clearing his land. But with the approach of fall and the family's meagre provisions nearly depleted, his obstinate nature and Mary's worrisome look overcame his misgivings and he went to work for Patrick O'Connor in Fitzroy.

"Tis a marvellous sight, Patrick," Carmichael said. They were standing at the perimeter of the field admiring the farmer's straight rows of wheat and barley.

"Yes, she's good land," O'Connor said. He hitched leathery thumbs into denim coveralls, rocked back on the heels of his leather boots and beamed with justifiable pride. "She's hard work! But the land rewards your labour." The men seemed transfixed as they gazed over the cultivated acres. "Well, the crop won't come in by herself. Best we get at er." They picked up scythes and were beginning to move into the field when the thud of horses' hooves drew their attention. They turned just as two men on a buckboard came rolling through the farmer's open gate.

"Friends of yours, Colin?"

"Nay, I dinna recognize them." The driver reined in his charges and pulled up beside the men.

"Is one of you Mr. Carmichael?" Authoritative in tone and with the trace of a British accent, the question came from the man seated beside the driver.

"Aye, tis I." The man stepped down from the buckboard and handed the crofter a grey document bound by a black ribbon. "What's this?"

"It's a *capias*, Mr. Carmichael, issued by the Attorney-General on a complaint by Chief McNab of McNab Township. You, sir, are under arrest. You will—"

"What? What do ya mean? I has broken no law! And who is ye?" The man pulled back the lapel of his jacket to reveal a badge pinned to his vest.

"I am Sheriff Jack Lyle. You owe, sir, as you will see stated in the *writ*, a debt to Chief McNab of 120 pounds. As proscribed by the *Imprisonment for Debt Act* under the Statutes of the Province of Upper Canada, by the authority invested in me I am placing you under arrest and I ask that you come peacefully and do not—"

"This . . . this is not right! Tis my passage money! Tis not due till the seventh year!" He thrust the *capias* back into the sheriff's hand. Sensing that the crofter couldn't read, the lawman untied the ribbon and browsed the document.

"I regret, sir, but the *writ* has been properly issued. Chief McNab's *affidavit* says you left his township without permission, and he has reason to believe you will leave the province and not return; I have no choice—"

"What reason? I've built me home in the township; I left only to provide for me wife an children; they is there this very minute; does McNab think I'll abandon them?"

Lyle shifted his strapping frame and pushed back the brim of his hat. "Mr. Carmichael, you will have an opportunity to argue your case before the magistrate in Perth. Now, sir, I implore you to come peacefully." The driver of the wagon, a man of similar proportions to the sheriff, had been sitting quietly through this exchange. Now he wrapped the reins of his team around the brake handle and jumped down to stand beside Lyle. The sheriff introduced him as Deputy Maule. Carmichael cast a pleading glance towards O'Connor.

"Perhaps tis best . . ." the embarrassed Irishman began, then paused. "Perhaps, Colin, you should go along and take the matter up in the court." The proud Scot bowed his head, but only for a moment. He pulled his shoulders back, elbowed his way between the officers and climbed into the wagon. The sheriff and his deputy hurriedly took their seats, bid O'Connor "good day," and galloped off, leaving the puzzled farmer blinking through a thin cloud of dust.

***

AT TIMES I feel tis a blessing, other times a curse, but I find myself with considerable leisure time. Tis by necessity, I know, but tis perplexing that the McNab conducts his affairs in this new land with much less formality than at home, my daily services limited to a repetitive routine.

A most dignified and disciplined gentleman, the Laird does his best to maintain order and respectability among his clansmen. Tis a principled tradition handed down through the centuries; a tradition that has made Clan McNab the distinguished family with which I am honoured to be associated, as were my father, grandfather and great-grandfather before me. Did ye know? Our families are blood relatives! The McNabs, too, are proud descendants of a son of King MacAlpin—Abraruadh, the eighth-century lay Abbot of Glendochart in Perthshire. Tis the meaning of "McNab" in the Gaelic—*mhic an Aba*—son of the Abbot.

"Time is of the essence," my grandfather used to say. Not a man to waste precious time, every day he practised a *piobaireachd* until his performance was up to his high standards. I was eight when he began my tutorial on the practice chanter. He lectured me on the necessity of dedication to the craft. I have never forgotten those homilies on discipline; I, too, practise every day. It fills my leisure time and ... dare I tell ye! I am being so bold as to try my hand at writing a *piobaireachd*!

Ah, but one practises alone, and in time the comfort of solitude wears thin. I am too gregarious by nature to lock myself away from the community. My disposition compels me to mingle among the settlers whenever opportunity presents itself. Our roads—if paths hacked through the bush can be called roads—are much in need of work. The McNab says he will assign statute-labour to build and repair the roads come spring. But now the township is once again cloaked in winter. Last winter was a bitter experience. Thus far this winter we have been fortunate; the weather has been mild. Travel is somewhat easier on the hard-packed snow. Lipsey, a squatter the Laird has engaged as an all-rounder— a strange but accommodating creature—is quite willing to saddle and bridle my Nellie so I may journey into the community. I try to time my arrival for mid-afternoon, when the men rest their weary muscles from clearing the timber and partake of tea and scones. Chief McNab has no objection to these visits: *au contraire*, he encourages me to mingle among the men and report back on how the settlers are getting on.

The other day I was visiting Walter Ross. Tis testimony to the innate fortitude of we Scots that Walter and Ann and their remaining child, Mary, have persevered to overcome the appalling tragedy that befell them. I know they have taken solace in their God. Walter told me they pray every day for the souls of their beloved children. It appears Ann is in a family way. Of course, I was discreet and said nothing, but tis a great blessing, a great blessing indeed.

Walter spoke of Colin Carmichael's long incarceration. Walter is loyal to his Chief; I dinna believe he would say anything to tarnish his good name among the settlers. But, in confidence, he told me he felt the McNab was being unfair. Of course I defended my Chief's actions. I explained that, by awarding him the township, the Lieutenant-Governor has placed considerable trust and responsibility in the McNab's hands. The Laird told me he would honour the clan by living up to that trust and responsibility. Aye, tis ingrained in the Scot to be good to our word, despite the sorry manner in which some Lowlanders have acted at home.

When I explained to Walter the necessity of maintaining discipline in the township, and that Mr. Carmichael should have asked permission to leave, he said the crofter *did* ask permission and the Laird denied it. Tis, of course, nonsense, and I told him so. But Walter insisted the McNab said "nay" to Mr. Carmichael's request for leave. Twas nothing to be gained by arguing, but I told Walter that if we are to be a civilized province, the law must be upheld. Tis not as if we are being governed by irresponsible men. *Au contraire!* Sir Peregrine has favoured our Executive Council with men of the highest quality, the highest principles. Ye will remember the McNab and I had the honour and privilege to entertain many of them in York. And the Chief meets with them on those occasions when he journeys to our provincial capital. Aye, he is intent upon . . . I know on his last visit . . . he said twas nae necessary for me to accompany him, but he told me he was honoured to dine with Sir Peregrine and Mr. Robinson, our much-admired Attorney-General.

Lately, I have heard the government referred to as the "Family Compact." I believe tis most fitting; we are fortunate to be all of one family and still be members of the British Empire; unlike those rogues to the south who turned on the Mother Country, and continue their efforts to convince us to do the same. Walter said he had no love for the English, but he did not wish to join the new union of the rebellious colonies. He said, all things being equal, he would like to return to his home in Perthshire. Alas, he knows that to be most unlikely.

On one point we were in agreement: there is embarrassment and shame among the settlers that one of our own—this fellow Mackenzie, a Highlander no less!—has been stirring up trouble with his newspaper, *The Colonial Advocate*, I believe tis called. Even though he is some distance away, word has reached us of his campaign for "responsible government"— some foolish notion that the

Assembly . . . ah, tis hard to fathom—that the learned men of the Executive Council should heed the advice of the majority in the Assembly. Those elected by commoners know *better* what is good for the province than those appointed to the Legislative Council by Sir Peregrine! Tis a silliness that will pass. Mackenzie is seldom spoken of in the community, but when he is, tis in hushed tones. The McNab told me Mr. Robinson dismisses him as nothing more than a conceited, red-haired, loose cannon. I am somewhat put out at the reference to his hair, my own being a ruby red—and I am nae a loose cannon!

Before taking my leave, Walter told me that Mr. Carmichael's neighbours at Flat Rapids saved and scrounged to pay his bail. The poor man was entering his seventh month of confinement. Walter said six of his neighbours journeyed to Perth and put up fifty pounds each. I must say I was impressed. Tis, of course, typical of the generosity and loyalty among Highlanders. Nevertheless, tis a considerable sum for crofters with little means; and a journey of some sixty miles would be a hardship, taking them away from clearing their land.

On my return to Kinnell, I reported on my visit to the McNab, as he had asked me to. He said he was most interested in the men who put up Mr. Carmichael's bail.

***

"TO YOUR HEALTH, gentlemen!" Colin Carmichael stood in front of his fireplace and gestured with his cup towards the six men who had put up his bail. On their return to Flat Rapids from Perth, Carmichael invited them in for refreshments. Each acknowledged the toast and sipped from his toddy. "I am grateful for—"

"Ah, tis what we had to do," Lorn McCaul said. "We must stick together."

"The Laird is a tyrant!" Duncan McDonald shouted, jerking his cup sideways and spilling some of his whisky on the planked floor. "We must fight him an we must—"

"Ah, Duncan, think of what you're saying, lad," Robert Miller said. The others were standing; he was sitting, nursing a bruised leg from a fall. "Fight him? He is our Chief, we are in his debt. If he had not paid our passage we would still be scratching—"

"Ah, Robert, spare me," McDonald said. "I's mighty tired uh hearin how we owe him our passage an we must be grateful an how we'd be scallags an—"

"Do ya think it otherwise, Duncan?" Hugh Alexander asked. "I knew when Angus got the notice . . . I knew we could be next. We is in no position—"

"We is nae his serfs, Hugh," Angus McLaren said. "Aye, it may be his township, but we's nae livin in the Middle Ages. The land is not what we was promised. I works me land every day an so far I's cleared only . . . at best five acres. And that's with all ye helping."

"So! What would ye have us do?" McDonald asked. The men's weathered faces registered puzzlement and frustration. Then Donald Cameron, who had been taking in his neighbours' arguments, broke the silence.

"I have an idea," Cameron said. He paused and tugged on his trimmed beard. "We could take up a petition and present it to the Lieutenant-Governor."

"A petition!" McDonald said. "McNab is Maitland's good friend! The Chief be a member of the Family Compact! A member in good standing! What good's a petition?"

"Aye, Duncan, tis true," Cameron said. "McNab and Maitland *are* good friends. But does the Lieutenant-Governor know how his good friend is conducting the township's affairs? If nothing else, a petition would put our grievances before the government."

"I agrees with Donald," Lorn McCaul said. "We's not livin in a lawless frontier . . . like them out west in America—at the mercy of the fastest gun. Tis true, the government treated us bad at home, but we is still British subjects, we still has rights."

"Rights!" Colin Carmichael said. "What rights? He throws me in gaol for *six months* for the crime uh providin for me family! We'll see what happens at trial, but if a man can be throwed in gaol for six months . . . jus for workin to feed his family . . ."

"I like Donald's idea," Angus McLaren said. "Cept on me bond and on me ticket, I have nae seen a scrap uh paper givin McNab the right to the quit-rent. Where be the government document? We is at least owed an explan—"

"The quit-rent twould be nothin if the land was fertile," McDonald said. He held out his cup for his host to replenish. "Tis simple. We was lied to . . . out-an-out lied to!"

"I still say he is our lawful Chief and we owe him our loyalty," Miller said. Favouring his injured leg, he pushed himself to his feet and limped closer to the fireplace. "He is strong-willed; I fear a petition will only raise his ire and bring more wrath upon our heads. I'm glad you're out of gaol, Colin, but when McNab denied ye permission ye should uh—"

"Shoulda let Mary and the young uns go hungry!" Carmichael said. "We may go hungry yet before the winter's over. I has barely three week's supply; what is we to do?

"Dinna trouble yourself with that," McCaul said. "If need be, we will share." The others muttered assurances, though they had little to share. "Where is Mary and the young uns?"

"They is at Walter's. I is grateful . . . Grateful to all of ye for carin for me family," Carmichael said, his voice breaking. "I is most grateful—"

"A petition could list our grievances, the quit-rent is only one," McLaren said. "Why does the Laird have timber rights on our property?"

"Ye know he sent John a bill for the timber he cut on his lot," Alexander said. "John says he's not payin it. I dinna know what he's gonna do, but I fear the worst."

"The worst?" Miller said.

"Aye. Ye know John; he be a hot-tempered lad," Alexander said.

"We can petition the government for fair treatment," McCaul said. "I say we take up a petition!"

"'Tis a good idea," Cameron said, as if he hadn't originated the idea. "I will write it up. I'm sure most of the men will sign it." Everyone offered to gather signatures, except Robert Miller.

THE SUN RISING red dissolved the vaporous crystals that hung in the frosty air as Harry Pinsell, Albert Hayes, and John Drummond took their positions around the base of the white pine. The stolid, scaly grey behemoth stood mute, tentacles anchored deep in the frozen earth. Each man hoisted his broadaxe and swung with his whole body. As the blades bit into the yielding trunk, muffled thuds and expelled grunts resonated briefly before dying in the thick silence of the forest.

"Whoa, boys!" Pinsell called out when he felt the tree shiver. "If she's to fall in the clearing, John"—the lumberjack nodded towards a long, narrow space mottled with rotting stumps—"we need lean er that way." Pinsell shoved wedged chips into Drummond's cut. "That'll keep er from fallin back on us." Because this was dangerous work, the veteran lumberman explained each step to the new man, who had hired on at the lumber camp the night before. Pinsell chopped further into his own cut. When the lofty pine began to lean, Hayes steered it towards the opening by stuffing wedges into his cut. Pinsell struck two more blows: a shattering crack ripped through the forest. "Back, boys, back! Timber!" The trunk splintered and the proud old

Goliath crashed into the clearing, its butt lashing upwards in one last kick before bouncing and settling on the forest floor. "Good job, boys." Pinsell wiped the sleeve of his shirt across his forehead.

They moved on to the next tree and by the time the sun was overhead, five pines lay along the clearing.

"Time for a break, boys," Pinsell said. They sat on stumps and took salt-pork sandwiches and jars of black tea from cotton sacks. They ate in silence. Intensely private men, lumberjacks were inclined to guard their secrets and reveal little about their lives away from the woods. But the imposed isolation of months separated from families often lowered that guard. And so there was a binding camaraderie in the Cambuse shanty, partly because of loneliness and partly because of necessity. Men worked in teams, each aware his safety was dependent upon the other. Albert Hayes was a quiet man who seldom spoke. Harry Pinsell was very much his opposite: outgoing and curious about others; an old hand who liked to joke that when he cut himself he bled sawdust.

The arrival of McNab's bill triggered the latent fury seething in John Drummond. He swore he would not pay. Isabel knew her husband; she didn't even attempt to persuade him. While many of his fellow settlers supported his decision, they warned him that the Laird would soon have him arrested. Drummond felt he had no choice but to leave his wife and children in the care of neighbours and hide in the woods. It was a hard decision, one he brooded over, but his Scots intransigence won the day. Late the previous afternoon, he had packed his saddle bags and ridden his mare to the lumber camp in adjacent Fitzroy Township.

"What brings you to the woods, John?" Pinsell asked. There had been little time to become acquainted with the crofter turned lumberjack. Now, unscrewing the lid on his jar of tea, Hayes cocked an ear towards Drummond, who seemed to ponder his answer.

"The Laird, I suppose."

"The Laird!" Pinsell said. "How's that?" Drummond explained his confrontation with McNab and his refusal to pay the bill. Pinsell said he had worked only in Fitzroy and for Philemon Wright in Hull, but he'd heard McNab was claiming timber rights for his entire township. "Who'd you sell to?"

"Ye probably knows him—Jack Brill."

"Aye, I knows Jack; a good man, Jack is."

"Well, Jack needed timber an I needed . . . the land's so poor I canna grow nough crops to feed the wife and young uns. I needed provisions, so I sold to Jack."

"What's the bill?" Pinsell asked.

"Eh?"

"How much does you owe?"

"Thirty-nine pounds."

"What is you gonna to do?"

Drummond looked at the ground and shook his head. "I dinna rightly know. I got wind he's gonna have me arrested, so I left. His toadies won't find me here." The men sipped their tea.

"You could take him to Perth," Hayes said. Startled by this rare interjection, his companions looked over at the lumberjack who was scratching his thick, black beard. "To the court."

"I has no means to go to court. Even if I did, the judges sides with him. He had a man throwed in gaol jus for leavin the township without his say so. He asked, but McNab said nay. The poor beggar was there six months. He'd still be there cept his neighbours put up bail." The men finished their tea in silence.

"Has he been tried?" Pinsell asked.

"Eh! Who?"

"The poor beggar who was gaoled."

"Nay, the trial's in the spring." Drummond stood and stretched. "I can provide better for me family workin here."

"How'll you get your wages to the missus?" Pinsell asked.

"I dinna know. My neighbours is good people. They'll see that—" Drummond's attention was drawn to the thump of heavy hooves and the rattle of chains dragging on the ground.

"Ah, it's Frenchie!" Pinsell said, as the skidder led a yoke of oxen around a bend in the clearing. "*Salut*, Jacques!"

"*Salut.*"

"We has five trees for ya," Pinsell said. "All trimmed cept this one. C'mon, boys, let's finish this one so Frenchie can haul er away." The men set to work with their axes, slicing off branches and tossing them aside. It took them only a few minutes to clean the tree. "She's ready, Jacques."

The skidder, who spoke almost no English, nodded and pulled the oxen in front of the tree. The fellers watched the skidder secure the chains around the end of the log.

"Gee!" the skidder commanded and the oxen lumbered forward, dragging their burden on to the skid road.

"Next log's jus round the bend," Pinsell shouted. The skidder raised an arm in acknowledgment as he guided his team along the rough trail.

***

TIS SPRING ONCE again, my favourite time of year in our township. I love to stroll on the grounds of Kinnell and bathe in the breezy, moist air rising off the Ottawa. Ah, but if I am to be honest with ye, the years roll by and still I long for the heather and juniper, the coarse moor grass and sweet turf of the Highlands. Tis home, and until we return my heart will forever bear this ache.

But then . . . these past few weeks . . . aye, I must admit, one canna help but be charmed by the flowers, the birds . . .

After a morning practising my new *piobaireachd*, if the weather be fair, I take my daily constitutional, careful not to step on the Spring Beauties with their delicate pink stripes and tapering green leaves. Trilliums! Ah, there are spectacular reds and whites! And we have alluring arrays of Blue Violets; some settlers use their blossoms in jellies and syrups. If lucky, one may spot a Scarlet Tanager or a Pileated Woodpecker—perhaps even a Red-shouldered Hawk! These of God's wild creatures make their home among our magnificent trees: coniferous Hemlocks with their tiny cones, Basswood, Birch, splendid Maples and towering White Pines, the favourite of the lumberman—and my own favourite! The Pine, the Scots Fir, is the Plant Badge of we MacGregors. Tis abundant. Always a fresh sprig adorns my bonnet.

I have not had the privilege of seeing it with my own eyes, but I know the squaws of a nearby tribe have shown the settlers' wives how to draw and boil the sap of the Maple to make sugar. Nay, I have not seen it, but I can attest to its sweetness. Tis most apparent in the delicious cakes and pies of which I am easily persuaded to partake on my visits. Tis gratifying to know we have not lost the touch of Scottish hospitality in this new land. Ah, but our roads. Abominable! The Laird keeps promising to see to their improvement. He says the statute-labour will be apportioned thus, but thus far I have seen scant evidence of this undertaking.

The McNab is forever espousing the great pride he feels for his township. He delights in introducing himself as "McNab of McNab." And I know he suffers much grief when duty calls him to court with one of his beloved settlers. This fellow Carmichael, he disobeyed his Chief. A Chief is like a parent, he canna tolerate disobedience. The man owed a debt of 120 pounds, a substantial sum. The Laird feared he would abscond without paying. Quite understandable. Others have. He told me tis why he denied the crofter leave.

It took us the better part of a day to travel to Perth, our poor horses near stumbling over rotting tree stumps. Fortunately, we have had little rain this spring, the footing was dry, and for that we were most grateful. While the Laird was an honoured guest at the residence of Mr. Justice Daniel McMartin, Esquire, I managed to find reasonable accommodation above a tavern on Gore Street. The next morning we met at the courthouse. I tell ye, I must take command of my sweet tooth: the staircase is steep and winding; I was panting when we reached the courtroom on the second floor. Ah, but the journey was for naught. The matter should have been settled between the parties. The proceedings were brief, indeed. Mr. Carmichael's neighbours had engaged Mr. James Boulton, a greenhorn. The Laird's legal Counsel was the portly Wilfred McRae. And the presiding Magistrate was the Laird's good friend, his host the previous evening, the sombre Mr. McMartin.

"Your Honour, Chief McNab regrets the unfortunate circumstances that bring him before the court," Mr. McRae said in his opening argument. He is a tall man with a hefty frame and an arrogant manner. He strutted before the bench with his long waistcoat pushed back and his thumbs tucked into his vest. "The defendant signed Chief McNab's bond in Perthshire and so . . . If it please the court, I have given the document to the clerk as exhibit A." His Honour nodded approval and motioned to the clerk to hand him the paper. "You will see the defendant's signature . . . his mark on the bond, signed in the presence of Dr. Hamilton Buchanan at Leney House in Perthshire. If necessary, I will verify the—"

"Your Honour, Mr. Carmichael acknowledges that he signed the bond," Mr. Boulton said. And then Mr. McRae continued.

"Your Honour will see that the defendant owes Chief McNab a debt of 120 pounds. That was the cost of Mr. Carmichael's passage . . . and that of his family. It was paid by—generously, I might add—it was paid by Chief McNab. I believe the bond—"

"The passage money was paid by Dr. Buchanan and it is not—"

"Mr. Boulton, you're out of order. Sit down," Mr. McMartin said. "Continue, Mr. McRae."

"I believe the bond speaks for itself. The defendant is in Chief McNab's debt and the Laird was concerned . . . from the conduct of other settlers . . . he was justified in believing—"

"Your Honour, Mr. McRae is conveniently forgetting that payment is not due until the seventh year," Mr. Boulton said. "And I wish to put on the record—"

"Mr. Boulton, you're out of order again," Mr. McMartin said. The Magistrate has a dour countenance, but his scowl at Mr. Carmichael's lawyer for this second interruption did not silence the novice.

"Chief McNab has reneged on his promise to settle the immigrants on their lots with adequate provisions and I wish to put on the record—"

"Sit down, Mr. Boulton, before I find you in contempt." This time the lawyer heeded the Magistrate's command. "Mr. McRae, you needn't continue. I have reviewed the facts of the case. It is not necessary for me to hear anything further. I have it on good authority that Mr. Carmichael left the township without Chief McNab's permission. And the Laird has informed me that other settlers have fled without paying their bond. I find for the plaintiff."

"But your Honour—"

"And furthermore, Mr. Boulton, you have been negligent in instructing your client on the appropriate date to surrender for trial. Because of your incompetence, the law obliges the court to forfeit bail."

"But your Honour—"

"Court will recess for fifteen minutes." The Magistrate gathered his robes around him and stepped down from the bench. The Laird, who was seated beside Mr. McRae, shook his Counsel's hand with such vigour he might well have dislocated both their forearms. I looked over at Mr. Boulton. He was standing at the defence table clutching a handful of papers, his expression that of a gentleman at the track whose horse did not finish.

I must say, although I believe the verdict be fair, my heart went out to the six poor men who each lost fifty pounds, a sum they can ill afford. Of course my Chief was very pleased with the verdict. He had a smug, satisfied look as he made his way towards the front of the courtroom, where he spoke to Mr. McMartin. While the Laird conferred with the Magistrate in chambers, I descended the stairs and wandered out into the fresh air where Mr. Carmichael and the men who had put up bail were discussing the proceedings. Tis understandable they would be upset and angry. Duncan McDonald was in a rant, threatening violence to his Chief. There was much fuming by the others as well: except for Donald Cameron. Mr. Cameron was doing his best to calm his fellow crofters. I tried to explain the McNab's position, but there was no reasoning with them, the verdict so close at hand. I thought it best to leave them to their bluster. I re-entered the courthouse and sat on a bench in the lobby. I detest this unpleasantness. Tis foreign to my nature. Tis a very simple matter: the McNab is to govern his township, the crofters are to work their land; together they will build a prosperous community. Tis the way of the clans. Has always been so. Except for a few rogues, Highlanders have always shown deference to their Chief. Why this defiance now? Alas, I had only a short time to reflect on the matter: the Laird emerged presently from chambers and we departed immediately for Kinnell.

***

IN LUMBER CAMPS in early spring, the felling of trees complete, skidders, with their teams of oxen or horses, drag the remaining logs to skidways where they're loaded onto sleighs and hauled to rollways beside the still frozen river. The camp foreman keeps a watchful eye for signs of warmer weather: geese flying north, chipmunks scurrying about, and, especially, the breaking up of black ice and the rising of the river. The expert lumbermen who stay on for "the drive" sharpen their cant hooks and pike-poles, anticipating the exhilarating and dangerous work of driving the logs to the boom on the big river. With their equipment at the ready, they pass the short time remaining in the Cambuse shanty playing cards and checkers and dancing to the jigs and reels of the French fiddlers from Lower Canada.

John Drummond was not among these men. When the tree-fellers finished their job of "hurling down the pine," they collected their wages and headed home. Drummond had been in the bush five months. He had had no contact with Isabel; he didn't know how his family had survived the winter. He was not, however, overly concerned; his neighbours promised to ensure that Isabel and the children had enough food and fuel to get them through the cold weather. Now, with money in his saddlebags, he was returning home. He wondered what, if anything, would happen when the Laird heard of his return. Perhaps the Chief, occupied with his numerous responsibilities, would no longer care about collecting the thirty-nine pounds. Perhaps his neighbours had taken up a collection and paid it for him. Perhaps . . . but it didn't really matter; the lumber camp closed for the summer, Drummond had no choice but to return to his lot. Not that it was a difficult choice; he missed his family. He had enjoyed the friendship of the loggers; they accepted him, tolerated his shortcomings and helped him learn the skills of lumbering. But each day—while sharpening his axe on the grindstone, or mending a tear in his jacket, or lying on his bunk to rest sore muscles—he wondered how Isabel and the children were getting on.

Drummond guided his horse over swampy trails, trying to keep the animal from becoming mired in the mud and stumbling on near-hidden roots, and trying to keep himself from being knocked out of the saddle by low-slung branches. He had packed his saddlebags and bedroll and left camp at mid-morning. Now, late in the afternoon, he rode into a clearing and onto the familiar trail that led over a knoll and down to his shanty. The crofter slapped his heels against his horse's flanks and the steed began a gentle trot along the hard-packed trail. At the top of the knoll, his shanty came into view. He brought his horse to a halt. Two of his fellow crofters were riding up the trail towards him. In front of his shanty he could see two horses tethered to a small fir tree. One he recognized: it was the Laird's big-chested, dappled grey mare. The men riding the last few yards signalled to Drummond to get back. The crofter moved his horse back down the other side of the knoll. Seconds later the two riders joined him.

"I wish we could say welcome home, John, but the Laird and the sheriff is at your shanty," Iain Storie said.

"I seen the Laird's dappled grey. How'd he know I was comin home?"

"We don't know," Donald Cameron said, "but he has ways of finding out. He says he's going to have you arrested unless you're ready to pay him the money you owe—with interest."

"I has enough in me saddlebags, more than enough. But I will not be payin it. I dinna believe he has the right."

"Then you're going to be arrested." Cameron turned in his saddle and watched Storie ease his mount back up the knoll to where he could see the shanty. Just as he returned his attention to Drummond, the crofter pulled his rifle from its sheath.

"If I's to be treated as an outlaw . . . goddam it! An outlaw I'll be!" Drummond waved the rifle above his head, startling his horse, who jerked her head up and whinnied.

"John, lad!" Cameron said. Drummond's dark eyes bristled like those of a cornered racoon. "Ye dinna . . . think of what you're saying, lad! You're no outlaw!" Storie rejoined them.

"Nay, I am no outlaw . . . but I am not gonna . . . We came to this colony . . . tis not right . . . We has to fight the land . . . We has to fight McNab . . . I am not gonna stand—"

"We all feels the same, John," Storie said. "But ye know we petitioned Maitland."

"Aye, and what come of it?" Drummond looked at Cameron.

"Nothing."

"Ye tried, Donald. Ye tried and we is grateful. But tis useless. We is nothin but serfs. Just like at home. I dinna know what to—" The men heard the hoof beats only moments before the Laird and Sheriff Lyle rode over the hill. The sheriff drew his pistol and pointed it at the fugitive.

"Drop your rifle on the ground, Mr. Drummond," Lyle said. The crofter appeared startled, as if surprised to be still holding the gun. He waved the barrel towards the sheriff, then wheeled his horse and galloped back down the trail.

"Shoot! He's getting away!" McNab shouted. Lyle fired a shot well over Drummond's head just as the settler disappeared into the woods. "Go after him! Go after him!" Cameron and Storie moved their mounts closer together to block the trail, but they could see Lyle had no intention of pursuing Drummond. "Why aren't ye going after the scoundrel? Tis your duty!"

"He cannot go far," Lyle said. "He will return home. Let us not make outlaws out of crofters, Chief." Although Lyle had to carry out the Laird's orders, as district sheriff, he reported to his superiors in Perth.

"Tis he who has made an outlaw of himself," McNab said. "Ah, Mr. Cameron, twas not wise to counsel Drummond to flee from the law."

"Nay, Chief, twould not be wise, which is why I gave no such counsel. John doesn't believe ye have timber rights on our land. Tis why he refuses to pay. Ye should show us the legal paper that gives you those rights."

"I am your Chief, Mr. Cameron. I don't answer to you or Drummond," the Laird said, punctuating his statement with a loud snort. Cameron frowned and shook his head.

"Tis almost dusk; Elizabeth and Margaret will be preparing the evening meal," Cameron said. "Iain and I should be getting on home. We'll stop at John's on the way and tell Isabel what happened." Sheriff Lyle tipped his broad-brimmed hat to the men, who tipped their hats in return. Then, without looking at the Laird, Cameron and Storie rode up the embankment and over the crest of the hill.

***

Tis NOW SUMMER and since our unpleasant journey to Perth in the spring, I am pleased to tell ye we have had no more incidents of disobedience. Ah, except for the rogue Drummond. Tis most lamentable the burly crofter has chosen to become an outlaw. There are rumours he has been home on many occasions. But whenever Sheriff Lyle visits the shanty, he is not to be found. At least that is what the good sheriff reports to the McNab. I canna help but wonder how much effort Lyle is making to apprehend the man. Alas, the Laird will see justice done—no matter how long it takes.

As tis his nature to be generous, Chief McNab did not demand the sum Mr. Carmichael owed him. Twould not have mattered; the man could not have paid. The poor soul spent more than six months in gaol. Tis enough.

But the Laird is most upset with the malcontents at Flat Rapids who put up Mr. Carmichael's bail. He said their time would have been better spent collecting the 120 pounds and

paying the crofter's lawful debt. Aye, the McNab has good
reason to be upset with these Jonahs! Last winter they got
up a petition and sent it by post to Sir Peregrine in York. Of
course, our astute Lieutenant-Governor dismissed it out of
hand, as was proper. The McNab has dubbed these
complainers "black sheep."

Sir Peregrine has seen fit to appoint the Laird a
Magistrate, a common practice throughout the province.
Without delay, Chief McNab used his new authority to issue
summonses against the six scoundrels. The Chief's judgment
is usually impeccable, but, dare I say, it failed him on this
occasion: he appointed Alex Yulle to guide Deputy Maule
into Flat Rapids where he was to serve the *writs*. Now Alex
is a fine fellow, but he has a reputation—a well-deserved
reputation—of being rather indolent. And I know from our
conversations that he sides with the settlers in these disputes.
Still, he is a good fellow, and so the Laird, given his
charitable disposition, uses him for the occasional odd job.
But to entrust him with the responsibility of a guide . . .

Twas several weeks after the incident when I extracted
the truth from Deputy Maule and from Alex's friend Henry
Rudd. Henry said he didn't know whether Alex had the
scheme in mind from the time of his appointment, or if he
devised it along the way. Whichever, he showed his true
colours and lived up to his reputation.

Twas a humid day when the men started out on
horseback just after the noon hour. Flat Rapids is a good
seven, eight miles from Kinnell. Some five miles out, Alex
got lost. That is, he pretended he was lost. He left Deputy
Maule in a clearing near the banks of the Madawaska. He
told the officer of the law he would inquire of a neighbour
as to directions and return shortly. Maule told me, in
hindsight, he should have insisted upon accompanying him.
Gadabout that he is, Alex rode off in the direction of Waba
Creek and on reaching Henry's shanty spent the remainder

of the afternoon and evening playing cards and imbibing homemade whisky. Alex said not a word to Henry about the task assigned to him by his Chief. And when his hospitable friend extended an invitation to stay the night, he gladly accepted.

In the meantime, Maule waited patiently in the clearing for his guide to return. But when dusk descended and mosquitoes from a nearby swamp descended upon him, he grew impatient, as one might expect. My father used to say, "He who hesitates is lost," and when the Deputy was plunged into darkness rather abruptly, he did not feel secure in his sense of direction and found it too late to venture back along the treacherous path by which they had journeyed. He gathered some punk and small branches and ignited them by striking a flint over the punk with the blade of his knife. He said tis a skill he had learned from a local tribe of Indians. By this means he was able to build a fire, which kept the mosquitoes at bay and provided some warmth, although the flames attracted a pack of howling wolves. Thus, the officer of the law spent a chilly and uneasy summer night wrapped in his saddle blanket.

At the break of dawn, the neighing of Mr. Yulle's horse awakened Maule when the guide rode into the clearing. Alex concocted a tale about losing his way and finding shelter in an abandoned shanty. This yarn was plausible to the good deputy, as he knows of settlers who have fled the township without paying their bond. Tired and hungry, for the deputy had only a few pieces of hardtack in his saddlebag, he followed Alex back to Kinnell, where the men told of their misadventure. The Laird was displeased that the *writs* had not been served, but seeing the dishevelled state of Deputy Maule, the McNab did not have the heart to send him out again. Aye, the scoundrels have evaded justice—for now.

***

DONALD CAMERON LEANED over his workbench and tried to concentrate on the task at hand. His adze chipped with loving care as he smoothed the maple rockers at the front and back of the sap-trough cradle. Elizabeth was pregnant. It was a sweltering summer's afternoon, but inside the shed the still, dusty air felt cool. Cameron felt uneasy. Although he hadn't aspired to the role, he had emerged as a leader among the settlers. He realized why: he had a rudimentary education; most of the settlers had none. Quiet by nature, he was a good listener who always considered what others had to say. As he stood back from his workbench to examine the finished cradle, he wondered about the meeting requested by Robert Miller and William Roddie. Their arrival was imminent.

Miller, a friend and neighbour in Perthshire, seemed caught in the middle of the conflict between the settlers and McNab. Although years of adversity had bonded their families, Miller was a staunch believer in clan loyalty: he saw the Laird's authority as paramount. Roddie, an émigré from outside Aberdeen, was a member of McNab's Cabinet-Council: five loyal settlers the Laird had favoured with the best locations. They, in return, ingratiated themselves with the naive crofters and informed the Chief about the growing discontent. Although they'd spoken on only a few occasions, it was apparent to Cameron why the Laird had picked Roddie: he found the man's kowtowing manner nauseating, his every word calculated to curry favour.

Cameron's thoughts turned to Elizabeth. He knew she was pregnant even before she told him. Despite her millstone of daily drudgery, he noticed a softening of the taut creases in her oval face; the revived sparkle in her blue eyes reflecting the life growing inside her. A fifth mouth to feed would be an added burden, but the child would also bring added joy to their family. He knew Elizabeth was hoping for a girl, a sister for Janet.

The slowing trot of horses told him his company had arrived.

"Come in out of the heat, men."

"Tis a scorcher, Donald," Miller said as the men entered the coolness of the shed.

"Tis that," Cameron said.

"The Laird still dresses in full Highland garb," Roddie said. "Tis only proper for the Chief. But he sweats . . . aye, he sweats."

"I asked Elizabeth to bring us some velvet tea," Cameron said. His visitors sat on a flattened pine log from which Cameron had removed the bark and placed against the wall to serve as a bench.

"Some tea would be welcome," Miller said. Cameron pulled his chair away from the workbench and sat facing the men. Each seemed to be waiting for the other to speak. Cameron reached over and took his pipe and tobacco pouch off the workbench.

"What can I do for ye?" Miller glanced at Roddie. Cameron sensed it was Roddie who wanted this meeting; that he had appealed to Miller for moral support. But it was Miller who spoke.

"Donald, there be trouble brewing. Most of us . . . ye know yourself most of us are peaceful and hard-working. But we're concerned . . ." Miller again looked at Roddie, who was squinting at Cameron as if trying to bring him into focus. Roddie removed his leather hat, revealing strands of thinning brown hair plastered with perspiration. He pulled a sweat-stained handkerchief from his pants pocket and wiped the band before putting the hat back on. The front of the brim circled his low forehead.

"The Laird is troubled by the disrespect," Roddie blurted out. "Aye, tis more than disrespect by some; tis disobedience by . . . tis *rebellion* by the likes of Drummond—and Carmichael!" Cameron drew slowly on his pipe. "You is their leader; they looks up to ye. We is askin you to put a stop to the disobedience—the rebellion. Tis not the way loyal clansmen should be behavin." Roddie smiled, as would a wolf baring its teeth. "Aye, I know ye had a run-in with the Laird about the quit-rent, but tis in the past. I can talk to the Chief. If ye promise to get the settlers under control . . . the Chief is most appreciative . . . most appreciative of those who are loyal and show him due respect." Roddie peered at Cameron. The crofter continued to draw on his pipe, but a flush had come to his cheeks and he tugged at his beard.

"Does the name Robert Gourlay mean anythin to ye?" Cameron said, his muscular baritone straining for control.

"Nay, it do not," Roddie said.

"I's heard the name," Miller said. "I dinna remember . . . Wasn't he a troublemaker?"

"He was an immigrant from Fifeshire," Cameron said. "He was a passionate man and his tactics may not have been wise, but he was devoted to making this a better home for those who settled here. In 1818—I read this in an old copy of the *Gazette*—he asked the settlers . . . he sent them a list of questions: he wanted their ideas on how to improve life in Upper Canada; he said he'd publish their answers in England. He wanted to encourage emigration to Upper Canada. Many were going to the new republic because they knew nothing of Upper Canada."

"Tis all very well," Roddie said, "but tis nothin to do with obedience to the Chief."

"If ye will listen, Mr. Roddie, ye will see it has much to do with obedience to McNab—and to his friends in York." Roddie sneezed, pulled out his handkerchief and blew his nose. "The settlers complained to Mr. Gourlay about the way the province was being governed; about the way the best land was reserved for the clergy and the friends of the Family Compact. He organized the settlers and planned to take their grievances to London. But Maitland—McNab's good and trusting friend had just been appointed Lieutenant-Governor—Maitland refused to consider the settlers' petitions. He had the government pass a law that made Mr. Gourlay's township meetings illegal."

"I still dinna see—"

"When this new law failed to silence him, Robinson—our sneaky and much revered Attorney-General—instructed a magistrate in Niagara to arrest him for sedition under an old law. The court gave him ten days to leave the province and when he didn't, he was gaoled for eight months. He was a broken man by the time of his trial at the summer assize. Of course he was found guilty and forced to leave the province." Cameron drew on his pipe. "Ye talk of loyalty, Mr. Roddie. This loyal Scot, who only wanted to bring the settlers of Upper Canada closer to Britain . . . this loyal Scot . . . the government—aye, Maitland and Robinson and the rest of their ilk—they persecuted him and drove him from the province. And tis *still* going on! This is not Scotland, Mr. Roddie. Tis no hope of rule by aristocrats here. There be no aristocrats. Not even McNab." Roddie sprung to his feet.

"Ye should be ashamed, Mr. Cameron! Ye are a disgrace to the clan! Ye . . . the McNab *is* an aristocrat! He *be* our Chief! He is due our respect! Ignorant crofters canna govern. Ye would have us—" Elizabeth stepped into the shed carrying a wooden platter with cups of tea and a small jar of maple sugar. She stopped just inside the door. The men stared at her for a second—as if struck by an apparition.

"Ah, Elizabeth, you're a welcome sight!" Cameron said. He and Miller stood up. Cameron walked over to his wife and took the tray.

"G'day, Elizabeth," Miller said, tipping his hat.

"G'day, Robert."

"This is Mr. Roddie," Cameron said. "Mr. Roddie, this is my wife, Elizabeth."

"I am pleased to meet ye, Mr. Roddie." The crofter removed his hat and returned the salutation with a bow. "I will leave ye to your business; I have chores to see to."

"Thank you, Elizabeth," Cameron said. She tilted her head towards the men and stepped out of the shed. Cameron set the tray on his workbench and placed his pipe beside it. "Let's have our tea while tis fresh." Each man picked up a cup. Roddie scooped in a spoonful of sugar. "You were saying, Mr. Roddie, that I disrespect the Chief. Nay, I do not. But McNab makes it difficult to respect a man who persecutes his settlers."

"Wha—"

"Many . . . aye, as Robert says, *most* of us are respectful and loyal. Tis ingrained in us as laddies to respect our Chief. It may be the Laird's township, but we crofters did not come here to be trod upon as at home. You ask me to stop the disobedience, and ye hint McNab will reward me if I do. Nay, Mr. Roddie, I will not become McNab's toady, he already has enough toadies."

"Who is ye—"

"The Laird himself can stop the disobedience. Treat the men with the same respect he would like shown himself. Tis the golden rule, and tis a good rule to live by." The men remained standing; Miller and Cameron sipped their tea. Roddie appeared to be groping for a response. Then the slits of his eyes opened wide, as if the appropriate rebuttal suddenly dawned on him.

"Ye talk of the troublemaker, Gourlay," he said. "I think the Reverend Strachan knows best, even if he be Church of England. The Chief told me the Reverend says some is born to rule and some is born to obey. Tis only natural."

"The Reverend Strachan is a pompous ass," Cameron said. "I have read some of his writing. He abandoned his Presbyterian faith and is insulting to those of other faiths. He and Robinson and the other arrogant fools in the Family Compact believe ye can impose home rule in the colony. Nay, it canna be done, neither British rule nor Scottish feudalism."

"Tis heresy, Mr. Cameron," Roddie said. "But ye's a stubborn cuss. Tis no reasonin with ye. I'll tell the Laird ye canna be trusted. Ye will rue the day." The men set their cups down on the tray. Cameron emptied the smouldering tobacco from his pipe by knocking the bowl on the side of his workbench. "Thank the missus for the tea, twas refreshing." Cameron nodded. Roddie glanced at Miller, who shrugged. The Laird's adherent stepped out of the shed.

"You're being foolish, Donald," Miller said. "The Laird is a powerful man. And his nature is vindictive."

"Aye, you are right on two counts: he is powerful and vindictive. As for me being foolish, I did not come here . . . *we* did not come here to be serfs. We could be that at home. As you said, the men are peaceful; we will take our grievances to court. But . . . I canna guarantee there'll be no violence. Scots . . . aye, especially we Highlanders . . . violence is in our blood. We will be patient; we will see what happens." Miller looked at the cradle and smiled.

"A new sap-trough! When be the blessed event?"

"We think tis a ways off; still seven or eight months."

"Congratulations."

"Thank ye. I hope he, or she, will be born into a peaceful community." Miller bid his host farewell and joined Roddie, who was already mounted.

As he listened to the horses' fading hoof beats, Cameron rocked the cradle and wondered: was it wise to defy the Laird? He had emerged as a leader, but he had neither the inclination nor the manipulative skills of a politician. What he did have was an uncompromising belief in fairness: a peaceful man who would not back down from a fight.

***

OUR GLORIOUS SUMMER is beginning to fade; the scent of fall is in the air and soon we will be cloaked in a splendid canopy of crimsons, golds and greens. Ah, but once again it saddens me to tell ye . . . the McNab is *most* distressed by the brazen insolence . . . the *contumacious defiance* of some of his beloved settlers. Sheriff Lyle has yet to serve the *capias* on the rogue Drummond. What effort he makes . . . And I was present when Mr. Roddie reported to the Chief on his meeting with Donald Cameron. I thought Donald a loyal crofter, but if Mr. Roddie's report be correct . . . I dinna care for Mr. Roddie's smarmy manner.

But then, despite the grumbling and fractious behaviour of some, we *are* making progress! There is much industry on the land. On my recent visits throughout the township, I was most impressed. Tis quite evident the settlers have persisted in their labours. This fall's crop promises a generous harvest to tide them through the winter. And a good many have acquired livestock, much needed to augment the diet.

It was during one of these visits I learned of the betrothal of Mr. Matthew Barr to Miss Elizabeth MacAulay, daughter of Mr. Francis MacAulay, our township's most elderly resident. I was riding near Dochart Creek when I came across the banns, the notice of their marriage fixed to three conspicuous pine trees for all to see. Twas delightful news! This marriage the first in the township since our arrival.

I must tell ye . . . the impending nuptials rekindled memories of my own star-crossed romance. Twas only months before our departure. I canna help but wonder . . . Her name was Colleen, her father an O'Malley from County Leitrim. We met at a social. Some of the elders frown upon the playing of the Great Pipes on frivolous occasions, but fashion is forever changing, and so I was delighted when the ladies organizing the gala invited me to partake in the entertainment. I first sighted her standing behind a table from which she was selling baking. Ah, she was a bonnie lass! Thick and tangled scarlet hair. Wild and unruly! She was forever brushing out the tangles. I often think . . . I tell ye, twas not only her hair was wild and unruly! Ah, but I didn't understand . . . I went up immediately and purchased a delectable shortcake filled with fruit and cream. I struck up a conversation; introduced myself; told her I was Piper to the McNab. She did nae seem impressed, and so I went on my way, wandering o'er the grounds and taking in the activities. Sometime later I saw her watching the stronger men compete at "putting the stone." The brawny man in charge invited those observing this feat of strength to try to better the puts of the strapping competitors. Alas, when one is smitten ... I heard the crack in my spine just as the stone rolled off the heel of my hand. Twas a sharp pain and I was unable to straighten up. She was at once by my side. She massaged the painful spot. She had strong hands for a lass.

And so, I began courting her. At first, we seemed well-suited. Twas not that our temperaments were similar. *Au contraire*! But we seemed to complement one another's differences. She had a fiery temper, like her father. She said she was descended from Grainne Ni Mhaille—"Queen of the Irish Seas." I'd heard of the legendary Grainne: a sixteenth-century lass who pirated three ships with two hundred men and led them against the English. I know my Colleen's mother, a Perthshire matron, was often distraught by her shenanigans. I remember one auspicious occasion when I was asked to perform at a friend's wedding. Tis a custom when the newlyweds enter their new home to break a cake over the bride's head—the lassies scrambling for pieces and she who retrieves the largest portion is soon to be a bride. My Colleen thought this a foolish and contemptible custom, but instead of standing aside and letting the other girls scurry for the cake, she picked up pieces and threw them ... nay, I still canna believe!—she threw them at the groom! I tell ye, we had quite a row over that. She said twas degrading to have lassies on their hands and knees scrambling for a dirty piece of cake. She said she would nae marry to become a handmaid. I dinna believe she understood a wife's duties in the Scottish clan. But I was

much taken with her charms. And I was in love! At least I
thought I was in love. I canna pin down the precise moment
my feelings began to change. But twas after a few months of
courting; I noticed an uneasiness; not in her presence, but
when I was dressing to call upon her. I would be walking to
her home—twas less than a quarter mile—and my feelings
would churn . . . from eager anticipation to . . . angst. And I
could nae explain these ambivalent feelings. We would play
with whelks and talk of events in the community. She would
serve tea and buttered bannocks. I would play a simple tune
on the pipes. She would stick her fingers in her ears. In jest
of course. She assured me she admired my pipes. What a
strong mouth to suck with, she said. I said, ye dinna suck, ye
blow! In this manner, we'd spend a few pleasant hours
together. But as I made my way home . . . at first I didn't
want to admit . . . ah, but there was no denying . . . I had
feelings of relief I could not account for. Twas no big spat
that brought the romance to an end. When the Laird
informed me he was leaving for the colony and wished for
me to accompany him, twas then I realized . . . twas like a
heavy burden lifted from my shoulders. Still, a twinge of
guilt. I should have explained before my departure. But on
reflection, I dinna think I ever understood my Colleen, nor
knew how to manage her. Perhaps no one did.

Chief McNab performed the nuptials for Mr. Barr and
Miss MacAulay. Not only does the Chief hold the title of
Magistrate, he is also a Justice of the Peace. Francis insisted
the marriage be on a Tuesday. Tis an ancient Scottish belief
that those who marry on a Tuesday will live a long and
happy life. Alas, tis not practical to carry out an elaborate
Highland ceremony in this wilderness. But we did make the
best of it! The livery colours of the two families were
prominently displayed on each side of the Clan McNab
crest. When Miss MacAulay, now Mrs. Matthew Barr, flung
her badge-plant of pine and cranberries to the guests

gathered on the banks overlooking the Ottawa, twas caught by Miss Adelaide Scott, daughter of Mr. Edward Scott and, I believe, a distant relative of Sir Walter.

We are still without clergy in this backwoods, so Francis, a devout Presbyterian, consecrated his daughter's marriage with this reading from the liturgy of John Knox: "The Lord sanctify and bless you, the Lord pour the riches of His grace upon you, that ye may please Him, and live together in holy love to your lives' end. So be it." Francis then led us in the singing of the 128th Psalm; the one that begins, "Blessed are they that fear the Lord . . ."

For my part, I had been practising tunes suitable for a wedding. I played "The Black Haired Girl with the Blue Eyes" and "Enlarging on Her Lover's Praise," before accompanying Arnold Miller, who is most proficient on the fiddle. Kinnell resounded to the joyful strains of the "Chez-mez Reel" and the "Homecoming Reel," although at home the latter would be played at the residence of the bridegroom. We dined on a scrumptious and plentiful meal prepared by the Laird's housekeeper, Miss Agnes Hunt. Our celebration was complete when the bridesmaid flung a garland of flowers around the neck of the bride. Francis then drove the happy couple home in his buckboard.

Twas strange; Miss Hunt was wearing a *mutch*. At home, tis a head covering worn only by a married woman. Alas, I dinna understand why . . . there be those who think it quite acceptable to take considerable liberties in this colony. Ah, but my heart is hopeful this delightful celebration be a good omen for our township. Twill not be long before the chill of winter is upon us once more. Aye, we *are* making progress! Despite the headstrong contrariness of some clansmen. And I know the McNab has not lost his resolve to found a colony of industrious Scots. We will persevere! We will persevere until the day we return in glory to our beloved home in the Highlands of Scotland.

PART THREE

FLAUGHTER SPADE IN hand, Dennis McNee was bent over, breaking up clods of dark earth, his backside exposed to the western ridge bordering his narrow croft. He didn't see the men coming over the ridge. Men brandishing clubs and unlit torches. An organized jumble marching with intent.

The Clearances in Perthshire continued to replace crofters with sheep. Two weeks earlier, McNee's landlord had sent notice ordering him to vacate his property. Although the *writ* was not unexpected, a surge of anger struck him with such intensity his steady hand began to quiver. He flung the paper onto the floor of his stone cottage and stomped off towards the house of his tacksman. He found the man in his barn tending to a cow in its stall. The tacksman heard the footsteps behind him just in time to glance around before McNee began pummelling him. The elderly and frail tacksman tried to ward off the blows, but he was no match for the younger crofter whose lean, muscular body stretched to just over six feet. The third punch broke his nose. Blood seeped into his greying beard and spurted onto McNee's jacket. Neither man said a word: both knew what this was about. The fourth punch caught the tacksman on the temple and he staggered backwards out of the stall. The fifth punch landed square on his jaw and McNee heard the unmistakable sound of teeth cracking. The tacksman went down. From the straw-covered, earthen floor, he looked up at his assailant—eyes pleading. The enraged crofter raised his boot above the man's chest, noted the terror in his victim's eyes, stepped over his head and strode out of the barn.

That evening, fleeting remorse discomfited the impetuous crofter. The tacksman, a cousin of the Laird's, was only carrying out his Chief's orders. The man also paid an exorbitant rent, his tenure on the land subject to the whim of his Chief. Flora McNee pleaded with her husband to abandon their croft, to take their seven children and resettle with other evacuees along the rocky coast. The headstrong Scot would not hear of it. He continued working the land cultivated by his father and grandfather before him.

Now, when he heard the approaching swarm he straightened up. The men halted some ten feet in front of him. The Chief's factor, who was holding a club, addressed him.

"Yez was givin notice. Yez was to be off the land nine days ago." McNee stared at him. "Yez assaulted MacLeod. Lucky for yez he be loath to bring a charge. Get the missus an young uns an be gone. Count yez self lucky to—"

"Get the fuck off me land!" McNee stepped forward and shook the spade in the face of his antagonist. The factor didn't flinch. He glanced at the posse behind him and immediately five men lit their faggots and moved towards the stone cottage. "Ye bastards!" McNee swung the spade; the factor raised his club to ward off the blow. Too late. The iron blade slapped him across the shoulder and he stumbled sideways. The other men surrounded McNee. A club across the temple knocked him to the ground. The men with the torches closed in on the cottage. One looked back towards the factor. He nodded. The man threw his torch onto the roof and the others followed. Flora opened the door; their eldest girl stuck her head through the window. Fire crawled across the thatched roof. Flora screamed and hastened the children outside, the older ones carrying the crying babies. The roof caved in, igniting their woollen blankets and heather beds. The flames spread like a wind-whipped bonfire. In only a few minutes, the blackened walls of turf and stone were all that remained.

"There be land for yez by the sea," the factor said. Clubs at the ready, the men had allowed McNee to regain his feet. The crofter stared at his smouldering home. Flora and the children huddled nearby, their hysterical weeping piercing the ears, if not the hearts, of their assailants. "Or yez can go to the colony." His business done, the factor led his men past the smoking ruins and on to the next burning. There, they encountered no resistance, the tenant and his family having departed days ago.

Evacuees who had dragged their broken spirits to the coast sent back stories of agonizing hardship: futile attempts to scratch out a living on the edge of a cliff; the soil so thin it slid into the sea, taking the planted seed with it. Salt water blasted the few crops that managed to grow; mildew shrivelled those on higher ground. Crofters fortunate enough to own cattle found their animals drifting onto the new sheep pastures, where the landlord impounded them. Fines were levied for their return. Since they had little if any money, mementoes were tendered as payment. Keepsakes treasured by families for generations were dropped, with tears, into soft, greedy hands.

But the factor was right: people *did* have a choice. Some refused it, many, reluctantly, gave in. Humiliating though it was, Dennis McNee swallowed his pride and asked the Perthshire Emigration Society for assistance. And so, like many before them, and many still to come, the McNees departed the land their ancestors called home for as far back as the family's recorded history.

JOHN DRUMMOND HALTED his mare at the top of the knoll. One hundred yards below, a steady stream of grey smoke curled from the chimney of his shanty. Behind his log house, a blistering spectrum of purples, reds and oranges splashed across the horizon as the sun retired for another day. Except for three hens in a wire coop, Drummond could see no signs of life outside his home. Isabel would be preparing the evening meal, the older children helping while the younger ones distracted their growling stomachs with one of their homemade games. As he had on other occasions during the past few months, Drummond walked his horse down the trail, alert to the possible appearance of the sheriff. Even though the Laird had no doubt issued a *capias* for his arrest, instinct told him Sheriff Lyle would not spend an inordinate amount of time attempting to serve it.

The survival skills he acquired as a lumberman had served him well as a fugitive. Throughout the summer and fall, he shot partridges, trapped black squirrels and feasted on plentiful berries. On his occasional visits home after sunset, Isabel filled his stomach as best she could from their limited stores. But when the icy temperatures and heavy snows of winter set in, his crude shelter afforded little comfort. Frosty nights beside his campfire listening to a wolf's plaintive howl gave him ample time to reflect on his situation. It did not take him long to realize his options were few. He considered returning to the Cambuse shanty. He knew he'd be welcomed back to work as a tree-feller for another winter. But come spring, he would again be faced with the inevitable. He did not have the temperament to be an outlaw. Fleeing had been an impetuous act. It was time to return home—regardless of the consequences.

***

LITTLE MORE THAN a fortnight ago, I had the opportunity to observe the manner in which our daily contentment is buffeted by events over which we have no control. On a clear, crisp, winter morning, having received word by post that the provincial government had extended his jurisdiction over the township until further notice, the Laird was, indeed, in high spirits. A few days previous, during an intimate gathering with a few clansmen at Kinnell—settlers the McNab calls his Cabinet-Council—he could no longer contain himself and, in a gleeful but confidential aside, hinted that this privilege would be granted. Now he had it in writing: in a letter from the province's Executive Council

signed by the Presiding Councillor, the Honourable James
Baby. The McNab told me this verification of his authority
will enable him to conduct the township's affairs more
effectively, although, except for our roads, I fail to see where
he has been negligent.

Alas, the very next day, still beaming from his good
news, the Laird was visiting me in my humble abode when
another correspondence arrived and was immediately
delivered by young John McDermid, a recent immigrant
whom the McNab has employed as his secretary. This letter,
too, bore the government seal. We were seated in cushioned
rockers on opposite sides of the hearth. I had begun to
disassemble my pipes for maintenance when the Laird
opened the letter. As his eyes moved down the page, his
complexion drained of colour and I watched his ruddy
countenance turn . . . how can I say . . . it became pasty pale,
like a still-warm cadaver. I knew better than to interrupt his
reading; I continued to pull through my pipes' drone bores
and wipe clean my blow-stick and chanter. Tis, perhaps, the
best cleaning they have ever had.

"The audacity!" The Laird pushed himself to his feet
and began to pace. "How cowardly! How reprehensible!"
His cheeks flushed the crimson of a fallen autumn leaf, his
leather boots thudded on the flat timbers. "The audacity!
The ungrateful audacity!" I tell ye, I canna recall ever seeing
my Chief riled thus. He paced back and forth across the
room, the letter grasped tightly in hand.

"If I may ask, my Laird, what news has so upset ye?"
The McNab came to an abrupt halt in front of me and thrust
the letter before my eyes. I hastily placed my pipes and
cleaning rag beside the chair and took it from his
outstretched hand. He resumed pacing and worked himself
into a rage, perspiration breaking on his brow. The writer
accused the McNab of being a tyrant; of ejecting him from
his land for no good reason; of being a cruel despot who

persecutes the settlers with the complicity of the government; of treating the settlers as no better than Russian serfs. The missive was unsigned and undated, thus twas not privileged communication. I did not recognize the handwriting, but I know that, under the law, the writer could be prosecuted—should he be discovered. The accompanying note explained why the letter displayed the government seal. The letter was not addressed to the McNab, but to our much-revered and honourable Lieutenant-Governor, Sir John Colborne, whom London sent out when Sir Peregrine returned home. Sir John, high-minded gentleman that he be, dispatched the missive to his friend with a note stating his outrage at such a vile communication.

"Tis libellous, seditious and treasonable!" the Laird shouted. He stopped before his chair. "Unsigned. How cowardly!" I thought he was about to sit down, when he turned and strutted the few steps to my door, only to turn around and march back to the hearth. "I will find him, MacGregor! Mark my words, I will find him! And when I do . . . he will pay dearly . . . his head shall roll for this . . . *this* inexcusable insult to his Chief!" I could think of nothing to say, so I said nothing. At that, the McNab snatched the communiqué from my hand, turned on his heel and departed.

While reassembling my pipes, I reflected on the McNab saying "his head shall roll." Tis how the clan came by its crest—a savage's head erased—and its motto in the Latin: *Timor omnis abestos*—Dread Nought. Early in 1613, Finlay McNab's son, Smooth John, retaliated against the MacNeishes, who had raided the McNabs. Smooth John had a well-earned reputation as a great warrior. The tale handed down says John and his brothers carried a boat through heavy snow and over a two-thousand-foot mountainous pass from the head of Loch Tay to the head of Glen Achern and down to the shore of Loch Earn. Tis an astonishing feat in itself! But then they rowed to the MacNeishes' hideout and slaughtered them. Tis said that when they returned to Eilean Ran, the lookout challenged John and his brothers to identify themselves and John did so by shouting out "Fear nought!" Then he removed a heavy sack from his shoulder and rolled out the heads of the MacNeishes, including the Chief's. That is how the McNab crest and motto came to be.

I am grateful we live in more civilized times. The writer of the appalling letter shall be punished—if he is found—but he shall keep his head. And yet, I canna help but wonder: what would possess a Highlander to libel and defame his legitimate Chief? To be a clansman is to be an honoured child of an aristocratic family. Aye, in the Gaelic "clan" means "children." Tis most upsetting that this wretched person has caused great distress to my Chief. He must be young; there is no gratitude among the young; no appreciation for the hardship of their elders.

A FEW WEEKS after receiving the anonymous letter, Chief McNab journeyed to York on township business. When I saw him again, the Ides of March were upon us. (Aye, I must confess to enjoying the Bard, even if he was an Englishman.) We were sitting in the living room at Kinnell, partaking of Miss Hunt's strong tea and delicious raspberry tarts. The McNab was telling me of his business in the provincial capital—something to do with apportioning the year's statute-labour. I was nae overly attentive. I do remember thinking tis time something be done about the roads. Even though most every hour of a crofter's day is spent working his land, some have taken it upon themselves to hack rough passages between concessions. Any means of being able to visit one another. Otherwise, the roads have seen scant improvement since our arrival.

When the McNab finished his monologue, I made so bold as to ask if he had discovered the writer of the anonymous letter. Just mention of the letter brought a flush to his cheeks. The Laird said his enquiries were inconclusive, but he determined it must have been Donald Cameron, because he was one of the few settlers who could read and write, and he had previously shown insolence and defiance. "He shall be severely punished for this cowardly act," he said, and then paused to wipe pastry crumbs from his chin. "I have ordered McDermid to draw up a summons. I will have Cameron before me to account for his scandalous behaviour. I will not tolerate this brazen impudence from these ungrateful recusants."

There are those in the township who would see this as persecution. But I fully understand the Laird's position. Our clan's welfare depends upon the McNab's authority. At home, when a Chief loses his authority, the clan falls into disarray and often disbands. Anarchy prevails, which causes much hardship and suffering. The McNab canna allow that to happen. Tis he who has the ear of the government at York; tis nae Donald Cameron. Thus, obedience to our Chief is paramount. He canna tolerate disobedience from his clansmen. The Laird is our protector and tis his responsibility to reward and punish. We owe him our devotion. Tis the way of the clans: an age-old tribal custom handed down over many centuries. I trust the Laird will deal with the matter and put this unpleasantness behind us.

Ah, but there be more unpleasantness ahead! Tis now apparent by her dress that Miss Hunt is in a family way. The child must be the Laird's; Miss Hunt seldom ventures out of Kinnell. Tis an indiscretion I can only attribute to the constant strain my Chief is under; the settling of his township a most onerous burden. The McNab canna make an honest woman of Miss Hunt; Margaret is still his legal spouse. I believe he asked for a divorce, but . . . ah, there will be gossip. Aye, much gossip!

**

AFTER RETURNING HOME, John Drummond remained on his property, ever wary of the sheriff's imminent appearance to arrest him. He and his oldest boy, seventeen-year-old John, spent their days clearing more acreage. They piled small trees and underbrush into heaps until several mounds dotted the landscape. Drummond knew smoke would attract attention—the settlers were constantly vigilant for fires— but the refuse had to be burned. Not long after the first stack was ablaze, his two closest neighbours, Lorn McCaul and Hugh Alexander, rode into the clearing. Drummond thanked them for watching over Isabel and the children during his absence and then asked if they'd seen Sheriff Lyle.

"Nay, I hasn't seen him in weeks," McCaul said. "But MacGregor says the Chief's still gonna have ya arrested."

"Someone wrote a letter accusin the Laird of persecutin us," Alexander said. "So now McNab has the sheriff gallopin round the township tryin to find him."

"I thought he was accusin Donald," McCaul said.

"Aye, that he is," Alexander said. "But ye knows the Chief, he thinks the whole township's agin him."

"Who wrote the letter?" Drummond asked.

"We don't know," Alexander said.

"I think tis someone who left the township," McCaul said. "There be plenty rumours, but nobody knows."

"Tis his own fault," Drummond said. "He treats us like criminals."

"Lyle's gonna show up sooner or later," Alexander said. "What is ye gonna do?" Drummond pushed back his leather hat.

"Isabel wants me to give myself up. She says I is no outlaw, and she be right. But it sticks in me craw . . . I didn't leave home to—"

"We knows how you feel," McCaul said.

"Aye, cept for a few who tremble when they hears his name, we all feel the same," Alexander said. "Can ye pay what ye owe him?"

"Aye, I can . . . but it sticks in—" From behind the back of the shanty, McNab and Lipsey rode into the clearing and out into the field where the men were standing.

"Mr. Drummond, I'm placing you under arrest," McNab said. "Lipsey, apprehend Mr. Drummond." The hunchbacked hireling dismounted, took the rope from his saddle horn, waddled up to Drummond and tried to put the lariat over his head. The burly crofter, towering over Lipsey, grabbed the rope and jerked it; the Laird's servant fell face down in the snow. "Resisting arrest, Drummond! Ye are only making matters worse for yourself! Mr. McCaul, Mr. Alexander, I'm appointing you temporary deputies; I order you to apprehend Mr. Drummond."

"Nay, Chief, I'll not be your flunkey," McCaul said.

"Me neither, Chief," Alexander said. "Ye is—"

"Enough!" McNab said. "Tis enough contumacy!" Having regained his feet, Lipsey gathered his rope and brushed the snow off his jacket. "Bind him, Lipsey!" The squat servant raised his rope and stepped forward. Drummond reached out, pulled the rope with his left hand and punched his antagonist square on the jaw with his right. Lipsey let go the rope, stumbled backwards and fell flat on his back in the snow.

"Ah, John, tis nae Lipsey's fault!" Alexander said.

"Ye is right, tis nae the poor flunkey," Drummond said. "Tis the tyrant on the horse!" Three giant strides and Drummond was beside McNab's horse. He grabbed the Chief by the cloak and pulled him to the ground. McNab lay flat on his back and looked up wide-eyed at the big man hovering over him.

"Nay, John!" McCaul and Alexander shouted. They pulled their friend away and helped McNab to his feet. The Laird quickly regained his composure.

"Ye have committed assault, Drummond!" McNab said. He brushed snow off his cloak and trews. "Ye shall pay dearly for—" Drummond stepped towards the Chief, but McCaul and Alexander stepped between them. "Come, Lipsey." The Laird and his underling mounted and rode off.

"That was not wise, John," Alexander said. Drummond removed his hat and wiped the sleeve of his jacket across his forehead.

"Ye can be sure Lyle will be here soon," McCaul said. "What is ye gonna do?" Drummond looked at his son, who had stood off to the side during the encounter. "Go an tell your mother to pack me camp . . . nay, don't. I'll not let the tyrant make me an outlaw agin. I'll not run."

WHEN DRUMMOND HEARD Sheriff Lyle and Deputy Maule ride up just before dusk, he met them at the shanty door— rifle in hand, the barrel pointed down. The officers remained on their horses. Maule glanced at Lyle, who took charge.

"Mr. Drummond, Chief McNab has issued a warrant for your arrest," Lyle said. "I order you to put down your—"

"Nay, sheriff. I'll not be leavin me family agin. Ye tell McNab to quit persecutin us."

"We have laws, Mr. Drummond, and the Laird—"

"The Laird *is* the law an he—" From behind the shanty a flash of reddish-brown fur darted between Drummond and the officers on its way to the chicken coop. Maule's horse reared on its hind legs. The deputy drew his revolver. Just as he fired, his horse reeled sideways; the bullet whispered over Drummond's left shoulder and lodged in the door frame. The crofter raised his rifle and pulled the trigger; the bullet caught Maule in *his* left shoulder, knocking the deputy off his horse. Lyle drew his revolver and aimed at Drummond. Isabel appeared behind her husband. The sheriff pointed his revolver in the air. Drummond lowered his rifle. The sheriff looked over at Maule, who had regained his feet. Blood was seeping through the deputy's cowhide jacket. The fox had disappeared.

"The wound need be bound quickly!" Isabel said. Lyle dismounted; he and Drummond helped Maule into the shanty. "Heat a kettle of water, Mary," Isabel said to her eldest daughter. Drummond ordered the other children, except for John, to play outside while Isabel removed the slug and dressed the wound. The crofter and the sheriff avoided each other's eyes as they examined Maule's shoulder and watched Isabel bind the wound. The shot had not done as much damage as first appeared.

When Isabel finished, Lyle handed Drummond the *capias*, which was rolled and tied with a black ribbon.

"I isn't goin with ye, sheriff."

"I will not force you, sir . . . under the circumstances. I realize you did not intend . . ." The men looked at Maule. The deputy was hunched over on a wooden chair, his left arm resting on the table. Isabel handed him a glass of whisky. "The Laird will not drop the charges." Drummond stared down at the *writ* grasped in his hand. Then he looked up at Lyle.

"Where is ye from, sheriff? Ye is nae a Scot, is ye?"

"No, I'm not. My family emigrated from outside London. My father was a British soldier. We settled in New York State, Westchester County. But he was not happy there and we left. It was the spring of 1812. He was killed in battle at Queenston, under Brock. Why do you ask?"

"We come from the Highlands of Scotland, where our land was taken from us. We was sold a bill-a-goods to come here. We's only poor, ignorant crofters tryin to make a new life in a foreign land. We's all known much hardship an we sticks together. But we . . ." Drummond looked again at the *writ*; his wide-set eyes narrowed and glistened.

"I will give you two days to get your affairs in order," Lyle said. "The Laird will demand an immediate arrest, but I can forestall for two days." Lyle asked Maule if he felt able to ride. The deputy said he was fine. The lawmen thanked Isabel and left.

- - -

DONALD CAMERON AND the Laird of McNab stood facing one another on opposite sides of the long table in the living room at Kinnell Lodge. John McDermid stood to the side and just behind the Chief. The Laird began by reading from a prepared statement.

"Degraded clansman," he shouted, paused and glanced at Cameron. The settler tugged gently at his trimmed whiskers, his face blank. "The honourable Lieutenant-Governor accuses you of libel, sedition and high treason. If you show a contrite and repentant spirit, and confess your faults against me, your legitimate Chief, and your crime against His Majesty, King George, I will intercede for your pardon." He handed the paper to McDermid, who handed the Laird his walking stick. "File that under black sheep." The appellation caused Cameron to wince: he envisioned black-faced ewes grazing on the pasture outside his Perthshire cottage. "What do ye have to say for yourself?" Dressed in the elegant attire of a Scottish aristocrat, shoulders pulled back, broad chest and square jaw thrust forward, Cameron saw a Highland Laird clinging to the hierarchy of the old country; a haughty, overbearing manner that had instilled fear and awe in most of the settlers. The crofter hesitated only a moment before answering.

"I say ye are mistaken; I did not write the letter; I have never written ye a letter." Cameron folded his arms over his chest and stared at McNab. Both men were of equal height.

"Mr. Cameron, ye do yourself more harm denying this. Ye have the faculty of writing. Ye are the *only* settler in the concession who can read and write!" McNab paused, as if anticipating a response. When none was forthcoming, he continued. "I will intercede with the Lieutenant-Governor for your pardon, my man, but ye must confess, ye must own up to this reprehensible . . . this *cowardly* deed!"

"Nay, Chief, I will not own up to something I did not do; ye have—"

"This is outrageous, my man!" The Laird slammed his walking stick down on the table and emitted a hefty snort. He strutted around the table and into the middle of the room. Cameron turned to face him. "I will have ye gaoled in Perth!" McNab pulled a sheet of paper from his sporran and waved it in the crofter's face. "This cowardly . . . tis beneath . . . tis appalling . . . aye, tis *shameful* to the honour and dignity of a clansman to wri—"

"May I see that?" Cameron held out his hand. McNab thrust the paper towards McDermid, who retrieved it and handed it to the settler. "Nay, I did not write this. It says here he was ejected from his land." Cameron glanced up and caught a twitch in his accuser's shaggy, black eyebrows. "Ye have not ejected me. I am still on my land; still clearing stumps and rocks and praying crops will grow in the poor soil." McNab emitted another noisy snort.

"A decoy. Tis a decoy to send me off the scent. I have considered that. None is capable of writing such a letter. Of course ye would try to disguise your hand. Nay, Cameron, you are the culprit; tis quite clear. If ye will not own up, you leave me no . . . I will see you gaoled in Perth, sir!" Cameron handed the letter to McDermid. "Well?" McNab paused. "I am giving you one last chance." Another pause. "As your Chief, I command you to own up, my man; make amends for this reprehensible deed."

Cameron held McNab's stare and spoke very slowly. "I will not own up to a deed I did not do. You are harassing the settlers. These are honourable men, hard-working men, trying to feed their families. You beat them down at—"

"Very well. I see your spirit is hard bound. I suspected as much. I have it on good authority twas you who drew up the petition against me. Ye will rue the day you opposed me; I assure you." He turned to McDermid. "Draw up a warrant for Mr. Cameron's arrest." He looked once more at the settler. "Bring it to me to sign and then deliver it to Sheriff

Lyle immediately." The diffident secretary nodded and scurried out of the room. McNab turned back to Cameron. "I order you to leave Kinnell. You have one hour to put your affairs in order. Good day . . . *sir*." The Laird wheeled and strutted out of the room.

✻✻✻

I AM GROWING weary of these journeys to Perth. We forgo the better part of a day riding some fifty miles over poor roads. And when the Magistrate dismisses the Laird's case out of hand, as he did the charge against Donald Cameron, the journey is for naught. I spend a most uncomfortable night in an ill-kept room above a tavern, awakened often by the roar and ruckus of drunken brawls below. My Chief, as title dictates, rests comfortably in the home of a Justice of the Peace.

I thought the Magistrate, a Judge Nichols, newly appointed, was rather short with the Laird: he did not accord him the respect due a Highland Chief. The McNab usually engages Wilfred McRae to represent him. But on the date of the Assize, the solicitor had business in York. Mr. Cameron had hired—I believe with donations from his neighbours—he had hired the Honourable Jonas Jones. The crofter took the stand, swore the oath and gave his testimony, which was brief and to the point. He confirmed that he had seen the libellous correspondence when summoned to appear at Kinnell, but he denied writing it and said he did not know who its author might be.

Judge Nichols then called upon the Laird to cross-examine Mr. Cameron. The Chief rose from the table as if air was being pumped into his capacious breast, and in a voice I suspect any passerby strolling along Drummond Street could hear, he asked the witness if he could read and write, to which Mr. Cameron replied in the affirmative.

"And are ye not the *only* crofter in the Flat Rapids' concession who can read and write?"

"I think I am," Mr. Cameron said. "I don't know of any others." The McNab spent a few moments parading back and forth in front of the witness, and then—to the surprise of everyone in the courtroom—he announced he had no further questions for the scoundrel. I tell ye, I was taken aback by the Chief's unapt language. I glanced up at the bench: from the Magistrate's grave frown, I thought he was going to chastise the McNab for his use of the word "scoundrel." Instead, he invited Mr. Jones to present his defence. This scrappy gentleman from Brockville served his King and country with pride and distinction during hostilities with the rebellious colonials in 1813. His be a boisterous manner, strutting before the court with arrogant confidence, presenting his short but compelling argument. Tis no wonder the people of Grenville have elected him thrice to our provincial legislature. The solicitor's contention was simple: there was no evidence Mr. Cameron had written the appalling letter. While that be true, officers of the court do not set a good example for lowly crofters when they mock the *writs* brought before the Assize. I overheard snickers and off-hand remarks that the warrant was "quaint" and "patriarchal." These insults seem most inappropriate. When Mr. Jones sat down, I thought Judge Nichols would render his verdict. But, nay, he did not. He called upon the Laird to rise and stand before the bench.

"Chief McNab, I am at a loss to know why we are here today," the Magistrate said. "But since we are, have you *any* evidence to justify issuing a warrant for the defendant's arrest and imprisonment? Imprisonment for *nine* weeks! And you denied bail!"

"He is an educated crofter, your honour," the McNab said. "He freely admits . . . his testimony before the court . . . he is the *only* settler in the concession who can . . . one of the

few in the *whole* township who can read and write. Tis quite
apparent that—"

"It is not at all apparent," the Judge said, visibly
incensed as he looked down at the Laird. "You cannot
assume a man has broken the law just because he is fortunate
enough to have some education. This is sophism of the
worst kind. You have been appointed an officer of the court,
sir. I find your language and conduct reprehensible for
someone vested with authority and responsibility. I trust
you will not appear before me again unless you have a case
with hard evidence."

"I would remind his honour that I am Chief of an
illustrious and distinguished Highland clan and I am due the
respec—"

"Sit down." The McNab's back was to the benches, but
I could see him stiffen as if the Magistrate had thrust a knife
into his side. When he turned to take his seat, the flush on
his face . . . twas like a man gasping for oxygen. "I find for
the defendant. You are free to go, Mr. Cameron."

I am loyal to my Chief, but I do feel there are times
when the Laird is blinded by his insistence upon justice. Tis,
of course, understandable. In his youth he studied the law
and was apprenticed to a solicitor for a short time. As
Patriarch of his clan, insubordination from his clansmen is
foreign to his nature. Alas, in this wilderness, clan tradition
is not so easily upheld, although that is clearly what the
Chief intends.

On our return journey, the McNab expressed
disappointment and what I feel to be a rather vindictive
attitude towards Donald. Truth be told, the man was only
defending his honour against unsubstantiated accusations.
But the McNab is convinced the literate crofter wrote the
scandalous letter, and he insists he must be punished. How
he intends to do that . . .

If the altercation with Mr. Cameron was not enough, Sheriff Lyle reports the rogue Drummond has disappeared again—this time with the wife and children. The Laird said nothing about the assault upon his person and that of Lipsey. I heard of this abhorrent occurrence from Hugh Alexander, who witnessed the incident. The McNab suffered no bodily harm. Twas his pride and dignity that suffered ignominy. I also heard about the near fatal confrontation with Sheriff Lyle and Deputy Maule. I am grieved that violence has poisoned our township. Ye would think men would learn from our past that disputes canna be resolved with violence. Nay, not a one! The sheriff says when he returned to arrest Drummond, the shanty was deserted—emptied of the family's few possessions. When I asked Lorn McCaul, his nearest neighbour, where Drummond had gone, he hesitated and then blurted out that he did not know. I am not so sure. I believe I detected an evasiveness in Mr. McCaul's answer. Ah, but the crofter would not be the first to flee the township, if that is what he has done. Others have quietly departed, reneging on their lawful responsibility to pay the Laird their passage money and the quit-rent that is his due. I dinna know what Mr. Drummond . . . does he think his Chief will forget about the assault—and the timber money? Nay, he will not. The McNab was most displeased with Lyle for not arresting the crofter on the night of the assault. Although it pains me, I have become aware of a spitefulness in my Chief that before was not apparent.

Ah, but all is not unpleasant news. We have had a blessed event! Two blessed events! Elizabeth Cameron has delivered a wee bairn, a baby girl, and Miss Hunt—some now call her Mrs. McNab—has given birth to a strapping baby boy. The Laird has named him Allan. *His* birth is the talk of the township! Some members of the Auld Kirk—

they be the God-fearing and righteous Presbyterians—have expressed their moral outrage and indignation at the Laird's scandalous behaviour. But others, those whose religious fervour is less binding—and less blinding—refer to the Scottish custom of handfasting. Tis an ancient tradition whereby a couple declare they will live together. At the end of a year and a day, if the lady fails to bear a child, they may part if that be their wish. But if the couple is fortunate and a child has been conceived, their declaration of marriage is looked upon as an acceptable and valid union. Alas, tis a most generous interpretation of the custom. The McNab canna marry Miss Hunt because he is still married to Margaret. Ah, but we will weather the gossip. The Laird has greater concerns than the sneers of the morally superior. My own conscience winna allow me to judge. Truth be told, my Colleen and I had many a romp in the heather. Aye, that lass could raise me kilt!

***

NEWS OF DONALD Cameron's acquittal spread rapidly throughout the community. The settlers were jubilant to discover the Laird of McNab was not omnipotent after all. Most didn't think the verdict a great victory, but encouraging nonetheless: one that revived their sanguinity and called for a celebration. On a sunny afternoon in early June, the pleasing warmth of a new summer hanging in the humid air, the Camerons' neighbours put aside their daily toil and arranged with Elizabeth to be at the shanty for Donald's return.

"Tis a fine day, Elizabeth," Iain Storie said. He and Margaret had arrived with a cauldron of boiled Indian corn and a hind of salt pork.

"Aye, Iain, tis that. How are ye, Margaret? A new bonnet?"

"Aye, Elizabeth, tis. I done the broidery last night. I hope tis nae crooked; the tallow hardly give nough light for these tired ol eyes. Do ye like it?"

"Tis very becoming; I must knit—" Just then the door opened. "Hello, Cathrine. Come in. How are ye, Angus? Colin, Mary, tis good to see ye. Are ye feelin yourself agin, Mary?"

"G'day, Elizabeth, I am, thank ye. Where be the wee bairn?" Their closest neighbours had been visiting often since the birth of the Camerons' daughter, but Mary Carmichael had been laid up with a fever and had not yet seen the infant. "Ah, there she be!" The women moved towards the corner of the shanty where Janet was rocking the sap-trough. "Ah, she's a dear one. A baby sister for ye, Janet! Put the kettle or smoothin iron agin the cradle, Elizabeth; ye knows till the christenin the fairies could snatch her for a changeling."

"Ah, Mary, we dinna believe in the ol superstition. And there be no minister to christen her. But never ye mind, the child be blessed, we will make do."

"Colin tells me ye named her Annabella."

"Aye, after Donald's grannie. I ne'r knew her, but Donald says she were a mighty strong woman." The opening of the door drew Elizabeth's attention and she went to greet Lorn and Jane McCaul. The shanty was soon crowded with neighbours and the pine table against the wall laden with dishes of fish, cold ham, salt pork, Indian corn, potatoes, yellow beans, carrots, cakes and two bread-and-butter puddings.

"Where be he, Elizabeth?" Duncan McDonald asked. He had brought a jug of brandy, of which, it was apparent, some had already been consumed.

"I spect he'll be home soon, Duncan." A short time later, lost in the rumble of conversations, his neighbours didn't hear the cantering hoofbeats of the crofter's horse.

"Tis himself!" McDonald shouted when Cameron entered the shanty. "Spake o the devil! Our hero! Welcome home, Donald. Have a toddy." Cameron waved his hat towards McDonald as he hugged Elizabeth. John and Janet threw their arms around their father, who gathered them in a long, warm embrace. One by one the settlers greeted him, saying how pleased they were he was out of gaol, how the Laird had been put in his place, how McNab wouldn't be so quick to lay charges for no good reason, how they were determined to keep fighting for their rights.

"Aye, tis good to be home," Cameron said. "Tis good to see you all again. I hope spring planting—"

"Ye showed him!" McDonald said. "We knew ye'd show him!"

"Ah, Duncan, dinna make more of this than tis. Tis but a minor setback for the Laird. I had time on my hands in the Perth gaol; time to think. I thought about the petition we got up. We must try again."

"Aye, tis a good idea," Storie said. "We'll take up a new petition." Expressions of agreement were unanimous. Almost.

"Lads, ye need to think . . . a petition will only raise his ire," Robert Miller said. "I said it before and I will say it again: he's our Chief, we are in his debt. And he is even more in league with Sir John than with Maitland. Nay, a petition will only anger him even more. Ye can be sure it will bring his wrath upon us."

"Nay, Robert," Storie said. "I used to feel the same. Tis true, he be our Chief and we owes him . . . we owes him his due. But we dinna have to put up with—"

"I feel no loyalty to the tyrant," Lorn McCaul said. "I agrees with—"

"He's a bustard" McDonald shouted, stumbling and grabbing the back of a chair. "I mean . . . a bistard . . . a bastard! . . . the Laird is a—"

"Duncan! Your language! There be ladies and children!" Colin Carmichael said. "I agrees with Donald; if we dinna fight him, he will persecute us even more."

"Tis the quit-rent," Angus McLaren said. "I has cleared near forty acres, but the soil . . . tis too poor; I canna grow nough to feed Cathrine and the young uns."

"Aye, Angus is right; this be a feast, a rare treat," Cathrine McLaren said, nodding towards the table burdened with food. "We lives on salt pork, Indian corn and potatoes. I thank the Almighty for our Bessie; at least the children has milk. But there be no crop left to pay the Laird his due."

"What would ye say in the petition, Donald?" Margaret Storie asked.

"The same as the first one; what Angus and Cathrine just said. The land is not what we were promised and we canna pay the quit-rent and we want our bonds and tickets cancelled."

"Ye think the Laird is going to let you live on *his* land without paying rent?" Miller said. "Ye are dreaming."

"Nay, we will pay rent, God willing," Cameron said. "But what is reasonable for the land."

"We should take an official name," Hugh Alexander said. "They is impressed in York if ye has an official name."

"A splendid idea, Hugh," Cameron said. "What shall it be?"

"The Scallags of McNab," McDonald said. A few crofters sniggered; others stared at their neighbour.

"You're drunk, Duncan," Angus McLaren said. "I say we call ourselves The Friendly Society of McNab. We want Sir John to listen to our concerns; we dinna want him to turn agin us."

"Aye, Angus, The Friendly Society of McNab would be a fitting name," Cameron said.

"Tell him we'll move to America," McDonald said. "We'll become repubs . . . republicas . . . repoos . . . Americans! Tell Colborne we'll become Americans!"

"Sit doon, Duncan, before ye fall doon," McLaren said, taking the crofter by the arm and guiding him to a chair.

"Men!" Cameron paused until he had everyone's attention. "The wives have prepared a feast. Enough talk of the Laird. We should not allow him to spoil our victory— small as it may be."

"Aye, Donald, lad, ye is right agin," Storie said. "We should nae allow the tyrant to spoil your homecoming."

"Tomorrow we will get up a new petition," Cameron said. "Today we will celebrate this small victory as a new beginning."

***

MY PAST HAS caught up with me! I canna believe . . . my Colleen be only a few miles away! In Pakenham Township. Tis a settlement of Irish. I made the discovery . . . tis a great surprise! Ah, my heart . . . I didn't know . . . I received the news from Andrew Richey, a Pakenham Magistrate who was visiting the Laird. He was telling the McNab about the arrival of new settlers in his township. When he mentioned the name "O'Malley," I asked and . . . twas no doubt he was describing my Colleen. Mr. Richey said she arrived alone. The men built her shanty. Ah, she would charm them into doing so, if need be. Tis a shock! My skin shivers when I think . . . there be a weight in my stomach . . . as if I'd swallowed a stone. Tis quite likely she knows I am settled nearby; the Laird's letters home, the word would spread to . . . our parting was . . . I should not have left without . . . ah, tis in the past. I will visit. We are having a glorious summer. Nay, nay, I dinna wish to rekindle the romance, but my curiosity . . . it winna allow me to . . . ah, she was a bonnie lass, a bonnie Irish lass . . . full of the mischief! But what brings her to the colony? And alone. My curiosity . . . I must know. Tis too late to venture out today. I will wait till morning, get an early start. I will ask Lipsey to saddle Nellie and I will ride to Pakenham.

I HAVE SEEN my Colleen! Ah, tis a sad story. Last year her father and mother were boating on the Firth of Tay—tis an inlet from the North Sea—when a violent storm erupted. Both drowned. The tragedy . . . of course, tis only natural . . . the loss of her beloved parents has taken a toll; her blue eyes misty as the morning dew. She greeted me with much kindness, a warm smile and a generous hug. But, as ye would expect, there is a lingering melancholy. She said she did not realize I was so close at hand until her arrival in Pakenham when someone told her McNab was adjacent. She talked incessantly about her parents. Her many friends in Perthshire would have been supportive, but . . . twas as if she had a compelling need to unburden her soul to me. I listened, consoled her as best I could; told her about life in McNab; about my duties as Piper, limited though they be; about the Laird and Miss Hunt, who is again in a family way; about the unrest and agitation among the settlers. We reminisced about the delightful times we had had together. The hours flew by, her spirit lifted, some of the cheerfulness I knew so well returned. Ah, but tis not surprising; she was always a resilient lass.

She said her decision to emigrate was a hasty one. When someone told her a ship was about to sail for the colony . . . twas an impetuous decision, but tis her nature. Twas surprising she was located. I told her the McNab will not locate single females. He says the government forbids it. She said Mr. Peter Robinson—tis he who founded Pakenham Township—located her and said not a word about her unmarried state. Ah, but Mr. Robinson is Commissioner of

Crown Lands and the brother of John Beverly, who has been appointed Chief Justice of the Court of King's Bench. The men built her a shanty and are helping her clear the land. She introduced me to many of them. Twas evident that at least one Irish is intent upon sparking her. I canna deny a pang of jealousy.

As I rode home—tis little over an hour's ride—I felt light in the saddle. Tis something because I have filled out in the midriff, a slight paunch perceptible on my stocky frame. But twas a temperate summer's day with a gentle breeze. Even our appalling roads did not irritate me. On my departure, my Colleen . . . aye, I still think of her as *my* Colleen, she made me promise to visit again soon. I promised, but I dinna want to rekindle . . . ah, tis no use, as soon as I saw her my heart swelled, and when she told of her great tragedy . . . when I saw the sadness in those blue eyes . . . aye, I will visit again soon—very soon.

***

FIVE WEEKS AFTER his homecoming, Donald Cameron sent the new petition to York. It met the same fate as the first one. It was ignored. Or perhaps it was just misplaced among numerous other petitions. Lieutenant-Governor Colborne and the Legislative Assembly were being inundated with petitions opposing Bishop John Strachan's prolonged and unrelenting attempt to establish the Church of England as the official church in Upper Canada. Had concern for their physical survival not overshadowed their spiritual needs, this, too, would have stuck in the craw of the McNab settlers. Some adhered to their strict religious upbringing, others were more lax; but, with few exceptions, all were Presbyterians—albeit without benefit of clergy.

While most settlers were willing to sign petitions—put their mark on them, since most could neither read nor write—a good many thought it a waste of time to appeal to the oligarchy known as the Family Compact. Political gamesmanship was superfluous to men whose days were consumed with the arduous task of cultivating their cleared fields, repairing their austere dwellings and tending to undernourished livestock—as well as to undernourished women and children. Many crofters had quit clearing more of their acreage: to do so would only add to the number of bushels they'd owe in quit-rent. A few discouraged souls broke under the yoke of helotism and followed John Drummond's example: they abandoned their lots and surreptitiously moved their families to nearby Beckwith or Fitzroy townships.

But under Donald Cameron's restrained but steadfast leadership, the settlers at Flat Rapids refused to give up. They continued to work their land as best they could. None had paid quit-rent—not a bushel. Every now and then McNab threatened to evict them; they kept constant vigil for the sheriff or bailiff. The threats, however, were mere bravado: the Laird's time was taken with more pressing concerns. To meet the government's expectations, McNab had to continually increase the township's population. He wrote to Dr. Buchanan requesting more families. When news reached Perthshire as to how his cousin was treating the emigrants, the principled doctor refused the request. The Laird had no choice but to journey to the port of Montreal where he met incoming ships and delivered elegant and convincing dissertations on the benefits of settling in his township. McNab's charming manner and persuasive rhetoric convinced many newcomers to take up his offer.

As summer gave way to fall, fall to the first snows of winter, the frustrated crofters waited patiently for a response. When it became apparent they were not going to receive one, Donald Cameron organized another petition.

McNab, 11ᵗʰ December, 1830

To His Excellency, Sir John Colborne,
Lieutenant-Governor of the Province of Upper
Canada:

<u>The Petition of the Undersigned Humbly Sheweth:</u>

Your Petitioners beg leave to address
your Excellency again with regard to an
answer to our Petition of July last. Your
Petitioners waited with patience expecting
an answer, and as we received no answer,
we thought that our grievous case had been
forgotten, and used the freedom of
addressing your Excellency a second time.
Several individuals of our Society made an
offer to McNab of £10 for each Individual or
Interest until we could pay him, which he
refused. May it therefore please your
Excellency to take our case unto your most
gracious consideration and take our
Humble Petition under your Excellency's
protection and deliver us from the last
remains of a Feudal system. God forbid that
true & loyal subjects should be under the
painful necessity of seeking an asylum under
a Republican Government. May your
Excellency return a favourable answer.
As in duty bound, your humble
petitioners will ever pray, &c.,

Donald Cameron & members of
The Friendly Society of McNab

This time the government responded. Or perhaps the
politicians were responding to the concern of the Home

Office that the influx of Loyalists from the United States was endangering the "Britishness" of Upper Canada. Whichever, the veiled threat that the colony might lose British subjects to the expanding republic tweaked the noses of Colborne and the Executive Council. The following spring, the Lieutenant-Governor appointed Arnold Hanson, Crown Lands Agent for Newcastle District, to investigate the settlers' complaints.

"I see what you mean, Mr. Cameron," Hanson said, as he watched a handful of sandy earth slip through his fingers. The two men were standing in the crofter's field, about fifty yards from his shanty. "Yes, the quality is quite inferior to what I've seen in other townships."

"There are some lots . . . the soil is much better," Cameron said. "But for many of us . . . especially here in Flat Rapids, we . . . tis simply not possible—"

"Yes, I can see that. I assure you my report . . . the Laird has been most co-operative with my investigation. He even offered to accompany me, but I thought it best . . . I thought his presence might inhibit the settlers in answering my questions."

"Aye, twould that for sure!"

"You're certainly not as far advanced as other townships; even those settled quite recently. I can see . . . as you say . . . at least for some of you it's not possible . . . or very difficult to pay your rent." The men walked back to the shanty where the agent's mare was tethered. "I will speak to more of your neighbours before submitting my report to the commissioner."

"I thank ye for your time, Mr. Hanson."

"I thank you for *your* time, Mr. Cameron—and your co-operation."

"I guess we can only hope York will see fit to address our concerns."

"I will submit my report, but I cannot promise what action the government will take—if any."

"Aye, I understand, sir." The agent mounted his horse and Cameron gave him directions to Lorn McCaul's.

When he had completed his inspection, Hanson recommended to Chief McNab that the settlers' quit-rent be reduced to a half-bushel per cleared acre. The Laird agreed to the proposal. Hanson then reported to Commissioner Robinson. A few months later, Colborne and the Executive Council endorsed the recommendation. To them, it was simply a personal agreement between the settlers and McNab.

"Tis at least a wee a victory," Iain Storie said to Cameron. It was a rustic, autumn afternoon when the courier delivered the post from York. The crofters were in Cameron's field harvesting his paltry crop of turnips.

"Aye, tis." Cameron scanned the single sheet of paper for the third time.

"Ye seems troubled."

"Nay, tis, as you say, a wee victory. But . . . just now it come to me . . . we were so concerned about the quit-rent, we forgot to ask about timber rights."

"Ah, I never thought—"

"No matter; tis another small victory to build on. We'll call a meeting to tell the others. The day is getting on; I would like to clear this acre before sunset."

"Aye, then tis best we get at er." The men began digging with their hoes. "Do ya really think twill make a difference?"

"I don't know." Cameron paused. "Nay, I don't know, but tis our only hope at present. At least we have their attention in York. Tis going to take patience, Iain. Let's see how McNab responds to the government order."

***

TIS AN ATTITUDE I have long observed in Chief McNab: he
be a staunch believer in the rule of law. When some
scoundrel fails to meet his legal obligations, the Laird has
stated unequivocally that the rule of law must prevail if we
are to be a community of civilized men. I must say I agree,
although I do believe leniency appropriate under some
circumstances. I am reminded of this because this morning a
man arrived on horseback just as I began the short walk
from my cottage to Kinnell. As I entered the living room, I
caught only the last few words of what the Chief was
saying—something about "bringing the scoundrels to
justice."

"The *writs* will be served, Chief, you can be assured of
that," the gentleman said in response. The Laird introduced
him as a Mr. Anthony Wiseman, an official from the office
of the Honourable Henry John Boulton, appointed
Attorney-General when Mr. Robinson ascended to the
position of Chief Justice. "I thank you for your hospitality,
but I have a full day's work ahead." At that he placed his cup
and saucer on the table and stood up. "If your guide is ready,
I should like to begin this rather unpleasant duty."

"Where is Lipsey?" the Chief wondered aloud just as
his bedraggled factotum entered the room. "Ah, there you
are, Lipsey." The poor soul is rather slow-witted. He
clutched his bonnet and near stumbled with an awkward
bow when the Laird introduced him to the government
agent. A short time later the men left and then, like an actress
waiting off-stage, Miss Hunt entered carrying little wee
Kitty. Aye, the Laird and Miss Hunt are proud parents of a
second bairn. And a beautiful child she be. "Would ye like
to hold her, MacGregor?" I took the McNab's question to
be more a command than a query. I am always a touch
nervous when holding a wee one, but I cradled her in my
arms and she stared up at me with her limpid, hazel eyes. I
inquired as to young Allan's whereabouts and the Laird

informed me his son was visiting the children of the Fishers.
Peter is one of the Chief's Cabinet-Council. Miss Hunt went
to fetch more coffee and cake. I was much relieved when she
returned and took Kitty from my tentative embrace. When
mother and child departed, the McNab and I sat down and
he explained the purpose of Mr. Wiseman's visit.

"I shall see those black sheep in court," he said. I had
near forgotten about the six who put up Mr. Carmichael's
bail those several years past. Twas the time the crofter was
gaoled for leaving the township after the McNab had denied
him permission. He had not pursued the matter since the
Alex Yulle fiasco, but the Laird does not forget a
transgression. Time should not lessen the pursuit of justice.
And now, these many years after they have settled their land,
their passage money is due. And they are in arrears with
their quit-rent. "They will rue the day they showed
disrespect to their Chief."

I thought it best to change the subject. I asked about the
Buchanans: two gentlemen he had met only three days
previous while recruiting new settlers in Montreal. Twas a
propitious query: the Chief's countenance brightened
considerably. He said the two brothers, George and
Andrew, are fine upstanding gentlemen who will make an
excellent addition to his township and a considerable
contribution. The McNab is not one to speculate with
regard to wealth, but he implied that the Buchanans brought
capital with them and were prepared to build a much-
needed sawmill at the mouth of the Madawaska.

"And we have made a most delightful discovery!" I
looked at the Laird with what, I'm sure, was a quizzical
expression. As usual, he paused to dramatize his
announcement. Tis a habit I find annoying, but . . . that is the
Chief. "We are distantly related; they are cousins, or perhaps
second cousins, of Dr. Buchanan. They, too, are of the
House of Arnprior!" I said, that is wonderful news my

Laird. "I have not had an opportunity to inform you; business has so occupied my time since returning from Montreal, but I am planning a *soiree* to officially welcome the Buchanans." Ah, this news was joy to my ears. I revel in every opportunity to don my finest Highland garb and perform the glorious music of my beloved Scotland.

***

LORN MCCAUL PLACED a winch under a boulder at the edge of his cleared acreage and almost had the obstruction hoisted out of its hole when a horse's whinny disturbed the still summer air. The overhead sun told him it was noon, the time of day his neighbours would be working their land—not visiting. He let go the rope and the boulder slipped comfortably back into its resting place. He straightened his aching back and cocked an ear. Moments later he heard the distant neighing of the horse a second time. Somehow he knew—his instinct told him it was the process server. Rumours had abounded the previous winter and spring that, come summer, with the passage money due for the bond signed in Perthshire, the Laird would demand payment. McCaul ran back to his shanty, threw open his trunk and pushed and pulled at picture frames, wicker baskets, crockery and various utensils.

"What be the matter?" Jane asked.

"McNab has sent the processor! Where is it?"

"What is ye looking for?"

"Ah, here tis!" He yanked out a dented old horn, rushed outside and started to blow. In Perthshire, crofters blew whistles and horns to warn their neighbours the evictors were coming. Now the blasts from McCaul's horn echoed across Flat Rapids and within moments the air resonated with the shrill of whistles, the blare of horns, the clatter of pots and pans and the ricochet of gunfire.

McCaul handed the instrument to his wife, who was standing in the open door. He scampered across the field and disappeared into the bush. Moments later Wiseman and Lipsey rode into the clearing and pulled up in front of the shanty.

"Afternoon, Ma'am," Wiseman said, reining in his horse and tipping his hat. Jane stood motionless and attempted to conceal the horn behind her back. "I'm looking for Mr. McCaul." Jane stared up at the processor. "Is your husband home, Ma'am?" Jane shrugged. "I have business with him."

"*Chan eil beurla agam*," Jane said. Wiseman leaned forward in the saddle and pushed his hat back. Lipsey's horse sneezed and the processor twisted his torso to look back at his guide.

"Do you speak Gaelic?" Lipsey shook his head rapidly from side to side. "You're from Scotland, aren't you? You must speak Gaelic!" The servant again shook his head, this time more violently. Only then did it dawn on Wiseman that Lipsey hadn't spoken a word since they'd left Kinnell. He returned his attention to Mrs. McCaul. "Husband, Mr. McCaul," he shouted down at the woman whose lips were pressed tightly together.

Jane shrugged and repeated, "*Chan eil beurla agam.*" Wiseman dismounted, stood before the aloof woman and peered over her shoulder into the shanty. Jane stared at him. Wiseman shifted to his left, Jane shifted to her right. The processor glanced from side to side before strutting the few steps to the corner of the log house. He looked back at Jane, who was following his every move. Then he continued around to the back. Jane looked up at Lipsey, who was slouched in his saddle. She thought she detected a grin. Wiseman came around to the front, having circled the shanty.

"Tell your husband . . . tell him . . ." Jane's sallow features remained immobile, her emerald eyes intense.

Wiseman released a deep sigh, turned away and mounted his horse. He tipped his hat to the woman and rode off. Lipsey tipped his hat and this time Jane was certain she saw the hint of a smile. The guide then spurred his horse to catch up to the processor.

∗∗∗

I SAVOURED EVERY moment of preparation for the *soiree* to celebrate the arrival of the Buchanans. Twas, indeed, a rare opportunity for such festivities. I canna recall . . . not since dining with Sir Peregrine in York those many years ago, have we had an occasion I looked forward to with such eagerness. I dinna mean to imply these gentlemen are of the same rank as our esteemed former Lieutenant-Governor. Nay, they are not. But when the McNab introduced them, they struck me as men of noble character.

I polished my black brogues to a lustre and pinned to my bonnet a sprig of freshly cut pine—the MacGregor plant badge. I took great care in hanging the sporran at the front of my kilt and my breast swelled when I tossed a freshly laundered plaid over my shoulder and secured it with the silver brooch bequeathed to me by my grandfather. Tis a large brooch engraved in the Gaelic with our clan's motto: *'S Rioghail Mo Dhream*. My Great Pipes—the pride of my life—I decorated with the distinguished colours of Clan McNab, dangling from the drones kenspeckle ribbons of green, crimson and red. On their arrival at Kinnell, I piped "Buchanan Castle," a most appropriate greeting for our honoured guests.

Both gentlemen were dressed in their finest apparel. George, the younger, sported trousers of soft cowhide, apparently quite fashionable now among our youth at home. The older brother, Andrew, was attired in traditional regalia: his clan's multi-coloured tartan set off this tall, sturdy gentleman's striking figure. To partake in the festivities, the Laird had invited his Cabinet-Council: the five loyal and dutiful men he has chosen from among his settlers. It was pleasing to see everyone had taken great care in their toilette.

Ah, the feast! Kinnell's mahogany table groaned under the weight of our repast. Miss Hunt adorned her finest linen cloth with venison, roast suckling pig, boiled leg of mutton, beavers' tails and fresh pike—the last caught by Lipsey that very morning. Just as we were about to be seated, the McNab bid us raise our goblets of Burgundy in a toast to the newcomers. Then Miss Hunt complemented our Lucullan banquet with dishes of steaming yams, yellow beans, braised carrots, squash and Indian corn. Aye, the Roman General would have been pleased! I knew, from having spoken to her in the afternoon, she had prepared my favourite dessert—gooseberry tarts, to accompany a pudding of bread-and-butter and, of course, a substantial rice pudding.

Twas a great pleasure to witness the men in such good spirits. Tis hard work settling this wilderness. It wears on the mettle. One needs to partake in an evening of gaiety to replenish one's fortitude. And that we did! The McNab delights in such occasions. Be they of humble means or well-to-do, loyal friend or stranger, tis well known my Chief be a generous soul, forever extending an open hand to all who arrive at his door. While the settlers complimented one another on the progress of their holdings, the Laird was most attentive to the Buchanans' news from home. Conversation at table flowed as freely as the good wine, which has a way of loosening the tongue.

" . . . the malcontents at Flat Rapids stirring up the others," I overheard Alex Anderson say to Roy McCallum, who was seated beside him.

"Tis Cameron," Mr. McCallum said, as he reached for one of Miss Hunt's gooseberry tarts. "He be their leader. Tis he who writes up the petitions."

"Aye, that be true," William Roddie said. He was seated next to me and across from Mr. Anderson and Mr. McCallum. I had been eavesdropping on Andrew Buchanan, who was seated to the right of the Laird at the far end of the long table. I wanted to hear his plans for the sawmill, but now I shifted my attention to the men seated near me. "He be a stubborn cuss, that one."

"He got Colborne to support a reduction in the quit-rent," Mr. McCallum said.

"Aye, but the Laird ignores it," Mr. Roddie said. "He only agreed to be rid of the agent, Hanson; he was meddling in township affairs."

"Colborne appointed him," Mr. McCallum said.

"Aye, but only to satisfy the radicals in the Assembly," Mr. Roddie said. "I dinna think . . . I think Cameron will keep sending their grievances to the gov—"

"Grievances!" Alex Anderson said. "What grievances?" I glanced towards the head of the table. The Laird, whose hearing I believe is failing, was engrossed in conversation with the Buchanans and Jack McDonnell and Peter Fisher. "These ungrateful wretches . . . they'd be scallags combing the beaches of the River Tay were it not . . ." Mr. Anderson glanced towards the head of the table; he lowered his voice, ". . . were it not for the Laird's generosity." He then began massaging his right thumb, a habit he has when agitated.

"Perhaps, Alex, but tis nae only the Flat Rapids' settlers who are discontent," Mr. McCallum said. "There are rumblings everywhere in the township. The grievances . . . I canna say, perhaps they are petty at best, but there *is* discontent."

"And Drummond," Mr. Roddie said. "I hear he has returned home, but Lyle has not arrested him. Why? The man assaulted the Chief."

"Nay, William, ye didn't know?" Mr. Anderson said. "The scoundrel has taken his family and left the township."

"Nay, I didn't—"

"Aye," Mr. Anderson said. "At least that is what Lyle says. The sheriff could still go after him, but . . . I don't know . . . I think the sheriff . . . I don't think he likes carrying out the Laird's orders."

"Tis his duty," Mr. McCallum said.

"Aye, tis that," Mr. Roddie said. Mr. Anderson drew a cigar from his breast pocket. I prayed he would not light it. Foolish of me. He lit the foul-smelling thing. Mr. Roddie got up from the table and we all glanced towards the party at the end. Andrew Buchanan had their rapt attention.

"We'd be more comfortable in the living room," Mr. Roddie said. We followed him through the short hall; I brought what remained of our third bottle of wine.

"What are they plannin to do next, William?" Mr. Anderson asked when we were seated.

"I don't know," Mr. Roddie said. "But they have the ear of the agitators in York: Mackenzie, Rolph, Bidwell, the Baldwins, Ryerson. There is even talk . . . foolish talk, but there is talk of the men on the Council havin to be elected. And now that London has passed the *Reform Bill*, I don't know what—"

The swell of voices from the dining room drew our attention. A moment later the McNab led the others into the living room.

"Ah, there you are, gentlemen," the Chief said. "Our ears caught your animated conversation; what subject has so engrossed your interest?"

"We were . . . we were discussin the progress of your settlement, Chief," Mr. McCallum said, somewhat hastily. "I must say that was a fine dinner. My compliments to the missus."

"Thank you. I will pass on your compliment. We, too, have been discussing the settlement." The Laird paused. I could tell his beaming countenance was due to more than just the consumption of wine. "I have an important announcement to make." The McNab was in his realm, parading his flair for the dramatic. He looked at each of us to ensure he had our undivided attention. "Perhaps MacGregor has told you that our honoured guests are proud descendants of the House of Arnprior." As a matter of fact, I had not. I said I thought it more appropriate the news come from the Laird. "I have suggested to Messieurs Buchanan they name the site of their new enterprise 'Arnprior Mills' after their village at home and in honour of their historical House, and I am *most* pleased to tell ye they have agreed to do so!" The Laird gestured towards the two men, who sported broad grins, although Andrew's smile was obscured somewhat by his bushy moustache.

"We believe tis a fitting tribute," George said.

"And a growing village should have a name, don't ye agree?" Andrew said, opening his long arms in a gesture of acceptance.

"Absolutely!" Mr. Anderson said. "Tis magnificent news!"

"Aye, tis for certain!" William Roddie said in that obsequious tone of his. After Mr. McCallum added his voice in agreement, a prickly stillness shrouded the room, as if further comment would distract from the Laird's proud announcement. I decided it was time to pipe up—pun intended.

"Gentlemen, if it would please ye, I would like to pay tribute to Chief McNab's announcement and to our distinguished guests. If ye will do me the honour, I have been practising a new *piobaireachd*; it would give me great pleasure to perform it for you." The tense ambience dissolved with enthusiastic "ayes" to my offer. While I retrieved my pipes from the table near the door, the Laird distributed the last of the wine. I positioned myself in the middle of the room before a most attentive audience, and the remainder of the evening was light-hearted indeed.

PART FOUR

BEFORE LEAVING PERTHSHIRE, Dennis McNee decided he would not settle his family in Upper or Lower Canada. Several years before, a cousin who had emigrated sent back reports that the budding republic of the United States of America afforded many more opportunities for the aspiring farmer. So instead of venturing west from the port city of Montreal, McNee headed south to the village of Berne, in the county of Albany, in the state of New York. There he purchased one hundred acres "in fee"—a perpetual lease—on the manor of Stephen Van Rensselaer, a retired army general who inherited a feudal domain along the Hudson River: land granted in 1629 by the Dutch West India Company to his father, Kiliaen Van Rensselaer, an Amsterdam jeweller and company stockholder.

The crofter's daily routine was the same as that of his fellow Highlanders in McNab Township—with one substantial difference: he did not have to struggle to grow crops in barren soil. From his shanty, he looked out over fields of rich loam capable of yielding an abundant harvest.

As at home, he paid rent; not to a tacksman, but to the Manor House in nearby Watervliet. But compared to the crushing rents in Perthshire, his annual dues were a mere pittance: a tithe of wheat, one day's labour with carriage and horses on the landlord's estate, four fat hens, and, if he sold his land, twenty-five per cent of what he received was to be paid to his landlord.

But McNee had no intention of selling. Each spring he added more ploughed acres to his croft—and Flora added another child to their growing family. The annual rents came due on New Year's Day. But after four years, he quit paying, as did many throughout the county. It wasn't that the tenants couldn't afford the grain or poultry, but after an exhausting journey with teams of horses over treacherous roads, they found themselves waiting in a convoy of wagons at the Manor House for Van Rensselaer's haughty agent to call their names. This infuriated the men: time away from their farms was time lost, and these obliging but proud immigrants were made to feel like serfs—the feeling many of them had left home to escape.

"I'm nothin but a serf!" John Shafer said to McNee and the others who were gathered around a campfire amid their circle of wagons. "Payin tribute to the Pharaoh! Fillin his lordship's storehouse! Pray tell, what does he *do* with all these hens?"

The first three years, McNee was fortunate: his name was called the morning he arrived and by mid-afternoon he was on his way back to Berne. But the fourth year, he lost more valuable time and incurred additional expense: he had to stable his horses, pay for a room and meals at the hostelry, and wait until the following afternoon to unload his cargo. He was not alone. Among those also furious at being detained were his Berne neighbours Lawrence Van Deusen and Isaac Hoag. Both men vowed they would never return and encouraged McNee and the others to do likewise.

On New Year's Day, in the years that followed, many of the farmers didn't show up at the Manor House. To their surprise, Van Rensselaer didn't send the sheriff to collect the rents. Their landlord had a reputation of being a kind-hearted, benevolent gentleman, but by not enforcing payment of the annual rents, his negligent tenants assumed he didn't care whether or not they honoured the terms of their leases. For awhile McNee fretted over possible consequences. But with the arrival of yet another spring, the remaining patches of snow melting away, work on the land pushed all other concerns aside.

A MUDDLE OF hoarse, leathery voices rippled through the cramped confines of Angus McLaren's shanty. As was now the custom each January, the men had gathered to discuss township business for the coming year. The government at

York had bowed to the Reformers' demand that officers for
the Quarter Sessions be appointed by elected
representatives. But York held a veto over those
appointments: agents of the Family Compact—Chief
McNab among them—still maintained control.

"I was talkin to a lad from Fitzroy," Hugh Alexander
said. "He was visitin a relative, and he says to me, he says,
'your roads is pitiful,' and I says, tell it to McNab. Tis a
disgrace for a settle—"

"Ye shoulda said, what roads do ya mean?" Duncan
McDonald said, twisting the yellowed curve of his new
handlebar moustache. "They is nae fit to be called roads."

"Tis first thing on my list before the Quarter Session,"
Donald Cameron said. The meeting had just elected him to
represent the township. "The main roads will be worked on
this spring. Tis for certain we canna go on like this."

"I wish ye luck, Donald," Angus McLaren said, as he
handed Cameron a mug of black tea. "McNab still holds the
purse strings and ye know Perth is gonna decide the statute-
labour accordin to his wishes. Aye, I wish ye luck, but I dinna
believe the election will make a difference—not a whit."

"We shall see," Cameron said. "We've made some
progress; we mustn't stop now; we must continue to press
the government to address our grievances."

"Would ye like a hot scone, Donald?" Cathrine McLaren
said. The robust, gregarious woman delighted in preparing
food for the meetings. To make room in the shanty, she had
sent her four children to visit the Alexander children.

"Aye, Cathrine, I'd be daft to turn down one of your
buttery—" Their attention was drawn to a commotion
outside the shanty. Shouts of "git along!" intermingled with
the neighing of horses and moaning of cattle. Angus
McLaren was the first out the door, the others right behind
him. Sheriff Lyle, Deputy Maule and seven bailiffs were
driving McLaren's cattle off the lot.

"Eh! What is ye doin?" McLaren shouted. The wet snow caused him to slip and slide as he ran towards the posse. "Where is ye takin me cattle?" Lyle drew his horse up in front of the crofter, cutting him off. From inside his buckskin jacket the officer pulled out a piece of folded paper.

"I have a *writ*, Mr. McLaren," the sheriff said.

"A *writ*! A *writ* for what? I has broken no law!"

"It says you owe Chief McNab 252 bushels of Indian corn or barley for unpaid quit-rent, and 120 pounds for your passage; the bond you signed in Scotland; passage for you, the missus and the young ones has been overdue for—"

Cries of "Hey! Stop! What is ye doin'?" came from the entrance of the nearby shed. The sheriff twisted in his saddle; the view of the other men, who were standing behind McLaren, was partially blocked by the sheriff's horse. They moved around the animal and stood mesmerized by the scuffle taking place before them. As the bailiffs hauled farm implements out of the shed, Cathrine McLaren ran amok thrusting a wooden pitchfork at them. The men dropped their bounty and raised their arms to ward off the blows. Finally, a burly man emerged from the shed, wrestled the pitchfork from the stout woman's hands and flung it aside.

"Place that woman under arrest," Deputy Maule said. He'd been watching the fracas from a safe distance. Her pitchfork gone, McLaren stood her ground and stared up at the big man who had taken it from her. Then, with both fists, she began pummelling the husky bailiff on the chest. The man quickly applied a bear hug and looked around for help. Seeing her subdued, another bailiff found his courage, grabbed a rope from his saddle horn and, with the help of a third man, tied her arms to the side of her body.

"What is ye doin to me missus?" Angus McLaren shouted. The settlers approached the melee, the startled look in their eyes declaring their bewilderment. "Undo her, ye heathen. Where d'ye get the right to—"

"Mr. McLaren, your wife has assaulted an officer of the law," the sheriff said. "I cannot allow this violation to go unpunished." Lyle turned towards Cathrine and the men holding her by the arms. "I am placing you under arrest, Mrs. McLaren. Take her to Kinnell; the Laird will deal with this." Two of the men pushed the woman forward.

"Wait!" Cameron said. He stepped to the front of the settlers and addressed the sheriff, who remained mounted. "Your men have suffered no harm. There is no need to arrest this woman. One of us will go to Kinnell in her place."

"That is very gallant of you, Mr. Cameron. But the law does not allow me to take another for the one who has committed the wrongdoing. No, Mrs. McLaren must answer for this breach of the law. The Laird is a compassionate man; he will—"

"Haw! Compassionate!" Duncan McDonald said. "Ye use fancy words, sheriff. Me thinks that fancy word means he cares. Aye, he cares for his friends; we sees that clear nough. But his crofters—us he treats like . . . like peasants! We is no better than Russian serfs!" McDonald's outburst provoked a dissonant chorus of barking and grumbling, but the men seemed uncertain what to do. Then Robert Miller stepped forward.

"Angus, perhaps tis best Cathrine go with the sheriff," he said. "I'm sure she'll come to no harm." McLaren sought guidance in the faces of his fellow settlers. None was forthcoming. A few men shrugged, all appeared astonished, as if they could not believe what they were witnessing.

While the crofters were distracted by the bedlam, Maule had ordered two of the bailiffs to hitch McLaren's sleigh to one of their horses. Now Lyle nodded towards the men guarding Cathrine: they lifted her on to the plank seat and scampered up behind her. With the woman secured between them, they began to drive away.

"Wait!" McLaren shouted. "She has no coat! She'll catch her death uh cold!"

"One of the men will lend her his coat," Lyle said, "if need be." By then the sleigh was pulling around a bend in the road.

***

THIS MORNING WHEN I entered Kinnell by the back door—my usual entrance in keeping with my rank—I caught a glimpse through the kitchen of Angus McLaren's wife, Cathrine, sitting on a stool by the hearth in the living room. I was delighted to see the woman who makes the finest scones in the township, and I was about to go over and extend a warm welcome when McDermid came down the back stairs and, in hushed tones, informed me that this gentle woman was a prisoner at Kinnell. I found this news astonishing until the Laird's secretary related what had happened at the McLarens' shanty. That is, he related what Sheriff Lyle had reported to the McNab the night before. I remained dumbfounded at the report of her actions. Perhaps tis understandable the woman would be arrested, but I believe the McNab might contemplate the trying circumstances and exercise a degree of tolerance. Of course he was not present when the incident took place. But a reasonable person could surmise that impounding a man's cattle and farming tools—impounding his livelihood—even if it be justified, might cause a violent reaction—especially in a Scottish lass!

I was mulling over whether or not, under the circumstances, twould be appropriate for me to address Mrs. McLaren when the Laird and his solicitor, Wilfred McRae, came down the front stairs and entered the living room. Without so much as *"adieu,"* McDermid left me to join them. My conscience nudged me to return to my humble dwelling, but curiosity—some would call it nosiness—is a shortcoming I have battled throughout my life. My attempts to curb this deficiency have met with little success. Against my better judgment, I cocked an ear to hear what was said.

"Mrs. McLaren, I regret the unfortunate circumstances that have brought you to Kinnell," the McNab said. The woman did not look up, but kept her head bowed and—I had only a partial side view—appeared to be shivering, despite the hearth's good blaze. "I canna allow . . . ye assaulted officers of the law; tis a serious matter." I had only a partial side view of the McNab as well, but I saw him pause and adjust his plaid, as if he was uncertain what to say next. After a moment he turned to Mr. McRae, who rocked his portly frame back and forth on his heels. He seemed unruffled standing before the woman. "Mr. McRae advises that you should be released." The solicitor hawked, as if clearing phlegm from his throat. He appeared about to speak when the McNab turned to his secretary. "Tell Lipsey to hitch the mare to the McLarens' sleigh." McDermid scurried from the room and the Laird turned back to Mrs. McLaren. "Lipsey will take you home." Without a word and with her head still bowed, the despondent woman rose from the stool, pulled her shawl around her shoulders and ambled towards the front door. The Chief and his solicitor pivoted slowly watching her go. Just then I heard Miss Hunt's footsteps at the top of the stairs. I thought it prudent not to linger, and so, quietly, I let myself out the back door.

LATER THAT DAY I rode over to Pakenham to visit my Colleen. I have been visiting whenever the McNab can spare me, and, aye, the romance rekindled as if . . . ah, I am a soft touch, tis no doubt! She opened the door of her shanty and threw her arms around my neck. I returned her warm embrace and twas then I realized that under her loose smock . . . twas *only* my Colleen! Her ample bosom pressed against my tunic and she . . . she is nae petite; I dinna care for a skinny girl. When her eager hips thrust against my sporran, I hastily pulled it aside and my kilt rose slightly. As she pulled me towards the quilted bed in the corner, I said, Colleen, tis the middle of the afternoon and she said, aye, that it is. The woman has a generous mouth and her tongue . . . tasting of butter . . . the thought of her buttered bannocks made my stomach growl and for a moment I thought I would ask . . . but only for a moment, because she had slipped out of her smock and was tugging at my . . . easy lass, I said, it don't detach! She laughed and snuggled down on the feathery mattress. Tis a hearty laugh, full of the joy of living. She is nae a Presbyterian, that's for sure. I hastily removed the remainder of my garments and we frolicked on top of the quilt. I canna seem to get my fill of her voluptuous body.

Afterwards, we sat by the hearth and she served black tea and the buttered bannocks that had intruded upon our lovemaking. Aye, she rekindled our romance as if the years apart had been no more than a natural interval, no more than a refreshing pause. Perhaps tis the new setting; I don't know how else to explain, but . . . I have no more misgivings. As I say, I visit as often as time permits, which is considerable, there being less and less call for my duties. The Irish lad who came courting on her arrival, she must have given him the mitten, for I have nae seen him since my first visit. Tis no doubt my imagination, but I canna help but wonder if my Colleen knew where I was before sailing from Greenock and planned to carry on the romance. Ah, such nonsense! Tis terrible of me to think such thoughts. Twas the tragic loss of her beloved father and mother that brought her to the colony. Then why the feeling I am not in charge? I have asked her to come and live with me in my humble cottage, but she says she likes her independence—no surprise—and is content on her small acreage. Tis certainly more fertile land than most in McNab. And the Irish are at her beck an call, always willing to help with the crops. Ah, but her dazzling smile could charm the petals off a petunia!

***

"I BELIEVE AND confess my Lord God eternal, infinite, unmeasurable, incomprehensible, and invisible, one in substance and three in person, Father, Son and Holy Ghost, who by His Almighty power and wisdom hath . . ." As he led the congregation in "The Confession of Faith" from the John Knox Liturgy, the Reverend George Buchanan cast dark, zealous eyes over the throng of Scottish immigrants gathered before him. Unlike his parishioners in nearby Beckwith Township, the people of McNab had yet to build a church. There'd been no need, since their numerous requests to the Glasgow Missionary Society to send out a minister had gone unheeded. To help quench their thirst for spiritual nourishment, they formed a township Missionary Society and appealed to the United Presbytery of Upper Canada. The Presbytery responded by asking Buchanan to journey to McNab every few months.

The minister was conducting the Sunday service in a new settlement west of the Madawaska River. The immigrants had named their virgin community Canaan— invoking the land God promised to Abraham in the Book of Genesis. It was a soft summer's morning: a torrential downpour the previous night had purified and freshened the air, the verdant grass still damp with dew. The neophyte arrivals gazed heavenward, gaping and gasping at the lofty forest containing them: the impassive trees, like Vatican sentries guarding nature's chapel, transformed the clearing into an arbour of devout worship. The minister rested his psalter on the high, flat stump of a massive oak. The settlers had drawn logs in front of the make-do pulpit to form rows of pews. Men, women and children sat upright with heads bowed, clasping prayer books in callused hands. The man commanding their attention was of average height and compact build, his black suit frayed, his white shirt immaculate. Sweeping one arm over his devoted flock, the reverend leaned into his scripture and his lucid baritone proclaimed the Word of God. ". . . for we shall all know Him from the highest to the lowest. To Whom, with the Son and the Holy Ghost, be all praise, honour and glory, now and ever. So be it."

The confession finished, the minister's daughter, Jessie, who often accompanied her father, served as precentor. Because a woman would not be permitted to take on this responsibility in the old country, a few disgruntled voices could be heard among the elderly. Miss Buchanan paid them no heed as she led the congregation in singing the One Hundredth Psalm: "All power is given unto Me in heaven and on earth . . ." In a book she would write sometime later, she noted that "tears flowed down the furrowed cheeks of hoary listeners, to whom the service and the language brought back vividly the scenes of their youth in Scotland. Heads white with the snows no July sun could melt bent low to weep silently. Every heart was stirred and every eye moist."

The service had drawn people from every part of the township, many risking their lives on a slippery barge to cross the Long Rapids of the Madawaska at Johnson's Rock. The settlers had been agitating for a bridge for quite some time, but to no avail. The Camerons, McLarens, Rosses, McCauls, Carmichaels and Stories were among those in attendance. Duncan McDonald, not known for his piety, had hitched a ride with Hugh and Kate Alexander in their new hay wagon. These neighbours had travelled in procession, crossing the river where it narrowed at Flat Rapids.

At the conclusion of the service, the minister baptized four young children whose parents he had examined and instructed on his arrival. Others sought spiritual guidance in coping with their daily trials, not the least of which was their constant struggle with the Laird of McNab. The reverend advised them to "bear up" under the burden the Lord had asked of them. As he recited John Knox's "Prayer in Time of Affliction": "Just and righteous art Thou, O dreadful and most high God . . ." Scottish peasants, inculcated with a strict religious upbringing, nodded acceptance of their cross.

At home, the remainder of the day would be spent in prayer and quiet reflection. Many still adhered to that practice; others relaxed their mores. They beseeched God to bless their labour six days a week. Away from the tyranny of tradition, they did not think that, on the seventh day, the Lord would mind if they put aside their cares and socialized with their fellow man. Stung by memories from their upbringing, but rebuffing the guilt cast by pinched frowns and glances of disapproval, those remaining bid farewell and a safe journey to those preparing to leave, including the minister and his daughter, who had promised to conduct afternoon services in adjacent Horton Township.

It soon became apparent why Duncan McDonald had roused himself to attend the service. Betty Frood, a young widow whose husband had succumbed to a fever on the voyage over, had attracted his attention. His courage bolstered by a few nips from the flask evident in his pants pocket, he sidled over to the log where she sat reading a book by the Perthshire poet, Carolina Oliphant.

"Tis a fine day!" he said, removing his leather hat. Startled, she looked up. "Ah, I didn't mean to frighten ye!"

"Nay, ye didn't frighten me." She closed her book. Her rubescent, oval face was bordered by a paisley *mutch* tied under her chin with scarlet ribbons.

"I'm Duncan McDonald from Flat Rapids."

"I'm pleased to meet ye, Mr. McDonald; I'm Betty Frood." The befuddled crofter twisted the yellowing ends of his handlebar moustache and plunked himself down on the log about two feet away from her.

"How is ye gettin on?"

"Fine, thank ye. I's livin with the Browns. Chief McNab promised George . . . my late husband, God rest his soul . . ." she clasped her hands and bowed her head, "he was promised a lot. Chief McNab says he's nae supposed to locate widows, but he says I can settle on George's lot—if I can pay the quit-rent."

"Aye, the Laird would settle a nanny goat if she could pay the quit-rent."

"Do ye think I'm a nanny goat, Mr. McDonald?" Betty Frood's impish grin surprised him.

"Nay! nay! I only meant—" Betty Frood laughed. "I knows the Laird, he likes his quit-rent."

"Aye, tis what I hear. The men's buildin me shanty tomorrow, if the weather be fair. I can only stay on me land . . . on George's land . . . as long as I dinna marry agin."

"Aye, tis the law. If ye . . ." He dangled his hat by the brim and swung it like a pendulum. "If ye needs help . . ." His sheepish glance begged the question.

"Why, thank ye. Tis generous of ye. But tis a long journey from Flat Rapids. The Browns . . . and my neighbours—"

"Aye! Good neighbours is best! Perhaps I . . . I could lend ye a hand on a Sunday. Tis not the custom but . . . tis not easy to hold to the old ways."

"Thank ye agin, Mr. McDonald." They fidgeted and feigned interest in settlers clustered nearby. Then McDonald shifted on the log and pulled the flask from his pocket.

"Would ye care for a nip?" Shock exploded from Betty Frood's violet eyes.

"Mr. McDonald!"

"Ah, I is sorry, Miss Frood . . . Mrs. Frood. I didn't mean . . ." She sprang to her feet and smoothed down the front of her long dress. "Tis good quality! I stilled it meself!" Her eyes and mouth popped open so wide, creases formed across her forehead. Then her angelic features broke into a broad grin.

"Ah, well then, that's diffrent . . . if ye stilled it *yourself*!" A lively laugh and her hand shot up to cover her mouth. She glanced around. No one appeared to take notice. She sat down closer to her would-be suitor. "But I dinna think twould be wise . . ." She again looked around.

"Nay, ye is right!" An agitated flush spread across McDonald's coppery face. He removed the cap on the flask and downed a swig. The cap slipped through his fingers; he bent over to pick it up and nearly slid off the log. Betty Frood laughed.

"We could take a stroll," she said, the impish grin returning.

"Aye! Tis a fine day . . . for a stroll!" he said, his voice stumbling in astonishment. They stood up. He slipped the flask back into his pocket and they walked side by side towards the perimeter of the clearing.

McDonald and Frood were not the only ones "sparking" on what had become a gloriously warm afternoon. At every opportunity during the past few years, John Cameron, who had grown into a broad-shouldered man of twenty-two, could be found courting Mary Ross, now a striking young woman of eighteen. They had excused themselves from their families, ostensibly to pick berries. Having ventured in among the bushes, their hands reached for one another more often than for the ripened fruit. But John and Mary's romantic solitude was soon intruded upon by the younger children playing hide-and-seek. And from the middle of the clearing they could hear the spirited grunts of their fathers: Donald and Walter had formed a team from Flat Rapids and were engaged in a vigorous tug-of-war with men from Canaan. Cheered on by those gathered round, the nine muscular crofters on each side of the line dug in with their leather boots. Shouts of "Pull!" and "We've got em!" bounced off the surrounding forest. The Canaan team was besting the Flat Rapids team—just another couple of feet— when the rope broke and the men on both sides toppled over. Everyone had a good laugh as the contestants got to their feet and slapped one another on the back. Donald looked around for his family. He spotted Elizabeth, Janet, and Annabella across the clearing where they were chatting with some of the other women and children. He began walking towards them.

"I has a challenge for ye," a raspy voice bellowed from close behind Cameron. He turned to face Charlie McNican, a barrel-chested, hulk of a man who had led the Canaan team. Cameron noted the sour smell of home-brewed *usque beatha* at the same instant a flash of apprehension surged through his body. His eyes were drawn to McNican's flared nostrils, the most prominent feature on his scoured face. "A wrestlin match, eh! Let's see whose man be strongest—Flat Rapids or Canaan. What do ya say? Will ye take the challenge?" Cameron was not opposed to wrestling; he had wrestled at social gatherings in Perthshire. But he remembered many of those matches degenerating into drunken brawls. He feared that might well happen here. McNican stood before him—sturdy as a primeval oak.

"I don't know, Charlie. Ye would make a worthy opponent, tis for sure. But I don't know if we have a man could match you." McNican's slack-jawed grin displayed a set of tarnished but remarkably even teeth. "We had a man, John Drummond, but he's left the township." Cameron tugged at his whiskers. "I'll ask the other men." He turned and walked away. McNican remained anchored to the spot, staring after him like an abandoned lover. Unsure of what to do, Cameron strolled over to the perimeter of the clearing where four of his neighbours were standing under the trees, shading themselves from the blistering sun. "There's a challenge to wrestle," he said to Angus McLaren, Lorn McCaul, Colin Carmichael, and Hugh Alexander. "Charlie McNican. If John were here—"

"Aye, John could match him," McCaul said. He passed a near empty bottle of whisky to McLaren.

"I don't feel good about him," Cameron said.

"He's a big un, that's for sure," McLaren said. "But I's no wrestler. Lorn, ye used to wrestle."

"Aye, when I was a young un," McCaul said. "I gets nough wrestlin workin the land, thank ye."

"I never seen ye, Donald, but I heard stories you was a good wrestler at home," Alexander said. He took the whisky bottle from McLaren. "If someone doesn't take the challenge . . ." Alexander didn't have to finish the thought. Scots did not back down from a fight—not even a friendly one. If the Flat Rapids' men did not take up this challenge, McNican and others would sully their reputations throughout the township. Cameron sensed the men were waiting for him to decide.

"I think ye could better him," Carmichael said. "The big uns is awful slow." Cameron's hand dropped from his beard, his shoulders lifted and he released a heavy sigh of acceptance. On his way back to where McNican remained standing, he dodged several youngsters bouncing in cotton sacks towards a tree stump where others were hollering for their favourites in the race. McNican and Cameron agreed to begin the contest as soon as both sides mustered their supporters. Donald walked over to where his daughters and a few of the other children had begun a game of *Peaver Lal*. He told Elizabeth of the match. She frowned. News of the contest spread quickly. Within minutes the Flat Rapids' settlers had surrounded Cameron. He looked back to where he'd left McNican and saw the Canaan settlers gathering round their man. Donald turned again towards Elizabeth; the misgiving in her blue eyes had given way to a steadfast confidence: she remembered watching her husband wrestle in Perthshire; watching him win most matches.

With the Flat Rapids' settlers trailing behind him, Cameron strode back to the middle of the clearing. McNican was waiting, already stripped to the waist. His opponent's arms, matted with hair and hanging by his sides, reminded

Donald of the image he had once seen on a daguerreotype of
an African gorilla. Cameron peeled off his shirt. Neither man
spoke. Both knew the rules. Surrounded and urged on by
their supporters, the wrestlers bent forward and circled
cautiously, eyes locked and alert, waiting for an opening.
Under the relentless heat of the afternoon sun, their torsos
soon glistened with sweat. McNican lunged. Cameron
sidestepped him. The crowd hollered for action. The
wrestlers moved closer, feet apart for balance, arms pawing
the air like mimes in slow motion. McNican lunged again, he
gripped Cameron's shoulders. Donald grimaced at the man's
brutal strength and recoiled from the stench of his whisky
breath. McNican wrapped his opponent in a crushing bear
hug. The Canaan residents cheered their man. Donald could
not break the man's hold. McNican expelled a loud grunt and
tried to throw his opponent on to his back. In so doing, his
grip loosened and Cameron, slick with perspiration, slid
down and out of the man's grasp. McNican's broad face
reddened. The wrestlers again began to circle.

"C'mon, Donald, the brute canna wrestle!" Iain Storie
shouted. "He's nae a match for ye. Take him like ye did at
home."

"Dinna pay him no heed, Charlie," one of the Canaan
men replied. "He's a scrawny one—and the Laird says he's a
troublemaker."

"Who is ye callin a troublemaker?" Angus McLaren
said to the Canaan man standing across from him. McLaren
had just opened another bottle of whisky. He waved the
bottle in the face of his antagonist and some of the burgundy
coloured liquid spilled on the ground. "Donald is fightin for
our rights and ye should—"

"Ah, shut your trap, will ye?" another Canaan man said.

"Who is ye tellin to—" The Canaan supporters erupted
into loud cheers. McNican had manoeuvred behind his
opponent and had him in a full nelson. Cameron's face

contorted with pain. He could not break free. But the lumbering Canaan wrestler couldn't throw the Flat Rapids' crofter, who had a slight advantage in height. Fingers entwined, McNican thrust down on his opponent's neck. Cameron was forced to stare at the ground and was about to concede when he saw the familiar stride of a neighbour who had elbowed his way through the crowd. With a swipe of his leather boot, Duncan McDonald tripped McNican who, feeling his feet going from under him, released his hold and fell to the ground. That provocation, fuelled by the day's consumption of liquor, turned the wrestling match into a free-for-all. Fists began flying. Grunts and curses followed. Bodies reeled and fell. Mothers gathered their children and scurried out of harm's way. They watched Cameron pull combatants apart and exhort the Flat Rapids' men to stop fighting. Cameron was surprised to see McNican doing his best to end the ruckus by lifting Canaan men off their feet and tossing them aside like branches. But the wrestlers had no sooner separated one pair of pugilists when several more began pummelling one another. In the midst of the chaos, Cameron and McNican bumped into one another. They turned face to face, blank looks of bewilderment registering their futility. They were about to be jostled by more whirling bodies when the piercing shrill of bagpipes blasted through the humid air. All fisticuffs came to a halt. All eyes turned to behold a thickset man of middling height positioned on a stump some thirty yards away. Attired in full Highland regalia, cheeks huffing like bellows, Malcolm Kenneth MacGregor flooded the clearing with the searing, full throttle roar of the pipes. The settlers gawked at the interloper. Then, blending the steady closing notes on the chanter and drones, the piper brought his piece to an end, lowered his instrument and stepped down from his platform. The throng, as if awakening from hypnosis, began moving *en masse* towards him.

"That is nae the way to keep the Sabbath!" MacGregor said, as the settlers drew near, a quaver in his usually stout voice. "I am nae a believer, but the Kirk at home . . . aye, the Elders would be disgraced!"

"Malcolm, ye are a welcome sight, laddie!" Cameron said. "We were just having a friendly match when some . . ." Cameron glanced around, but McDonald was nowhere to be seen. "Someone . . . I don't know who—"

"Aye, Donald, twas Dunc—" Alexander said, cutting himself off when he caught Cameron's "hush up" look.

"Aye, ye are a *most* welcome sight!" Cameron said. Just then McNican came up beside them. "Charlie, ye know the Laird's piper!"

"Aye, we met at Kinnell," McNican said. "Twas a rousin bit uh pipin!" He turned to Cameron. "I has another idea." Cameron looked askance. "Nay," McNican said with a hearty chuckle. "Tis nough of the rough an tumble. We has a piper, an I seen another man with a fiddle. Let's have a dance!" Boisterous cheers erupted among the gathering. A few of the more belligerent scrappers shot menacing glares and barked empty threats at one another. Their spurious honour was saved by wives and older children tugging at their shirt sleeves, guiding them to campsites, where they nursed bruised knuckles and jaws beginning to swell. The heart had gone out of the fight; a sense of "forgive and forget" spread through the assembly. The fiddler, Arnold Miller, was soon found, and MacGregor, who never needed coaxing to perform, returned to his perch. The musicians got the revelry under way with "The Reel of Tulloch," composed, MacGregor believed, by one of his ancestors. The whisky abstainers registered frowns of dismay as they watched men, bottle in hand, trying to bend an elbow while linking arms with a dance partner. Liquor splashed everywhere: on themselves, on the ground—and on their partners.

"Did ye ever see the like?" one of the Canaan women said to Margaret Storie.

Aye, that I have!" Storie said. "More times than I care to remember!"

"I'll no dance with ye, Colin, till ye put down that bottle!" Mary Carmichael said to her husband, who had twice tripped over his feet. "Tis a disgrace! Look at Donald and Elizabeth! And Hugh and Kate! See how lively they step!" Carmichael soon relinquished the bottle in favour of the reels and Strathspeys, as did most of the other men. A few settlers, while willing to participate in games, drew the line at dancing on the Sabbath. They gathered their belongings and departed. But close to one hundred remained, Duncan McDonald and Betty Frood among them. Both were the object of scornful glances from some of the Canaan settlers: McDonald for tripping McNican and depriving their man of certain victory; Frood for behaviour deemed inappropriate for a woman recently widowed. Neither gave a whit for the disapproval. They twirled each other to and fro on the trampled grass, generous grins openly displaying their infatuation.

As the day wore on, the dancing burned off the home-brew. And when the setting sun blinked through the tops of the tall trees, shifting late afternoon into a hazy twilight, the piper and fiddler put down their instruments, mothers called and beckoned their exhausted children, while hung-over fathers, clutching their heads and wavering with an unsteady gait, made their way to family campsites where they devoured the baskets of food brought by their wives. Revived by sustenance, those from afar bid farewell to their new acquaintances and loaded their wagons for the journey home. Those on foot, who had crossed on the barge at Johnson's Rock, prayed for their safe return over the hazardous Long Rapids.

Before his departure, Reverend Buchanan had appointed Francis MacAulay as Elder. Guilt is a potent incentive, so the township's senior resident heard little grumbling when he asked for donations to fund yet another application requesting that the Glasgow Missionary Society send out a permanent minister. The United Presbytery, fearful that people were losing their faith, had relaxed its rules and allowed Elders to conduct devotional services. MacAulay undertook this responsibility with great zeal in the weeks that followed.

Reverend Buchanan returned to the township in late August, at which time the faithful gathered to worship at the shanty of Robert Miller. Scolded for their sins and praised for their good deeds, the fear of the Lord inherent, the settlers raised their voices in humble gratitude for the fall crop now ripe for harvesting: *"O Lord God, most merciful Father and Saviour, seeing it hath pleased Thee to command us to travail, that we may relieve our need; we beseech Thee of Thy grace to bless our labour . . ."* And with the final "Amen" of the "Prayer Before Work," men, women and children picked up scythes, hoes, and sacks and tramped into the fields. As in years gone by, the yield varied greatly from farm to farm: those located on fertile soil cast grateful eyes over acreage bountiful with oats, barley, and rye, among other crops; those whose lots fell on dusty, rocky terrain gathered what the land offered—and were thankful to have neighbours who would share in their time of need.

***

WE ARE BEING pounded by the fury of a bitter winter, the severe cold and brutal wind relentless most days. I am soothed in fair weather by the translucent blue of the Ottawa, but when the north wind churns the water into white-capped mounds of dark foreboding, I canna help but long for the shelter of my Perthshire home. Tis only my Colleen that makes the winter bearable. I need only think of her lusty body next to mine, my head nestled upon her dimpled bosom. Ah, but we are miles apart; many days, travel is not possible.

Alas, I tell ye, tis not only the Ottawa being whipped into a rage this winter! Last week the McNab returned from another visit to York. That is, Toronto: our provincial capital has been incorporated as a city and renamed. To our astonishment, the elected officials have chosen the rogue Mackenzie as Mayor! There be no accounting for the actions of politicians! I regret not accompanying the McNab, but, to my chagrin, there is less and less call for ceremony on these visits, my services as Piper not required. The Laird says the government has finally granted him adequate money to build proper roads. Tis not advisable to contradict my Chief, but the House of Assembly appointed and then granted the two hundred pounds to three commissioners: tis they who are responsible for its expenditure. Of course, the McNab nominated the men; they are loyal clansmen, members of his Cabinet-Council. Ah, politics!—tis nothing but deception and manipulation.

A portion of the money is earmarked to build a much-needed bridge across the Madawaska at Johnson's Rock. The Laird is settling the southwest side of the river with new arrivals from home. Tis only natural they wish to become acquainted with their fellow crofters on the more settled northwest side. But unless willing to journey many miles out of their way to cross the river at Flat Rapids, there be no passage across, except a perilous venture by Indian canoe or barge over the Long Rapids.

Two days after his return, the Chief summoned the commissioners to meet at Kinnell. That same day I happened upon Donald Cameron in Arnprior Mills. He told me the commissioners had discussed with the settlers how the remainder of the grant should be spent. From my conversations with the Laird, I anticipated a disagreement.

Shortly after two o'clock, I made my way through the blustery snow and entered the lodge. Twas earlier than usual to partake of Miss Hunt's delicious tea and tarts. As I walked into the living room, the McNab's resonant baritone warmed my frost-bitten ears.

". . . and thus, my good men, we have at last—ah, MacGregor, ye are early for tea; please join us; we were just relishing our good fortune." The Laird was seated in his high-back leather chair behind the mahogany table. The commissioners were seated in front. I acknowledged their salutations and took a chair near the side. "I was about to tell my men that with the grant . . . aye, the Assembly *insists* half be used to build the bridge, and so I shall carry out their wishes. But I am most pleased . . . *most pleased* indeed that Sir John and the learned men of our esteemed government have shown great wisdom: they have left expenditure of the other half in my hands. I have decided to make much-needed improvements at White Lake. Not only the roads, but there are—"

"Excuse me, Chief," Peter Fisher said. Although a loyal clansman, I have noticed Peter does not kowtow to the Chief. He be . . . what is that saying? his own man. "We have discussed this with the men and we have agreed there are many parts of the township that need—"

"Thank you, Peter, but I will be the judge of what is best for my township. I will engage those negligent scallywags who have failed to pay their rents; they may work off a portion at Whi—"

"Excuse me for interrupting again, Chief, but Roy and Jack and myself, we were . . . twas us the government appointed commissioners and tis us who they'll hold responsible for how the money is spent. So we have decided to spread it—"

The McNab bolted from his chair and cut Mr. Fisher off with a honking snort. He fidgeted with his dirk and began pacing back and forth behind the long table. "Mr. Fisher, are ye questioning the authority of your Chief? Would ye have us abandon centuries of honourable clan tradition? Abandon honourable custom because of the imprudent and misguided liberties of this province?" The Laird came to an abrupt halt and glared at the three men. They remained seated, albeit rather stiffly.

"Chief," Roy McCallum addressed the Laird, a cautious tone in his voice. "Tis nae our intent to oppose your wishes." The McNab raised his chin and stared down his nose at Mr. McCallum, who glanced at the commissioners seated on each side of him. Then Mr. McCallum appeared to compose himself. He stood up. "The road to Flat Rapids be in dreadful shape! The same be true of the road to Goshen! The men—aye, and the wives—are in bad need of a gristmill! Tis a long, tiring walk haulin grain to Pakenham and back. The township—"

"Very well then, I see ye are pig-headed! Very well then, ye will get *none* of the money! I will return it to York!" The McNab stared at the commissioners. I'm sure he expected them to submit to his authority. Most do. Then Jack McDonnell, a taciturn man by nature, rose slowly to his feet.

"Chief, we know White Lake needs work," he said. His colleagues nodded agreement. "But *other* parts of the township are even *more* in need of work!" The commissioner paused, the McNab did not flinch. Then Mr. Fisher stood and shifted his woollen bonnet from his left hand to his right. He spoke.

"We are prepared to spend fifty pounds at White Lake if tha—"

"Nay, not a farthing! Not a farthing shall be spent! Not a farthing, my men! The money shall be returned to York! I appointed ye, my good men; tis on my authority ye hold the title of commissioner—at the pleasure of Sir John." The Laird was again pacing back and forth. "Had I suspected ye would . . . ye would turn against . . . ye shall pay for this . . .

this unconscionable contumacy towards your Chief! My township—"

"Excuse me, Chief," Mr. Fisher said, "but we know tis not your township." The McNab halted near the end of the table. I have never before seen such a dazed look on the Laird's face. Mr. Fisher stared at his Chief; his colleagues appeared to hold their breath. For an instant, the scene reminded me of the wax figures at Madame Tussaud's in London, where I once had occasion to visit.

"What? What say ye?" the Laird shouted, his voice cracking. "Mr. Fisher, have ye lost your senses, my man?"

"Nay, Chief, my senses are fine." I detected a renewed confidence in Mr. Fisher's voice. "George Buchanan was in York on business and spoke to someone in the Assembly. I don't know who, he wouldn't say. But he told George you were an agent the government appointed to settle the township, but tis nae *your* township." The McNab threw his arms in the air and muttered something I could not make out.

"My men, I am sorely disappointed with such . . . such inexcusable disrespect from men I believed to be loyal clansmen." The McNab was in a state, astounded at Mr. Fisher's charge, as was I. He adjusted his plaid, although it did nae need adjusting. "I will . . . I will send the money back to York. That is all! Good day—*gentlemen*."

The Laird turned on his heels, marched out of the room and stomped up the front stairs. The commissioners looked at one another with blank faces. I felt most uncomfortable. Loyalty to my Chief has been instilled in me since childhood. Aye, it has been instilled in MacGregors down through the generations. But the McNab . . . was it *not* his township? I was most distressed. While the commissioners mulled over their quarrel with the Laird, I bid them "good day" and departed through the back door. My stomach's queasiness could not have accommodated Miss Hunt's gooseberry tarts—succulent as they are.

PART FIVE

ISAAC HOAG, DENNIS McNee's closest neighbour, rode over
with the news: their landlord was dead. His passing might
not have been cause for alarm, except the tenants knew from
their dealings with the sons of Stephen Van Rensselaer that
the two young men were much more business-minded than
their amicable father. The Berne farmers, as was true of most
farmers across the manor, had not paid their annual rents for
several years. That laxity had contributed to their landlord's
leaving his estate in considerable debt. His vigilant sons,
having kept detailed records of accounts in arrears,
calculated that their father's tenants owed an enormous sum
in bushels of wheat, several days' labour on the manor and a
myriad of fat hens—or their equivalent in some four
hundred thousand dollars.

"Do ye think they'll try to collect?" McNee asked
Hoag, who said there was a rumour the heirs intended to
collect the rents to pay the estate's debt. He was right. Their
father was hardly in the ground before the Van Rensselaer
boys demanded full and immediate payment. Hoag,
Lawrence Van Deusen, and a few others organized a meeting
of tenants. With Van Deusen as chairman, they appointed a
committee to approach Stephen Van Rensselaer Jr. in an
attempt to settle the matter peacefully. Their new landlord
refused to meet with them. Instead, he sent Van Deusen a
letter demanding full payment of the back rents. The
farmers—now tagged "anti-renters"—met again.

"I'm not payin im a penny!" Paul Vincent said. "My
farm ain't worth the half of what I owe!" Many of his
neighbours voiced the same opinion, while others, whose
farms were large and prosperous, simply refused to pay. In
turn, the Van Rensselaers refused to back down, or even
compromise. They sent Sheriff Michael Artcher to serve
writs on their headstrong tenants.

"It's the tar an feathers, boys!" Hugh Scott said to the
tenants preparing to resist. The men decided to confront the

sheriff on the outskirts of the village. "We best disguise ourselves." "Injins" had always been a convenient scapegoat, and so the upstart outlaws put on masks of sheepskin decorated with feathers and, to their wives' chagrin and dismay, clothed themselves in calico dresses, thus gaining the moniker, "Calico Indians." The sheriff escaped the tar and feathers, but his *writs* did not: the mob surrounded him and forced him to throw the papers into the tar barrels, which they then set on fire. The men knew the Van Rensselaers would persist, and so they took turns guarding the roads into Berne. Sheriff Artcher, accompanied by three deputies, continued his attempts to serve the *writs*, but each time large bands of "Calico Indians" forced the officers to retreat before they could enter the village.

Violence, however, was now intrinsic in the American character. The war for independence, the degradation of human beings through slavery, and the attempted genocide of North America's aboriginal peoples had disseminated and entrenched a culture of violence throughout the nation. Thus, each altercation between the sheriff and the tenants escalated until riots ensued. The state's governor called out the militia in an attempt to put down the mounting insurrection. But the violence of the militia only provoked more violence, which led to the inevitable: a bullet struck a deputy sheriff in the temple, killing him instantly. In the maelstrom, McNee couldn't be sure, but he thought it might have been his bullet that felled the lawman. The governor ordered an intense manhunt. This time the obstinate crofter listened to Flora's pleading. Under cover of darkness, the family abandoned their prosperous farm, retraced their steps to Montreal and travelled westward until they arrived in McNab Township.

ON A MILD day in early January, the commissioners were conducting the annual township meeting in Angus McLaren's shanty. The memory of having his cattle seized and Cathrine arrested kept their host on watch at the window. It had taken McLaren the better part of a year to replace the cattle. McNab sold them for the rent and passage money owing him. But the sale did not pay the full amount, so the struggling farmer was forever wary of the sheriff's return. Even after several weeks confined to her bed, Cathrine McLaren complained of feeling "a chill in me bones." The hardship of being arrested had whipped her spirit. Not until she attended Reverend Buchanan's summer service at Canaan did this robust woman appear to emerge from her melancholy. Angus McLaren harboured an intense anger for several months following the ordeal. A temperate man by nature, he threatened violence to the Laird. His fellow crofters indulged his ranting and over time brought him to his senses.

Cathrine delighted in preparing food for the annual meeting. But since the ordeal of being arrested, she was easily persuaded to leave that task to some of the other wives. This year she and her children were spending the day with Elizabeth Cameron and her children.

The meeting under way, McLaren dropped his surveillance and turned to listen to Peter Fisher. He was explaining to the gathering that, despite their pleas, the Laird refused to hand over the money the government had allocated to build the bridge at Johnson's Rock. For that reason, they could not hire workmen to begin construction.

"Did he not return the money to York?" Hugh Alexander asked.

"Nay, he did not," Fisher said. "He threatened to, but John McDermid told me he still holds the full amount."

"And in his possession it shall remain," Donald Cameron said. "He's become a boon companion of Sir Francis Bond Head; the views of our new Lieutenant-Governor make Colborne appear as radical as Mackenzie. Aye, these two are well-suited."

"It don't make no diffrence anyway," McLaren said. "Look what happened to our last petition: the government says 'aye' to a reduction in the quit-rent and the Laird ignores it. He still demands the full bushel."

"I's beginnin to think petitionin is useless," Iain Storie said. "Angus is right. We sends a petition, the government says 'aye' and McNab pays it no heed. And Donald is right. Head will do nothin agin the Laird." Cameron was about to speak when the door flew open and Lorn McCaul rushed in.

"The Laird is here!" McCaul said.

"Eh!" McLaren said. He moved back to the window and the others crowded in behind him.

"He's no more than a quarter mile behind me," McCaul said. Moments later McNab reined in his dappled grey mare.

"If he thinks he's welcome . . ." McLaren said. "I will throttle—"

"He be so bold," Walter Ross said.

"Tis his township," William Roddie said. "Tis his right to attend our meetings." Scowls were directed towards Roddie, and Duncan McDonald was about to say something when the door opened and the Laird stomped in.

"Good day, gentlemen!" McNab said. "Tis a fine winter's day! I trust your meeting is going well."

"Aye, Mr. McNab," Cameron said, "we have been doing just fine without you."

"Ah, Mr. Cameron, I see your manners have not improved since our last meeting." The Laird handed his heavy cloak and wool bonnet to Roddie. "Ye know very well ye do not address me as 'mister.' I am McNab of McNab; I am nae mister." Cameron maintained a stony countenance. The others stood as if their boots were nailed to the rough timbers. McLaren remained near the window.

"What can we do for you, Chief?" Fisher said. The Laird reached into his sporran, pulled out a roll of bills and waved it above his head.

"My men, they have lost their senses in York—in Toronto," McNab said. "The rabble with their wild ideas of reform have the ear of the Assembly. Tis the influence of those scheming connivers in America who stick their noses in everyone else's business. They would do well to look after their own affairs. Ah, but we are fortunate to have Sir Francis; he will control the shenanigans. Our new Lieutenant-Governor is a man of high principle. But the law is the law, and ne'er will it be said the Laird of McNab broke the law. So I am giving ye one last chance to come to your senses, to obey your lawful Chief, to honour our noble tradition of clan loyalty." McNab paused. A spark from the hearth exploded; the men standing near it lurched forward. "The government . . . I don't think it wise, but since they have appointed commissioners to oversee the expenditures . . . aye, I question the judgment of such a . . . Sir John, before London called him home . . . I believe he had no choice . . . so he asked me for men who would be up to the task. Tis an idea ill conceived, but tis the government's right." McNab paused again. "Sir Peregrine, in his wisdom, saw fit to make *me* responsible for settling the township. As your Chief, I *will* fulfil that responsibility!" The Laird again waved the roll of bills above his head. "Tis *my* township! This vicious rumour . . . tis I the government holds responsible! So the money will be spent where I believe it appropriate! I will use half to build a bridge at Johnson's Rock—as the Assembly wishes. Aye, tis sorely needed. But with the remainder . . . I will see much-needed improvements at White Lake. I trust the commissioners will come to their senses and obey the will of their lawful Chief. If ye will not, I will return the money to York." There was a brief, awkward silence. Then Fisher stepped forward.

"Chief, I believe I speak for Roy and Jack," Fisher said, turning towards McCallum and McDonnell, who nodded assent. "We will not be bullied this way. We—"

"Bullied?" the Laird shouted. "Bullied, Mr. Fisher? I did not *bully* you to leave Perthshire and come to my township! I loaned ye money for your passage; I gave ye the land free of rent for three years; I sheltered your wife and children while ye cleared the land and built a home. Nay, I did not bully you!" The Laird cast his eyes over the men, many of whom had their heads bowed. "None of you!"

"Aye, Chief, ye did the things you say," Fisher said. "And, tis true, we owe ye allegiance. But we canna . . . improvements are needed *everywhere* in the township! The road between here and Kinnell is—"

"Tis piss poor for a road," McDonald said. Several men muttered agreement.

"Very well, my men, I see there is no reasoning with ye." McNab thrust the roll of bills into his sporran. "Your fathers, aye, and your grandfathers before them will . . . they will turn in their graves at the defiance . . . this appalling recusancy ye are showing your lawful Chief."

"Chief," McCallum said. "We—"

"Nay, Mr. McCallum, I will hear no more; I will return the money to York. When ye come to your senses, I will have the treasurer pay it over." McNab reached for his cloak and bonnet, which Roddie handed to him. "Good day, *gentlemen.*" He whirled on his heels and left the shanty.

"What's a recus . . . a recusa . . . ?" McDonald asked. "What the Laird called us."

"Tis someone who refuses to submit to authority," Cameron said. "McNab believes he has complete authority over us. That's how he was raised and tis not easy for him . . . men, we have to remember that the Chief is under pressure from the government . . . as he says, tis he the government holds responsible."

"We isn't in the old country," McDonald said. "The commissioners was given the job—"

"We are within the law," McDonnell said.

"Aye, ye are right," Fisher said, "we're within the law, but the Chief holds the money, and if he returns it to his friends in York . . ." Fisher threw his hands in the air.

"I have an idea," Cameron said. He paused to ensure he had everyone's attention. "Jack is right. We are within the law. And since the Laird is fond of litigation . . . he takes us to court for a penny, why don't we play that game, too? Let's sue him for the money!"

There was a smattering of uncertain, half-hearted "ayes."

"Ye is only diggin yourselves in deeper," Roddie said. "Ye canna fight the Laird's authority. Ye will bring his wrath upon your heads—"

"Ah, shut the fuck up," McDonald said. He tried to move towards Roddie, but Cameron and Alexander blocked his way. Then Cameron addressed the Laird's flatterer.

"Mr. Roddie, I have little good to say about our Chief Justice, but I read in the *Gazette* that he charged a grand jury in Picton last fall. Mr. Robinson told the jury that the rule and force of law was critical to deter or restrain human nature. Those were the very words of the Chief Justice of the Court of King's Bench." Cameron paused to gather his thoughts. "I don't know why, but, unlike those in the republic, those of us who have chosen to settle in Upper Canada . . . for some reason . . . for some reason we are more law-abiding. Whatever the shortcomings of British law— and, aye, there are many—tis still a means for poor crofters to address our grievances." Cameron turned towards McDonald. "Duncan, we all feel your anger, but doing violence to Mr. Roddie will not settle our grievances with the Laird. It will only bring on more violence, as violence always does. Tis no great observation; tis simply a lesson of history—a lesson we men canna seem to learn." Cameron gestured to take in the whole gathering. "So I ask again, should we take the Laird to court for the bridge money?"

This time the shanty resonated to a raucous chorus of "ayes." "Good! I see we are agreed. Peter, will ye talk to Thomas Radenhurst about how we should proceed?"

"Aye, I will; tis a fine idea, and Thomas is partial to defending those of little means," Fisher said. The commissioner presented the men with a few minor concerns, which they quickly resolved. He then declared the meeting over. "The wives have sent food, so let's eat."

"Did ye bring one of Mary's mincemeat pies?" Iain Storie asked Colin Carmichael.

"Aye, that I did," Carmichael said. "But ye best go easy, Iain; ye's gainin a paunch."

"Never ye mind my paunch," Storie laughed. "I's makin up for the hungry years."

"Ah then, we has a lotta makin up to do," Carmichael said. "A lotta makin up."

***

WE HAVE LEFT Kinnell.

The Laird has had a falling out with the Buchanans and has gone to litigation. Tis ostensibly over the supply of timber to their Arnprior sawmill. I canna help but suspect it has more to do with George Buchanan spreading the calumnious rumour that the McNab does not own the township. To be frank, I do not care. I am wearied hearing about litigation upon litigation. But tis, apparently, the reason we have left Kinnell and moved to White Lake in the rear of the township, some twelve miles away. I say "apparently" because there is gossip among the settlers that William Roddie told the Chief he had discovered an excellent tract of valuable hardwood around the lake. The McNab's intent—alas, I trust it remains his intent—is to accumulate sufficient wealth so that, someday, we may return home in triumph and reclaim his Highland estates.

Tis only natural he takes advantage of every opportunity for economic gain. While I applaud these undertakings, I regret he has become selective with his confidences in me. He has said little about his quarrel with the Buchanans. When he informed me of the move to White Lake, I sensed an evasiveness in his explanation. Of course, I do not question my Chief, but . . . I canna help . . . I canna help but feel a weakening of the bond between us.

Perhaps because twould necessitate passing close to Flat Rapids, but since the vicious attack by John Drummond, the Laird has rarely visited the southwest concessions of his township. Now he has built a rugged stone cottage on the north shore of this magnificent lake. And he has built for me a similar, though more humble, dwelling nearby. Both residences, my own in particular with its pavilion roof, remind me of my Perthshire home. While I am still pining over my splendid view of the Ottawa, my feelings are assuaged somewhat by the bustle of the new community.

Not since I was a wee lad in Perthshire have I seen the Fiery Cross invoked. Twas used to summon our clansmen to gather, perhaps to celebrate the birth of the Chief's first son, or perhaps to defend against an intruder laying claim to our lands—and to do battle if need be.

Chief McNab, himself, supervised Lipsey in nailing strips of pine together to form a hand-held cross, charring one end of the cross piece and attaching a square of white linen to the other. In keeping with our more civilized time, the Laird did not ask Lipsey to slaughter a goat so he might have blood in which to dip the linen. Aye, the servant would have obliged quite willingly! The McNab selected his runners: two athletic young men from among the new arrivals. With crosses held high, one sped off to the southwest, the other to the northeast shouting out the Laird's summons for Clan McNab to gather at White Lake. There is nae historical record on how the Fiery Cross came to be. There be many stories, but tis believed twas adopted when the Roman religion was dominant. We Highlanders show great respect and awe for sacred icons. Tis sheer speculation, but tis likely why the Fiery Cross passed from generation to generation. It shames me but . . . we were . . . at times still are . . . a violent people: a clan would attack another clan at any time—provocation nae apparent; perhaps because of some long past grievance. Twas always necessary to be on the watch. If a seer foretold of imminent danger, the Chief would summon his clansman to rendezvous—and to prepare for war! Aye, I remember the stories of my father during the Rising of the '45. He said the Fiery Cross was used by both Jacobites and Hanoverians. Lord Breadalbane—the father of the rascal who seized the McNab's estates—the Viscount secured his tenants' loyalty and prevented them from joining the Jacobites by sending the Fiery Cross round Loch Tay. And this primitive symbol has given rise to many superstitions. Perhaps handed down from the Druids, the ancient Celtic sect. If a runner bearing the cross met an armed man, twas a good omen. But if the men marching to the rendezvous happened upon a bare-footed woman crossing their path, she was seized and blood drawn from her forehead.

It was most gratifying to see the hundreds who obeyed the call of their Chief. I have no doubt childhood memories held their own persuasion. I am sure every last settler can recall stories when failure to heed the command of the Fiery Cross was punishable by death.

I sported a new kilt woven by my Colleen and positioned myself on a flat rock by the lake. Twas with great joy that once again I piped the rousing strains of *Co-thional Chlann an Aba*. Settlers, new and old, came in droves: by horse, on foot and piled into buckboards, the latter a perilous journey bouncing over rutted trails while weaving through copious pines. In the days that followed, the

industrious nature of the Scot transformed this wild
backwoods into a bustling commune of new arrivals. A
strong current flows from the mouth of the lake into Waba
Creek, so named by a tribe of Algonkin Indians. I think it
most appropriate the Laird has christened his new home
"Waba Cottage."

"MacGregor, look here, lad," he said to me one
afternoon while we strolled along the rocky shoreline.
"Here, ye see how the creek flows from the lake. Come
spring, I will hire men to build a dam across; it will provide
power for my sawmill." The McNab had said nothing about
plans to build a sawmill. Ah, but his entrepreneurial spirit is
forever vigilant.

**

LATE ON A blustery winter's afternoon, Sheriff Lyle and
Deputy Maule rode away from Waba Cottage determined
this time to carry out the Laird's orders. They timed their
arrival in Flat Rapids for shortly after dusk, when Lorn and
Jane McCaul would be sitting down for the evening meal,
not expecting company. So as not to warn their quarry, the
lawmen tethered their horses in the bush, fastened
snowshoes to their leather boots and trekked the quarter
mile to the shanty. After years of failed attempts, the officers
finally served the *writ* for McCaul's passage money. The
arrest took place without incident. Jane insisted upon
accompanying her husband to Kinnell where they were
housed overnight. They did not see the Laird, who made
only sporadic trips to the lodge since moving to White Lake.
The next day, Maule took them by horse and sleigh to Perth.
Jane went with her husband to the gaol where her stoical
nature betrayed her: pinched teardrops squeezed from her
puffy eyes as she left the gaol escorted by a cousin who had
settled in Perth the year before.

The arrest heightened the tension already rampant throughout the township. Others feared the same fate would soon befall them. Donald Cameron called a hastily organized meeting at his shanty.

"We has no rights, Donald," Iain Storie said. "Nay, not a one!"

"We's no better than peasants," Angus McLaren said.

"I canna grow nough grain to pay McNab his rent an feed Ann an Mary an the young lad," Walter Ross said. "There be nothin left for market; nae money to pay the Laird our passage. What is we to do?"

"I say we shoot the bastard," Duncan McDonald said, prompting a jumbled chorus of angry voices. "We has taken enough; we was better off at home."

"It doesn't matter if ye has money for the passage," Hugh Alexander said. "Me uncle at home died and left a few pounds. I got the money a few days ago. So I offers the Laird me passage money with interest and, would ya believe, he refuses!"

"Wha? He refused!" Storie said. "Pray tell, for what reason?"

"He said it be too long owing. He said the time for payment is past. So I says, 'Do that mean the debt be forgiven?' He says, 'Nay, it do not,' and he left the room. I left White Lake shakin me head."

"John Macdiarmaid—ye know, John, at Canaan—he worked off some of his debt at Kinnell," Robert Miller said. "So I don't understand why he would—"

"I asked if I could do that too," Alexander said. "He said, 'Nae, nae will I have black sheep workin me land.' Indeed, he be a tyrant!"

"Tis still a rumour McNab is only an agent," Colin Carmichael said. "Do ye know if it be true, Donald?"

"I don't know," Cameron said. "I only know what the commissioners said George Buchanan told them."

"Perhaps . . . tis possible George is spreadin a false rumour to make the Laird look bad," Storie said. "He's furious at McNab for suing over the timber rights."

"I think not," Cameron said. "Tis no shame being sued by the Chief."

"What of our suit for the bridge money?" Carmichael asked.

"Peter spoke to Mr. Radenhurst," Cameron said. "He says we have a good case and he's asked the Quarter Session clerk to add it to the docket. But he could not say when it will come before the magistrate."

"Ye can be sure the Laird will stall as long as he can," Carmichael said. "Where is Peter?"

"He's in Pakenham," Roy McCallum said. "Visitin a sick cousin."

"I say we shoot the bastard," McDonald said.

"Listen to me, men!" Cameron said. "I said it at our last meeting. Tis not the American West. We are a law-abiding community. We will keep petitioning the courts; they canna dismiss us forever."

"And what is we do about Lorn?" Storie said.

"Tis why I called this meeting," Cameron said. "We will raise his bail. Tis ninety-three pounds."

"Why ninety-three pounds?" Alexander asked.

"Tis their passage money plus eleven years' interest. Each of us should give what he can to get Lorn and Jane back on their land." To this suggestion there was unanimous agreement. Cameron adjourned the meeting with the understanding they would meet again to plan further legal action.

***

SPRING IS BUDDING out all over, but for me its salubrious scent is tempered by the dour atmosphere at Waba Cottage. The Laird's disposition, usually robust and gregarious, is sombre and mean-spirited. Tis understandable, of course: he is most upset at the rumour he does not own the township. I asked about his arrangement with the government. He assured me Sir Peregrine *gave* him the township, and his lawful possession of it was confirmed by his successor, Sir John, and by our present Lieutenant-Governor, Sir Francis. I have no reason to question the word of my Chief. I am confident he believes tis *his* township. But each day the rumour is spreading and gaining credence.

Most disturbing was my conversation last week with Commissioner Fisher. Peter accused the McNab of persecuting his settlers. He said the Laird was intolerant and sought revenge on anyone who opposed him. He said, by now his book of "black sheep" must be overflowing. And he said the McNab acts as if he were at home—Lord of the manor and Patriarch of the clan. I interrupted Peter's tirade to make the point that, as a Scottish Highland Chief, the Laird *is* Patriarch of his clan. But I thought Peter rebutted me rather well: he said we are not living in the Scottish Highlands; the Laird has no right to impose feudal dependence upon his settlers, and much of the land canna sustain adequate produce. On his last point, we are agreed. Tis most certainly difficult for some crofters to pay their rent.

I have tried, diplomatically of course, to raise the settlers' contentious issues with the Chief, but he will hear none of it. He pooh-poohs the very idea that these ungrateful wretches, as he calls them, have any grievances. And I must confess, though it saddens me to do so, the Laird confirmed Mr. Fisher's point that he seeks revenge on anyone who opposes him. He said he will "punish the whole township" for spreading this rumour that denigrates his honour and the honour of his illustrious forefathers. How he intends to do that, I do not know. In his vigorous grasp of life, the Laird is sometimes given to hyperbole. No one has said anything to me—the settlers are too courteous—but my reception in the community . . . tis chilly. I no longer feel the neighbourly good wishes to which I have become accustomed.

Ah, but tis not the only place where the welcome is frosty. I have apparently offended my Colleen. How? I do not know. She will not say. She will not even say I have offended her. Nay, tis what they call the "cold shoulder." I am left to puzzle over what grievous transgression I have committed. Two weeks ago, when I departed for home, she saw me off with a deep kiss and a crushing hug. And we had had a splendid roll in the heather that afternoon. She will not allow me to stay the night. She says she doesn't care what the Irish think, but she needs their help with her acreage. I did not ask what she thinks they think we are doing when we spend hours in her shanty on a beautiful spring day. Last week . . . I knew on my arrival something was amiss. Twas nothing she said, but her embrace was tentative, and when I tilted my head for a kiss—she being a few inches taller—twas like that of a sister. Here is the conversation that followed:

"Is something troubling ye, Colleen?"

"Nay."

"Ye seem to be bothered."

"Nay."

"Have I offended ye?"

"Nay."

But, as ye know, I like to talk. And so, hopeful my nattering would thaw the chill, I told her of the rumour about the McNab and whether or not tis his township and about the unrest among the settlers over the bridge money and about Sheriff Lyle and Deputy Maule finally serving the *writ* on Lorn McCaul and how his neighbours raised his bail and . . . Twas all for naught, the chill remained. She served tea and freshly baked bread. Twas delicious. But we ate in silence. I asked again if something was troubling her, which roused her fiery temper and she said just because she was feeling melancholy didn't mean she was troubled. I did not mention it again. And so this week I have decided not to visit the settlers nor my Colleen. I will devote the time to writing a new *piobaireachd*. Alas, I am grateful to have my pipes as refuge from these perplexing . . . these bedevilling foibles of human nature.

***

AFTER THE LAIRD'S move from Arnprior Mills to White Lake, Andrew Richey had a more difficult journey from his home in Pakenham Township. While the hard-packed snow of winter made the roads passable, come spring the magistrate feared for his safety and that of his horse as he navigated through muddy ruts, over hazardous mounds and around rotting tree stumps. The journey, however, was necessary: the Quarter Sessions' court in Perth had decreed the two magistrates responsible for apportioning the statute-labour. Richey was not about to criticize his fellow officer, but it was obvious to him the Laird was a poor administrator: that his inexperience in developing a farming community combined with his egotistical nature was resulting in decisions of pure self-interest, not decisions for the benefit of the whole community. Having arrived at Waba Cottage, safe but exhausted, Richey promptly went along with McNab's proposal to build a road from White Lake to Bellamy's Mills, a hamlet near his home. The magistrates filled out the formal papers and had Lipsey deliver them to the home of Jack McDonnell, where the commissioners were playing cards and discussing township business.

"Ah, now, will ye look at this!" McDonnell said to Roy McCallum and Peter Fisher as he browsed the order paper.

"What's he doon now?" McCallum said.

"He's ordered a new road from White Lake to Bellamy's Mills," McDonnell said.

"I told ye!" Fisher said. "Ye didn't believe me, but I told ye that's where he wanted—"

"Nay, nay, I didn't believe ye because . . . I didn't think he'd . . . tis a good ten-mile journey for the men on the west side of the Madawaska," McDonnell said. "And their own roads are in frightful need of repair."

"Then we'll tell the pathmasters to lay out the statute-labour in their own divisions," Fisher said.

"We'll be in plenty hot water with the Chief if we do that," McCallum said.

"We're already in hot water," Fisher said. "A touch more ain't gonna scald us."

WHEN McNAB LEARNED the commissioners had directed the pathmasters to have the men work on roads near their homes, his temperature soared to match the oppressive summer heat. He invoked his love for litigation and subpoenaed the thirteen pathmasters to testify against the commissioners at the next Quarter Session. In the midst of their fall harvest, the sixteen men journeyed to Perth and paid for four days' accommodations before being examined by Attorney-General William Henry Draper and dismissed: he could find no grounds for McNab's charges.

"Mr. McNab, will you please stand, sir?" Draper said. The Laird always took exception to being addressed as "Mister." He stood abruptly.

"I will have ye know, sir, tis nae proper to address me as 'Mister'; I am McNab of McNab, and I demand the respect due a—"

"Excuse me, sir," Draper said. "*You* demand respect? You have a reputation for wasting the court's time; this hearing is further proof that the reputation is well-deserved.

If this were more than a hearing I . . . your subpoena is contemptible. I trust that any further actions you undertake will have legal substance." McNab appeared about to speak, but Draper called the proceedings to a close and strutted out of the courtroom.

"This has been a costly journey," McDonnell said to Fisher and McCallum. They were standing outside the front door of the courthouse. "Costly indeed."

"Aye, costly for the pathmasters," McCallum said. "They'll be hard-pressed to finish harvestin before their grain goes to seed."

"Perhaps our time need not be completely wasted," Fisher said, drawing quizzical looks from his colleagues. "I saw Thomas Radenhurst in court. Since he got us the road money from the treasurer, why dinna we ask him to get the clerk to subpoena the Chief? Maybe we can get the balance of the money right now. He's holding it illegally."

"Ye know the Laird's been gettin his friends on the bench to put off the trial," McCallum said. "Donald told me just a few days ago he was talkin to Thomas an he—"

"Aye, but everyone's here," Fisher said. "The magistrate will have no excuse for ignoring a subpoena."

"Ah, Peter, you're always thinking," McDonnell said. "Tis an excellent idea, since we are here." But by the time the commissioners found Radenhurst and obtained the subpoena, McNab had left Perth. So once again the Quarter Sessions' clerk scheduled a trial, this time for the fall session.

"Suppose we award the contract for the bridge?" Fisher said, after discovering the subpoena could not be served.

"And how will we pay the contractor?" McCallum asked.

"With the money we already—"

"Tis not enough," McDonnell said.

"Nay, but tis enough to get the contractor started," Fisher said. "It'll be the new year before he's finished; by then we'll have the balance from the fall session."

"You're puttin a lot of faith in the Quarter Session magistrate," McDonnell said. "We dinna know who twill be, but he's likely to be thick with the Laird."

"Aye, but tis a risk worth taking," Fisher said. "We are in the right, and if the work is already started . . ." Although apprehensive, his fellow commissioners agreed.

**

"I AM AT wits end with these . . . these . . ." The McNab was pacing back and forth across the living room of Waba Cottage, a space considerably more confining than he was accustomed to at Kinnell. I was seated in a cushioned armchair beside his beautifully varnished new pine table. It has been no pleasure to visit the Laird these last few weeks—no pleasure at all. He is once again furious with the commissioners; this time because they awarded a contract to begin construction of the bridge at Johnson's Rock. The Laird came to a halt in front of me. "Francis, John, aye, all the proud Chiefs of Clan McNab would turn in their graves if they could see the disobedience, the disrespect . . . what do ye make of it, MacGregor? Tell me, my man, what do ye make of it?" I fidgeted with my sporran; I was most uncomfortable. I have always sided with my Chief in these disputes; tis my duty.

"My Laird, the commissioners . . . the government has seen fit to make the commissioners responsible for the road money. They are—"

"Ah, tis nae the road money. I am Chief of Clan McNab; tis *my* township; the settlers are *my* children; they are in *my* charge." I was about to continue my explanation when, to my relief, the McNab resumed pacing. I had visited the settlers quite often this past summer. I decided that, welcome or not, I would resume my casual visits. At the beginning of summer, I argued for the absolute obedience of loyal clansmen. But as the weeks wore on, their rebuttals grew stronger. By the time the leaves were showing their fall colours, my arguments did not convince even me. Alas, tis most troubling, but I canna defend the McNab unconditionally, as once I could.

"Tis Cameron!" the Laird said when he stopped pacing. "He is the instigator. The commissioners are good men; I, myself, chose them. Nay, tis the rogue Cameron! I will stop him, stop him before he destroys my years of toil." Just then young Allan entered followed by his mother with a tray of tarts and lemonade. "Ah, Agnes, my dear; MacGregor, let us talk no more of these . . . these . . ." The Laird threw his hands in the air and snorted. I bit into one of Miss Hunt's butter tarts and nodded my approval, which she acknowledged with a cramped smile before departing with the stride of a marionette whose strings are being held too tightly. "And how is my boy today? Your mother tells me ye are doing well with your studies." Allan nodded in the affirmative and stood quietly in front of his father. He knows better than to interrupt. "Keep at it, my boy. Ye do me proud, my lad. Go along now and see if your mother needs help." Allan gave a perfunctory bow— first to me, then to his father—before departing. At last the McNab sat down with a tart and his glass of lemonade. Between butter tarts, I made so bold as to ask how he proposed to stop Mr. Cameron.

"Ah, ye shall see, ye shall see! The rascal escaped punishment for that vile letter. Unsigned. How cowardly. But I will trap him, I will trap him with his own defiance. Mark my words, ye shall see."

I felt a sharp twinge at the McNab's unwillingness to confide in me. But perhaps the Laird was still devising a scheme. Or perhaps he *had* no scheme. Whichever, I knew twas all the explanation I would receive, which was no explanation at all. I deemed it best to drop the matter.

"How are ye and the Colleen getting on?" I had confided in the Laird about the ups and downs of our courtship. I was pleased to tell him that, at present, we are getting along just fine. Ah, but she be a moody lass. I canna know from one visit to the next what my reception will be. I must say the Irish are very good about helping her with the land. But I dinna believe altruism be their only motive. During my last visit, a new Irish came around and asked if he could take her excess produce to market in Bytown. Twas evident, at least to me, his interest was more than neighbourly. My tummy churned with a queasiness. Tis jealousy, I know, but I canna help . . . On the ride home, I thought of Othello. Nay, there is no Iago spreading a nasty rumour, and I don't have a murderous soul, but . . . my Colleen likes to control. When we are making love . . . tis not only the position of missionaries she favours! She be a lass of voracious appetite, and matching her . . . aye, I am doing my best. I tell her of the beauty of White Lake; I have asked her again to come and share my humble dwelling. Tis not that I don't trust her with the Irish; tis just that . . . But she says, nay, not at present. She always leaves me with a morsel of hope.

The Laird and I passed the next hour in conversation about his children, and the growing unrest in Toronto. It seems the agitator Mackenzie is again stirring up the people. Some say he is trying to rally the people to oppose the rule of the Family Compact—with violence if need be. I canna help but wonder if men will ever learn . . . When I finished draining my glass . . . my third glass of Miss Hunt's sweet lemonade, I rose to depart.

"Have the last of Agnes's tarts before ye go." Twas a command I was most willing to obey; I plucked the scrumptious pastry from its silver platter.

**

DONALD CAMERON WAS walking his chestnut mare into the barn when he heard the dying thud of axes behind him. He peered through the woods and could see a man holding a compass while directing two axemen in blazing trees. The crofter assumed McNab had ordered a survey for a new road and was about to continue into the barn when he realized the men were blazing a path directly towards his property. He tethered the horse and walked over to the tree line. Intent upon their task, Cameron's "Good day" startled them.

"G'day!" the man with the compass said, his voice spiking to a falsetto.

"What can I do for ye?" Cameron said. The man took a deep breath.

"We's . . . we's blazin a road to Muskrat Lake," he said, spitting out the words. "The Chief hired us." Cameron noted the shamefaced slouch of the other men, who were dangling their short-handled axes at their sides. There was an awkward pause; the man with the compass appeared to be waiting for Cameron's response.

"Aye, I can see you're blazing a road. But you're awful close to my property."

"We's goin through it," said the man with the compass. "The Chief said to." He squinted at Cameron from under the brim of his leather hat. "It's where the Chief wants the road laid." He tried to assess the look of disbelief on the settler's face.

"Nay, ye are not going through my property." Cameron crossed his arms in front of his chest. The man averted the crofter's eyes, dug the toe of his boot into the fallen leaves and examined his compass as if he didn't know what it was for. "Who are ye?"

"Manny Nowlan. I'm a . . . I'm a surveyor from Carleton Place. The Chief hired me. He showed me where he wants the road laid. If ya opposes me, ya'll be in the Chief's bad books. We don't want no trouble, so step aside." His confidence bolstered by his brief oration, he stared at Cameron whose cheeks, atop his brown whiskers, were burnished with the sheen of polished apples. The crofter strode towards the surveyor, who took a step backwards and flinched at the intensity of Cameron's gaze.

"Ye are *not* going through my property." The two men stood toe to toe. Nowlan glanced at the axemen; one shrugged, the other lifted his felt hat and wiped his forehead with his sleeve.

"We's only . . . we's only carryin out the Chief's orders! We don't want no trouble. Ya can take it up with the Chief. Now we has work to do." The surveyor tried to step around Cameron, who moved sideways to block him.

"I'm tellin ye for the last time, McNab is not putting a road through my property. Go around it, because ye are not going through it."

"Yous is breakin the law, now step aside." Nowlan again tried to manoeuvre around the farmer. Cameron placed a hand flat against Nowlan's plaid shirt and gently shoved the surveyor whose boot heel caught on the underbrush, causing him to topple backwards and sit down in a manner comical enough to elicit suppressed chuckles from his colleagues. The crofter turned towards the axemen, the grins left their faces.

"We don't want no trouble," said the shorter of the two. "We's jus followin orders." The tall, angular farmer took a menacing step towards them; they broke into a run, dodging trees and heading back the way they came. Nowlan had regained his feet.

"Tell McNab not to try to run a road through my property again. And tell him not to try to run a road through the property of the other settlers either." Cameron stifled a smile when Nowlan tipped his hat. The surveyor then turned and hurried back in the direction taken by his axemen.

AT MID-MORNING THE next day, Cameron was chopping logs for firewood when Sheriff Lyle rode into the clearing. They acknowledged one another with a nod as the officer dismounted.

"I have to place you under arrest, Mr. Cameron."

"Eh! For what, sheriff?" Lyle pulled a sheet of rolled paper from his saddlebag.

"Chief McNab has issued a warrant for your arrest." Lyle handed the paper to Cameron. "It says you assaulted the surveyor, Manny Nowlan, that you stopped him from completing his survey of the road to Muskrat Lake."

"I stopped him from trespassing on my property. What is unlawful about that?"

"The law says you must file a complaint before the Quarter Session; you cannot stop a legal survey." When Cameron didn't respond, Lyle added, "That is the law."

"Fuck the law!" Surprise flashed in the sheriff's eyes. Surprise at hearing the expletive from this gentle man. "Ye know, sheriff, there's only so much harassment we are willing to take; *I* am willing to take. Ye say tis the law! Who makes these laws? McNab's cronies in Toronto? They're laws for the wealthy! But what about us? This is not Scotland! We are not serfs! Aye, we are *treated* as serfs, but, nay, we are not serfs!" Cameron tugged at his beard, a rare, heated rage in his eyes. "Mackenzie is right; we are governed by . . . by pompous asses! The English who think they have the God-given right to rule the world. Tis a government to benefit those of privilege. McNab . . . he is nothing but a toady for the Family Compact. He cares not a whit for his settlers." Over the years Sheriff Lyle had learned patience in dealing with the settlers. He reminded himself his job was to enforce the law—not pass judgment on its fairness. "In Perthshire we were driven from our land to make way for sheep. Old men, women and children . . . families whose fathers and grandfathers fought for . . . fought and *died* for their Chiefs . . . forced to leave their homes . . . forced to watch them burn to the ground. Forced to find shelter in a ditch. Pulled out of their homes and beaten by the Laird's factors. And for what? Because greedy Lowlanders and English noblemen . . . those who put money before people;

because there's more money from sheep than men! Sheep! The Laird's four-footed clansmen! Tis only greed in their hearts! And there is no end to it!" Although not as articulate, the sheriff had heard similar rants from other settlers. He thought it best to listen before making an arrest. "We didn't cross an ocean to be put upon as at home."

"If you will come peaceful, I'll take you to Waba Cottage and ask the Chief to allow bail. If he agrees, you can return home." Cameron's anger drained away, a heavy weariness streamed through his body. His quarrel was not with the sheriff. He had always found the lawman resolved in carrying out his duties, but courteous in doing so. He sensed that Lyle did not always agree with the law, but as a former military man, he saw its authority as absolute.

"Aye, sheriff, I'll come peaceful. Let me tell Elizabeth, and I'll have to saddle the mare." Lyle nodded and the farmer walked towards his shanty.

When they reached Waba Cottage, the sheriff left his prisoner outside the door while he went inside. Cameron dismounted and stood next to the window where he could hear the men talking.

"Do not bring the fellow here," McNab said. "I smell the air foul already. I dinna want my house contaminated with his presence."

"Chief, Mr. Cameron is not a threat to abscond from the law," Lyle said. "It is not necessary to imprison—"

"Nay, take the black sheep to McVicar in Pakenham and order him not to allow bail."

"Chief—"

"Do your duty, sheriff. I dinna wish to discuss it further." Cameron mounted his horse and seconds later the sheriff emerged.

"He says 'nay' to bail, Mr. Cameron. I'll have to take you to Pakenham." To the sheriff's relief, the farmer turned his horse towards the Pakenham Road.

PART SIX

FOR QUIT-RENT OF a bushel per cleared acre, Chief McNab located Dennis McNee on a lot of one hundred acres—one hundred acres of mostly rocky terrain, nothing like the rich soil of Van Rensselaer Manor.

But luck, or good fortune, seemed to be with the forsaken American. While purchasing supplies in Isaac Gregory's General Store, he met George Watt, a recent arrival from Lochiel. Their topic of conversation was the topic of all the settlers: "How are ye getting on?" Watt complained that he wanted to open a tavern, but McNab had located him just outside Flat Rapids on a lot of arable loam surrounded by woodland: good land for farming, but a poor location for a tavern. Together they came up with the idea of exchanging lots: each would then have the land best suited to his purpose. When they sought McNab's approval, he agreed with the proposal: the arrangement was of no consequence to him. He sanctioned the exchange of location tickets and, at the request of the two settlers, ordered McDermid to register the exchange with the Crown Lands Office.

The legal transaction completed, the men moved on with their lives: Watt built a well-stocked tavern; McNee built an addition to Watt's shanty to house Flora and the children.

At first the crofter gave little thought to the timber on his new land; his neighbours assured him that the Laird held timber rights to the whole township. But once again destiny intervened. During a cattle-buying trip to Perth, McNee came across the Crown Lands Office at the corner of Foster and Gore. No harm in making an inquiry. To his surprise, he discovered McNab had not taken out a patent for timber rights on his acreage. The enterprising Scot immediately registered a patent and, on returning to the township, arranged with the Buchanans to provide timber for their Arnprior sawmill.

Of course, news of the arrangement infuriated the Laird. A few months previous, the government had granted the Chief timber patents on all unoccupied lots. He already held patents on the lots of the earlier settlers. But he'd neglected to register patents for recent settlers. McNab refused to acknowledge his mistake: McNee's audacity must be punished. The Laird applied to the Lieutenant-Governor to cancel the exchange of lots and register the location ticket for McNee's lot in his name. Without determining whether or not the request was legal, Head issued the patent to his friend, who then began the lengthy proceedings necessary to evict the irascible crofter.

***

ALAS, IF THE relentless discontent throughout the township was not enough, now we are becoming more like the rogues to the south. It saddens me that recent events threaten the people's desire for civility and the rule of law. We have received news that Mackenzie and his band of rebels attempted an armed insurrection on our provincial capital. But the good people of Toronto—loyal supporters of the government—drove them out of the city. When word of the uprising reached us, the McNab showed me the hasty letter he wrote to his good friend, the Lieutenant-Governor:

Waba Cottage, 15ᵗʰ Dec., 1837.

My Dear Sir Francis, — The spirit of my fathers has been infused into my soul by recent events, and has roused within me the recollection and memory of the prestige of my race. The only Highland chieftain in America offers himself, his clan, and the McNab Highlanders, to march forward in the defence of the country — "Their swords are a thousand, their hearts are but one."

We are ready to march at any moment. Command my services at once, and we will not leave the field till we have routed the hell-born rebels, or — "*In death be laid low, with our backs to the field, and our face to the foe.*"

I am yours sincerely,
McNab

Within days the Laird received his commission: Sir Francis appointing him Colonel of the 20th Battalion of Carleton Light Infantry. Twas a proud moment, a rare, joyful respite from the squabbling and ill will that permeates the settlement. My Chief was to command and . . . I detest this violence . . . but, if duty calls, the Laird will lead into battle all able-bodied men in the townships of McNab, Fitzroy and Pakenham.

The first order of business was brief: the McNab assembled his Regiment at Pakenham, where he appointed Captains for each township's Companies. I spotted my Colleen standing amidst the wives of the Irish. She waved, but of course I could not acknowledge . . . twould not have been proper while standing at attention beside my Chief. I searched for her after the ceremony, but one of the ladies said she had already departed; that she'd come with an Irish lad and had ridden home on the back of his horse. As usual, a twinge of jealousy . . . tis torturous and I so wish I could purge myself of this feeling.

Before discharging his Regiment, the Chief ordered our township's Captains to muster their Companies at Sand Point on the fifteenth of the month ensuing. Twas *this* rite I so looked forward to! As I donned my finest tartan, my heart swelled with a great pride. A few weeks previous, I had taken delivery of a new chanter. My prized instrument finely tuned, my steps lively and light, I piped my Chief into the cavernous stone barn where the ranks assembled. The

McNab called the roll, read the *Articles of War* and addressed the Companies:

"Now my men, you are under martial law. If you behave well, obey my orders and the officers under me, you will be treated as good soldiers. But if you come under the lash, by the God that made me, I will use it without mercy. So you know your doom. Now I will call upon as many of you as will do so willingly to volunteer and go to the front, and I will lead you on to glory." To my astonishment, to the astonishment of the Laird, two—*only two!*—stepped forward. Two minor clerks. The ire of my Chief was apparent, but his resolve to serve his new country unwavering.

"What!" he said, gasping in stunned disbelief. "No more! Then I must ballot and force you!" From the barn's high ceiling, a pall of cold, musty air descended upon the gathering; my heart thumped against my tunic. Then a young man, a newcomer I did not know, he asked—I believe in innocence—what authority the Laird had to ballot the Companies. The McNab was caught short. He huffed with indignation, as well he might have, and then abruptly, and without ceremony, dismissed the men.

On our journey home to White Lake, the Laird did not speak—even once. Sitting beside him in the sleigh, I sensed a heavy disappointment, a bewilderment that McNab clansmen who for hundreds of years have borne proudly the motto, *Timor Omnis Abesto—Dreadnought*—that their beneficiaries would dishonour their ancestors; for that is surely how the McNab saw the refusal of his men to volunteer when duty called.

***

McNab, 22nd January, 1838

To His Excellency, Sir Francis Bond Head,
Lieutenant-Governor of the Province of Upper
Canada:

The Petition of the Undersigned Humbly Sheweth:

That the Carleton Light Infantry was
mustered on the 25th ultimo, at Pakenham
Mills, commanded by McNab of McNab, and
on the 15th current by Companies at their
Captains' respective places of abode.

That we, the undersigned, one and all of
us, consider ourselves true and loyal
subjects, and are willing to serve Her Majesty
in any part of British North America, where
your Excellency may think proper to call us,
under any other commander than McNab.

That a number of us have suffered
severely from McNab through the course of
the Civil Law, and are therefore afraid to
come under him in the Martial Law, being
harsh in his disposition, and also
inexperienced.

That we hope it may please your
Excellency to look into our circumstances as
misled people by McNab, who made us give
bonds for Quit-Rents, which we, not knowing
what the poor lands in this part of the
country could produce, gave without
hesitation; and not withstanding all our
industry and economy, with these bonds we
are not able to comply.

That we trust your Excellency will
endeavour to set us on the same parallel
with other loyal subjects in the Province, and

free us of those Quit-Rents, as we find them a heavier burden than we can bear. We beg to know from your Excellency whether the land of this Township is McNab's or the Government's.

And your humble petitioners as in duty bound will ever pray . . .

Loud cheers drowned out Donald Cameron before he could finish reading the new petition to the annual township meeting in Angus McLaren's shanty.

"Tis the best petition yet!" Iain Storie said.

"Aye, tis that all right!" Colin Carmichael said. "We has tried many times before, but this—"

"Tis a waste of paper," Duncan McDonald said. "We has petitioned and petitioned and what has we got? Nothin. How long has it been? I canna remember how many years since we was promised the quit-rent would be less. And is it? Nay, tis still a bushel, not a grain nor kernel less. I say we is foolin ourselves. The Laird is thick with the government an we's . . . we's wastin our time!"

Years of struggle had taken their toll and it took little to dash the hopes of the settlers. McDonald's outburst evoked despondent mumbling.

"Men, we must not give up," Lorn McCaul said. "Donald, tell them . . . tell them we must keep trying."

"Lorn is right," Cameron said. "Aye, Duncan is right, too. But Head will need us to fight if the rebellion spreads. And tis still . . . we still don't know if McNab owns the land. If he doesn't . . ." Cameron stroked his whiskers. "If we don't petition the government, what are we to do? Things will not get better, only worse. Most every able-bodied man is here present. If everyone signs, it will send Head a message we are determined to be treated fairly."

The men's emotions were as pliable as birch saplings. But these were Scots: a stubborn breed who throughout history had come back from adversity time and time again.

"Donald, ye is an opti . . . an optimis . . . ye knows what I'm tryin to say," McDonald said. "But he'd uh ruined your property with the road. And no bail! If Magistrate McVicar weren't a decent sort an took our word ye'd appear in the court, ye'd still be there. An ye still has to go to trial."

"Aye, Duncan, we understand how you feel, we all do," Hugh Alexander said. "But we should listen to Donald; he's right, Head canna ignore us forever. I say we send the petition; we has nothin to lose." Alexander gazed over the men's aged, leathery faces, his eyes pleading for support. From the disgruntled muttering came a few hesitant "ayes," followed by more "ayes" and then a groundswell of "Send the petition!"

"Very well," Cameron said. "There's a post leaving for Toronto in two days. I will send the petition with it."

∗∗∗

MY COLLEEN. I have received the Judas kiss. She has taken up with an Irish. The lad who took her produce to market in Bytown. I only learned of her infidelity . . . twas most painful. Of course I had no way of knowing before my arrival. I had had no opportunity to visit for a few weeks, my place being with the McNab. We have been awaiting Sir Francis's order; anticipating that any day now the Lieutenant-Governor will call upon my Chief to lead his Regiment into battle. We are still waiting. The Laird said he could spare me for an afternoon, and since twas a mild winter's day, I thought I would surprise my Colleen. I didn't expect when I rode up . . . a horse tethered outside her shanty is not unusual. I was about to knock when laughter from within stayed my hand. Then the rollicking screech of my Colleen was followed by the hearty whoop of a male. That was followed by a moment's silence, which was followed by a low moaning . . . and then my Colleen hollering out his name. There was no mistaking she was in the throes of ecstasy. I have heard my own name shouted with equal passion. Twas only then I realized I was still holding my hand as if about to knock. My fist clenched, my nails, in need of filing, cutting into my palm; my stomach . . . I felt I was about to vomit a large stone from its pit. I began to sweat profusely, as if someone had tipped a bucket from above. I turned away from the door and as I did I heard my Colleen . . .

I dinna understand. She gave no hint . . . I shamefully took my anger out on poor Nellie on the ride home; her chestnut shanks lathered as I pushed her hard; my own clothing slimy and sticky. I remembered when I was becoming a young man and noticing the lasses in a way I had not noticed them before. At sixteen I was smitten with a girl of fifteen. Jean was her name. When I was being instructed on the pipes, devoted as I was, often I longed for the lesson to end so I could be with her. She seemed besotted as well, and we spent carefree days romping about. Then, one day, for no reason—at least none apparent to me—she spurned my attentions. She didn't explain. Ever. Twas nae another lad; I would have heard in the village. I never said anything to the lads I went about with; I felt I was to blame, although I didn't know for what. I never grieved. I told myself it didn't matter. I applied myself to the pipes with even more dedication and made considerable progress. Twas almost two years before I gave my heart again. And then, uncertain and holding back; the pain, I didn't want to feel . . . And now my Colleen . . . There is a lump in my throat and I canna swallow.

***

Government House, Toronto, 13ᵗʰ March, 1838

Gentlemen: — Having laid before His Excellency, the Lieutenant-Governor, your memorial of the 22ⁿᵈ of January, I am directed to reply to the several statements contained in it to inform you that the arrangements made between The McNab and his followers are of a purely private nature and beyond the control of the Government — that Martial Law, which you apprehend will bring you more immediately under the control of your Chief, has not been proclaimed nor is it likely to be — and that in any military organization, which may eventually take place, the Government will take care in this, as in all other cases, not to put it in the power of any individual to treat Her Majesty's subjects harshly or oppressively.

J. Joseph, Secretary,
Lieutenant-Governor's Office
Toronto, Upper Canada

"Aye, I told ye!" Duncan McDonald said when Cameron finished reading Head's response to the petition. Harsh curses, boiling with rage and frustration, seared the air in Angus McLaren's shanty. "Shoot the bastard! Tis the only way to be rid the tyrant!"

"Aye, Donald, Duncan be right!" McLaren said. "I should uh shot him when he sent Lyle to raid me farm. The bastard."

"I dinna know," said Lorn McCaul. He was sucking on his pipe in a futile attempt to keep it lit. "I would like to be rid the tyrant, but I dinna know about shootin him."

"Ye dinna know, Lorn!" McDonald said, as he paced back and forth before the meeting. "He threw ya in gaol for your passage money. Ye'd still be there if we hadn't bailed ya out. The McNab has no heart; he'd uh let ya rot in gaol." McDonald turned to Cameron, who had moved off to the side of the room. "He'd uh let ya rot in gaol, too, Donald, if we hadn't given our word to McVicar. I say we shoot the bastard!" Mumbled exasperation followed McDonald's rant, some men voicing doubtful agreement, others voicing feeble dissent. "Beyond the control of the government, indeed; the bastard. McNab be the government!" Cameron stood back while McDonald vented the men's anger. But as the settlers' acknowledged leader, all eyes eventually turned towards him.

"We have good reason to be frustrated," Cameron said, pausing, choosing his words carefully. "Aye, we might be justified in doing violence to the Laird." Several "ayes" came from the men. "But do ye want to leave a legacy for our children and grandchildren that we settled our differences with violence?" Several "nays" were uttered. "I know, twas the way of our forefathers . . . but we are *not* in Scotland! These are *not* the Highlands! The Family Compact may rule us now, but they will not . . . they canna rule us forever. There's a rumour—tis *only* a rumour—but a rumour Head will soon be recalled to London. Remember . . . tis necessary to remind ourselves we live under the rule of law, we—"

"Tis the law of the Laird," McDonald said. "Tis nae the law of the land."

"Aye, Duncan, but we've been patient," Cameron said. "We should not lose patience now. Let us carry on as best we can; at least until we see if Head is to be recalled."

"Ye is bein reasonable," Iain Storie said, "but London will only send another scoundrel in his place."

"Perhaps, perhaps not," Cameron said. "Let us wait and see." The majority seemed relieved, if not satisfied, to heed Cameron's call.

***

WHEN I FIRST courted my Colleen, I cursed the distance between us. But since my serendipitous discovery of her indiscretion, I have been grateful for that distance. I have not seen her since . . . it has been several months past. Nay, I have not seen her, but I have not purged her from my thoughts—from my heart. She is ever present. And now . . . the McNab and I are preparing for another journey to Perth, to the Quarter Session. We will be away for a few days and so this morning . . . because Lipsey is ailing, my Chief asked me to ride into Arnprior and purchase supplies for Agnes and the children. While in Isaac Gregory's General Store, I met an Irish from Pakenham, an elderly gentleman my Colleen introduced to me shortly after her arrival. We exchanged pleasantries and I inquired as to his reason for journeying such a long distance. He said he'd been told Mr. Gregory had a fine stock of harness, which be true; Isaac keeps a first-rate stock of quality harness imported from America. And then my curiosity . . . I asked after my Colleen. He said he'd spoken to her just two days previous and she was fine now. And I said, "Now?" And he said she'd been stricken with bilious fever in the winter, but the ladies tended to her and being a robust and hearty lass, she shook off the fever. Ah, but I could not let the gentleman go without asking: Was she being courted? I could tell by the way the Irish raised his eyebrows he knew twas more than an innocent query. He said he didn't know. He said twould appear that plenty lads tried sparking her, but he thought she gave them all the mitten. Then he said he noticed a melancholy about her, but he thought it just the lingering effects of her illness. He said he would tell her about our chance encounter and extend my regards.

I rode Nellie hard back to White Lake, but not as hard as I rode my mind's eye. Was my Colleen's melancholy an omen that she missed me? Did she regret her peccadillo? Of course she didn't know I knew, and never having been to

McNab and having no means—she said she had no need of a horse because the Irish were kind and brought her her supplies—she could not journey here to find me and explain. And what did I hear outside the door of her shanty? Had she the bilious fever and was delirious, and that Irish scoundrel took advantage? Perhaps she was not . . . did not intend to be unfaithful. It's been several months and I am just now realizing . . . just now aware . . . she could not know why I have not come calling. What am I to do? I could ride over! I could ask . . . when he is himself again, and if the Laird could spare him, I could ask Lipsey to deliver a letter. I could . . . alas, I don't know what to do! Ah, but I miss my Colleen.

TIS THE DAY after our return from Perth. I tell ye, I hoped to awake this morning and find it all a bad dream. The Laird brought charges against Mr. Cameron for obstructing Manny Nowlan, a surveyor the McNab had engaged to blaze a new road from White Lake to Muskrat Lake. I found Donald's evidence most disturbing. When the McNab informed me of the incident, he failed to mention that the road was to run *through* the property of this industrious gentleman. Aye, tis true, Mr. Cameron should not have assaulted Mr. Nowlan. But he was justly provoked. I thought it most fitting that Colonel Fraser—he was on the bench for this spring session—I found it most fitting that the Magistrate instructed the Jury to ignore the outlandish charge of aggravated assault and bring in a verdict of simple assault. Of course the Jury complied. These twelve good men went even further and found the incident to be of a trifling nature under strong provocation. They recommended leniency; Mr. Cameron's fine was slight, as was appropriate.

To say I am distraught over what I heard in court . . . I am reluctant . . . I canna deny it any longer: the settlers are right: the Laird is mistreating them in a most foul and unjust manner. My Chief has lost his sense of fairness. He has overstepped the bounds of decency. Ye don't assail a man's property. Not without just cause. A man's property is his God-given right. To bring ruin to his property is to bring ruin to the man. The settlers may be in the McNab's debt—I am no longer certain even of that—but, nay, ye don't . . . a man's property is a man's soul!

Alas, if these distasteful proceedings were not enough, as we were leaving the courthouse, we encountered the crofter at the door.

"Ah, Mr. Cameron, I trust ye have learned the consequences of opposing your Chief," the McNab said.

"Ah, Chief, I trust *ye* will learn the consequences of not paying your debt," Donald retorted.

"Eh! What do you mean?" The McNab gestured towards Mr. Cameron with his walking stick. I feared he might strike the man and hasten our return to court.

"The Clerk has given the commissioners a warrant to seize your horse," Mr. Cameron said. "It will be sold for the road money ye are holding unlawfully." There was a smugness to his tone that seemed out of character for this benevolent gentleman.

"Pooh! What nonsense!" the Chief said. "They would not dare do that! And I warn ye! Do not get up another petition against me!"

"Another petition?" Mr. Cameron said. "That we will! And a dozen more if need be!" The McNab seemed taken aback. His only reply was to snort in that peculiar manner of his. I followed him as he strutted away from the courthouse. "Ye shall see," I heard Donald shout after us. When we reached John Craig's stable, it was with utter disbelief we found Mr. Cameron be telling the truth: the McNab's horse *was* impounded. Aghast and embarrassed—and despite my earlier feelings, I felt pity and compassion for my Chief—he had to borrow money from Colonel

Fraser to reclaim his horse. I have never seen the McNab so out of sorts. The Laird rode out of Perth like a man possessed. I followed at a distance. It was a most unpleasant journey to White Lake. I don't know what is to befall us next. Nay, I don't even care to think what it might be.

⁎

ANGUS MCLAREN'S SHANTY revelled in wild rejoicing as crofters slapped one another on the back, tossed their hats in the air and raised toddies to toast the news. Not only had the Home Office replaced Sir Francis Bond Head with Major General Sir George Arthur, but London was sending out John George Lambton, 1st Earl of Durham, as Governor-in-Chief of the Canadas and High Commissioner for British North America.

"Ah, Donald, ye dinna mean another petition, lad?" Duncan McDonald said, his silly grin revealing a gap from where a tooth had recently fallen out.

"Aye, Duncan, another petition it be!" Cameron said.

Prior to calling the meeting, Cameron had drawn up the new petition, once again asking the government to investigate the settlers' grievances. All the men signed it without hesitation. Fear of the Laird still kept a few settlers from signing, kept them from even attending the township meeting.

"If I may make a suggestion?" Iain Storie said.

"Aye, Iain, ye dinna need permission," Cameron said. "Ye have never been shy about making suggestions."

"Lord Durham will be in Montreal in three weeks' time," Storie said. "Why wait till he be in Toronto? Why not go to Montreal and present our petition to him when he arrives?"

"Tis an excellent suggestion," Cameron said. Several others voiced agreement. "Tis a pleasant spring we're having; I'd enjoy such a fruitful journey."

"Ah, who said ye is the one to go?" McDonald said, trying to hold a questioning frown while swaying from too much brandy. The men laughed good-naturedly. Everyone knew Cameron was the right person—the only person—for this mission.

THE WHARF AT the port of Montreal was crowded with people anxiously awaiting the arrival of loved ones from home. Donald Cameron, bracing himself against the wind, watched the ship dock and the passengers disembark. The petition, bound with a scarlet ribbon, he held tightly for fear of it blowing away. The settlers' envoy moved forward when he spotted Lord Durham. But as his lordship neared the end of the gangplank, a carriage pulled up and the new representative of the British Crown boarded without so much as an acknowledging glance at his surroundings. Cameron arrived at the carriage just as Colonel Basil Cooper, Durham's *aide-de-camp*, opened the carriage door and stepped onto the running board.

"Excuse me, sir." Cooper turned towards the crofter.

"Yes, what is it?"

"I represent the settlers of McNab Township."

"Ah, yes." Cooper stepped down and turned to face Cameron. "London knows of your grievances, but we did not expect . . . let us step over here." The men moved a few feet away from the coach. "You understand his lordship is exhausted from the long journey; I do not wish to trouble him with this matter just now."

"Sir, if I may be so bold, I have travelled from McNab, more than one hundred miles, to present this petition to his lordship. This matter is most urgent to us. We have been mistreated . . . aye, we have been treated as serfs. Many of us have endured this persecution since our arrival. I know his lordship—"

"Yes, his lordship has been fully briefed on your situation; you are?"

"Donald Cameron."

"Ah, yes, Mr. Cameron. Your name is well known in London. I am Colonel Cooper; I am pleased to make your acquaintance." They shook hands and Cameron handed the petition to Cooper. "I will see to it that his lordship considers your petition as soon as we reach Toronto. That is a promise. Now, sir, if you will excuse me, I must take leave; his lordship is impatient to be on his way. We have chartered the *John Bull*; I trust you understand we have a long and tedious journey ahead." Cameron thanked Cooper and watched the carriage pull away with the new Viceroy of Upper Canada.

Four days later, when the crofter returned home, Elizabeth handed him a single sheet of paper displaying the wax seal of the Governor-in-Chief of the Canadas. Cooper's brief letter said Lord Durham had appointed a commission to investigate the affairs of the township.

***

THE McNAB, BACK from Toronto only a few days, is in a terrible state. London has recalled his good friend, Sir Francis—the Home Office displeased with the way the Lieutenant-Governor dealt with Mackenzie's rebellion. They have replaced him with Major General Sir George Arthur. Ah, my Chief's timing was not good. He had sent by post an application for a trust-deed for ten-thousand acres. The McNab told me he wished to transfer ownership of their lots to those settlers who have discharged their obligations. The luck of it all! The application arrived two days *after* Sir Francis's departure. The Laird's friends on the Executive Council recommended granting the deed, but Sir George . . . tis understandable that our new Lieutenant-

Governor is scrutinizing his every decision. Much to the Council's chagrin, Sir George vetoed the recommendation and summoned the Laird to Toronto. Persuasive he be, but my Chief failed to win his Excellency's approval.

"Tis nothing, MacGregor, a minor setback," he assured me. There is no denying it: the McNab is a man of perseverance and wily cunning. If one means be stymied, find another. Before leaving the provincial capital, he dispatched by courier a new petition, a copy of which he showed me upon his return.

> *To His Excellency, Sir George Arthur, K.C.H., Lieutenant-Governor of the Province of Upper Canada, &c. &c. &c.*
>
> *The Petition of the McNab Sheweth:*
>
> *That since it appears to your Petitioner there are some difficulties entertained by Your Excellency and the Executive Council as to granting him a trust-deed for enforcing the terms of his agreement with his settlers for the present, and duly appreciating the motives, he humbly hopes there can be no objection to ordering him his patent-deed for the five-thousand acres granted this Petitioner originally for settling the Township. And your Petitioner shall ever pray, &c.*
>
> *Archibald McNab*
> *Toronto, June 28, 1838*

We shall see if Sir George grants the Laird his patent-deed. Ah, but our neophyte Lieutenant-Governor is not the only personage the McNab will have to contend with. Lord

Glenelg, our Colonial Secretary, believes many of the province's affairs have been mismanaged: he has dispatched the 1st Earl of Durham to assist Sir George in rectifying matters. The Laird says Lord Durham has the ear of the Reformers. If that be so, may God help us!

THE LUMBERMEN HAVE acquired a new saw they call a crosscut. Two men, one on each side of the tree felled by the broadaxe, whip it back and forth. These days, tis as if the blade of the crosscut is slicing into my heart: it, too, is being whipped about: one moment I am gay and jubilant, the next . . . I canna help . . . the McNab's quandary floods my muddled brain.

Ah, but tis so good . . . such a great relief to be once again with my Colleen. After I spoke to the Irish gentleman in Arnprior, I could get no release from her spirit, my mind relentless, a tangled mess. For weeks I wracked my tortured psyche trying to decide: Should I ride over? Should I send a note? Should I? . . . And then early one afternoon my contemplation was interrupted by the neighing of a horse outside my cottage. I opened the door and there to behold . . . I tell ye, she looked resplendent! As she dismounted, a glimpse of shapely leg from under her calico skirt jolted my loins and my heart . . . twas beating as if a wee sparrow was trying to escape the folds of my tunic. Ah, but my jubilation was cut short when I saw the scowl on those rosy cheeks.

"Where have ye been?" she said, standing in front of me, arms akimbo.

"I . . . I . . . come in, come in," I said, searching for a reply. But she stood fixed to the spot and then . . . I don't know what came over me, I blurted out, "Colleen, ye have been unfaithful an ye have hurt me very—"

"What? What do you mean? Unfaithful!" she said, her deep blue eyes glowering like those of a cornered fox. I could not take back my accusation, I had no choice but to explain.

"Last winter I rode over to surprise ye and . . . tis most painful . . . I was about to knock when I heard . . . I heard the sounds of lovemaking. There was no mistaking the voice of an Irish. I stood before your door and—" Twas like the torrent of Niagara, which I have not seen, but have heard about. Sobs poured from her shaking body. I have never seen my Colleen so distraught, so vulnerable. My heart . . . I put my arm around her shoulder and guided her into the cottage. She confessed; said she was sorry and begged my forgiveness. She said the Irish had brought her some of his home-made whisky and, being neighbourly, as the Irish are, they had a few toddies and she felt a surge of warmth and the scoundrel—she didn't call him a scoundrel—he patted her bosom and the whisky—she said twas a strong brew—and then she said the Irish put his arms around her waist and kissed her like the French and his hands caressed her bottom and their thighs rubbed . . . I looked at my Colleen and my Colleen looked at me. We quickly shed our garments and romped like ravenous mink on my feather mattress.

Afterwards, while we lay side by side, she again asked me to forgive her. She said it only happened the one time. I said I forgave her. Then I asked—twas a strange thing to think of at the time—where did she get the horse? She said another Irish lad gave it to her as a present. She had a quizzical look in her eyes when she told me. I said, as a *present*? And she said, for weaving him a quilt. And I said, ah, then, tis understandable.

But the hoof beats of her new mare had hardly faded when my mind again flooded with worry. Nay, not for my Colleen—for the Laird. The McNab may lose the township—*his* township! After months of quibbling, Toronto has refused to grant him his patent-deed. Tis on the recommendation of Thomas Radenhurst's brother, John, our Acting Surveyor-General. My Chief accuses the Radenhursts of waging a vendetta. I think the accusation somewhat overblown, but what is most distressing . . . nay, I simply canna believe . . . Donald Cameron told me Mr. Radenhurst—that be John—told Council that the five thousand acres the McNab requested under his patent-deed . . . ah, tis nonsense! . . . those five thousand acres be the land upon which he has located his settlers! Donald says had Council granted the deed, the Laird would have evicted his settlers from their lots! I told Donald twas poppycock; the McNab has told me of no such intention. And I dinna believe for a moment he would commit such a vile . . .

Ah, but tis nae the worst of it. Lord Durham has lived up to his nickname of "Radical Jack." He has endorsed his commission's recommendation that the Laird be stripped of his responsibilities. His settlers—those who signed a bond for their passage—they are to pay for their land at valuation. That is fair enough. But those who paid their own passage are to receive their lands free. The McNab's patent is to be rescinded, as are the quit-rents of the settlers. Why should this be? The Laird has devoted years to settling his township. Quit-rent is his due. Is it not? Even if he be *only* a government agent. Since coming to this new land he has put his life into his township. Aye, at times I believe his dealings with the settlers be rather harsh. And his litigation against Mr. Cameron over the road to Muskrat Lake . . . that still . . . tis most difficult for . . . aye, tis a harrying injustice that sticks in my craw. I have never asked my Chief to explain; I don't know why. Perhaps . . . but one chilly afternoon this fall, we were seated in front of the hearth at Waba Cottage, teacups in hand. I dinna recall our topic of conversation—twas nothing of consequence—when the McNab suddenly expounded on . . . twas a rare display of insecurity for the Laird, but he unburdened his feelings and told me he is troubled—most troubled—that his plan is taking much longer than expected. The McNab said he believed by now he would have acquired sufficient funds to return home and reclaim his estates. But, nay, the years roll on and tis still one skirmish after another. The Chief said nothing of Mr. Cameron, but he defended his governing of the township. Quite forcefully, I must say. Tis *he* who answers to the government! Tis *he* to whom Sir Peregrine entrusted responsibility! Aye, the heavy burden of *that* responsibility is the Chief's! Tis nae Donald Cameron's! Nor the commissioners'! I felt much sympathy for the Laird when he finished his outburst. I could see from his flushed countenance he was embarrassed by such a display of feeling. I consoled him as best I could and assured him many of the settlers are law-abiding and respectful men and have scant contact with the disgruntled crofters at Flat Rapids. Although I don't know if that be entirely true. Robert Miller told me every able-bodied man in the township signed the petition to Lord Durham. Even himself! And Robert has always been loyal to his Chief.

Twas a bleak day, indeed, when the commission's report arrived at Waba Cottage. I didn't know what to say to my Chief. I have been Piper to the Laird since he succeeded to the Chieftainship on Francis's passing in 1816. I take great pride in the honour bestowed upon me through my association with this illustrious clan. Now that honour has been tarnished—soiled in a most shameful and public manner.

AH, AT LAST! Some good news! The McNab has been given a reprieve. Lord Brougham has scandalized Lord Durham: he attacked his character and reputation in the House of Lords—something to do with his ordinance freeing the prisoners of the rebellion in Lower Canada. Word has reached us that Lord Melbourne's government has disallowed the ordinance. As one might expect from this impetuous and proud nobleman, the Viceroy has resigned his commission and sailed for England to defend his honour.

The Laird's spirits brightened considerably when we received word of the Governor General's departure.

"You see, MacGregor, the rascal has thrown up his commission and returned to England," the McNab informed me during a brief visit to my humble dwelling: a visit I believe was for the sole purpose of delivering this news. Ah, but we are not out of the proverbial woods just yet. Tis evident the Laird canna get a sympathetic ear from Sir George; he will have to lean more heavily on his friends in the Assembly. Tis what he has done, and to his relief the Assembly has agreed to defer the commission's recommendations. The government did not set a future date to deal with the matter. Tis a relief, indeed, but tis still hanging over our heads—hanging as sure as the executioner's axe hovered over the neck of the Laird's grandfather Buchanan, Chief of Arnprior, whom the English beheaded at Carlisle for partaking in the Rising of the '45.

I WISH MY news . . . tis most regrettable, but once again mayhem has afflicted our province. As ye might expect, tis the Americans again! "Patriots" they call themselves; "vagabonds" Sir George calls them. This time they crossed the border at Prescott and Windsor. I must tell ye I think the Laird was secretly pleased. The Assembly, preoccupied with this new invasion . . . the honourable members have no time to concern themselves with the grievances of settlers. And the McNab, that is, Colonel McNab, Colonel of the 20th Battalion of Carleton Light Infantry, called his Regiment to assemble in Pakenham. My Colleen was foremost in my mind as I polished my pipe's silver mounts. Except on one occasion in Perthshire, she had nae seen me partake in a formal ceremony. Keeping the proper distance from my Colonel, I shouldered my pipes and marched in a circle, my steps slow and deliberate. As wave after wave of "The

McNab Gathering" rolled over the open land, some nine hundred men amassed on the ploughed field commandeered by my Chief for a parade ground. Twas a glorious sight indeed!

Ah, but once again the pig-headed contrariness of the McNab's settlers fouled the day. When their legitimate Colonel stood before them and asked for volunteers, the proud companies of Fitzroy and Pakenham stepped forward to a man. But, nay, not one—*not one* of the McNab's settlers volunteered! I could see the frustration, the flush of embarrassment on my Chief's face. He quickly discharged the Regiment to their billet, supplied in a most generous manner by the good people of Pakenham.

It shames me to tell ye that we imposed upon their gregarious hospitality when . . . tis most distasteful . . . later that evening fighting erupted between our Highlanders and the Orange Irish. No one seemed to know who instigated the Donnybrook. Some unprincipled rascal spread an outlandish rumour twas the doing of the Laird! Nay, we learned the cause the next day. The proud, steadfast Irish called our Highlanders "disloyal cowards." Aye! That would start a row! The McNab and I were quartered outside the village, but my Colleen told us the melee went on into the night before both sides tired of the fracas. She said she helped nurse some of the men who suffered cuts and bruises, and someone told her at least one Irish had been severely wounded. The Laird inquired—and I sensed he was disappointed—but he was told none of the crofters from Flat Rapids took part. Tis not surprising: Donald Cameron would keep them in check.

On the morn, a courier delivered a dispatch from the front informing us that government troops had repelled the invaders. Twas good news indeed, not only for the security of the province, but the McNab was able to skirt further embarrassment. He called his Regiment to order, informed the men that the raiders had been routed, thanked them for their willingness to defend the province, reminded them it was their sworn duty to the Crown, and summarily dismissed them. I would like to have stayed with my Colleen, but duty called, my place being with my Colonel. We journeyed home by sleigh through extremely heavy snow. Although guarded in his comments, I sensed the McNab's relief that no further action need be taken with the Regiment. I also sensed a renewed determination to secure his hold on the township.

PART SEVEN

As IN PREVIOUS winters, some settlers left the care of their farms to wives and older children. They ventured into the dense forest to work as lumberjacks, felling pine for loggers who drove the booms down the Ottawa and St. Lawrence. Others, recent immigrants, worked with their neighbours in "bees," clearing their acreage of trees and underbrush, tossing the debris into piles for bonfires, stacking the remainder against the sides of their shanties and covering it with leather tarpaulins to keep dry for fuel. Old hands, who had toiled on the land since their arrival, spent the winter months repairing tools, caring for livestock, and travelling by horse and sleigh into Arnprior and Bytown, where they sold excess produce at market.

"G'day!" Donald Cameron was in Isaac Gregory's General Store selecting a new cooking pot for Elizabeth when he heard the throaty voice of Walter Ross behind him. He turned around.

"Walter! How goes it, lad? I haven't laid eyes on ya in weeks."

"Nay, I's been keepin busy. Has ye heard the latest?"

"The latest? I don't know. What's McNab up to now?"

"I didn't say twas McNab." Ross chuckled.

"Nay, ye didn't, but who else?"

"I was talkin to Duncan and he says Alex Yulle told him the Chief has sold the township and the settlers is to be thrown off their land."

"Ah, that. Aye, I heard that. Tis nonsense. Tis not his township to sell."

"Do ye know that for a fact? None seems too sure."

"Tis hard to say for a fact, but I was in Perth two weeks ago and John Radenhurst—ye know, the government man in Toronto—he was visitin Thomas and he told me twas for certain Maitland only appointed McNab an agent."

"He has nae been actin like an agent."

"Mr. Radenhurst says the government ordered McNab to stop cutting timber on our lots. But bein the Laird, he pays it no heed. He's gone and given Roddie a licence to cut on Hugh's and Colin's lots."

"That won't sit well with Hugh and Colin. What is they gonna do?"

"Hugh says when they told Roddie he was trespassing, he showed them the licence from the Chief. So now they've asked Thomas to take Roddie to court."

"Tis the Chief should be taken to court."

"Aye, but there's a better chance of winning against Roddie than the Laird." Ross shook his head.

Although weary of their struggles with McNab, and despite mostly hollow victories, the obstinacy of their Scottish temperament would not allow the settlers to capitulate. McNab's continual threats to take them to court wore down the resistance of some farmers who eventually gave in and paid what they could in quit-rent. But the Flat Rapids farmers and their closest neighbours would not be swayed: they held to the belief that eventually the government would act on Lord Durham's recommendations. That steadfast defiance was due largely to Donald Cameron's leadership. But now the unwavering crofter had another predicament: one not widely known among the settlers because it involved a reclusive neighbour.

ON A WOODEN chair in the corner of his shed, Dennis McNee sat hunched over a small pine table. Lying on the table were the Laird of McNab's notice of eviction and McNee's Brown Bess. He picked up the flintlock musket and a powder horn made from a hollowed deer antler. He poured a measure of powder down the barrel. He greased a patch of cloth and stretched it over the muzzle, centred a lead ball in the cloth, trimmed the edges and, with a hickory rod, rammed the ball down the muzzle on top of the powder. He put the rifle back down on the table and picked up the notice of eviction.

A quiet man, cordial enough with his fellow crofters, but inclined to keep to himself, McNee didn't attend township meetings and he took little notice of township gossip. He had, however, shown the eviction notice to Donald Cameron, who encouraged him to retain Thomas Radenhurst and fight for his land at the spring Quarter Session. But McNee didn't believe he'd receive justice in the district court. Nor did he have the patience for litigation. He hadn't come to McNab Township to fight again the battles of Albany County—nor the battles of Perthshire. He tossed the document onto the table.

McNee had prospered since he and George Watt exchanged lots. Not only had his arrangement with the Buchanans supplied him with additional income, but the brothers hired lumbermen to harvest the timber, which sped up the clearing of his land. The farmer had sixty-nine cleared acres. Despite having to plant grain around rotting tree stumps, the land yielded a bountiful harvest: enough to pay his quit-rent, feed Flora and the children, and still have plenty of bushels to sell at the Arnprior and Bytown markets. He had acquired several more head of cattle and, this past summer, he hammered together a wire coop and purchased a number of hens. For the first time in his life, McNee was feeling optimistic about his future. He was getting ahead, building equity in his land, and providing security for his family.

Then, with no advance warning, Lipsey delivered McNab's eviction notice. The crofter had no idea why he was being evicted; the notice didn't say. It said only that the government had granted McNab a patent on his one hundred acres and that he and his family had a fortnight to vacate the land.

A deep sigh escaped from his body as he pushed himself away from the table. He walked over to the shed door and looked out at his snow-covered fields. It was a mild day, overcast and calm. His saddled mare was tethered to a stump in front of his shanty. Some fifty yards away, his older children cavorted in a good-natured snowball fight. From inside the shanty, he could hear the playful voices of his younger offspring. He stood in the doorway, seemingly transfixed. Beads of perspiration broke on his brow. He removed his leather hat and used his sleeve to wipe the glistening sweat from his forehead. He looked back at the rifle lying on the table. With purposeful steps, he walked over, picked up the gun and the eviction notice and carried them outside. He mounted his horse and rode off.

HAD HE ARRIVED at the dog-leg in the road seconds later, Donald Cameron would not have spotted the rider several yards ahead who was turning his horse onto the snow-covered trail to White Lake. Cameron halted his mare. He couldn't see the rider's face, but he recognized his neighbour's cowhide jacket with the American eagle embroidered on the back. The crofter had failed to convince McNee to fight the eviction in court, and now, instinct, intuition, whatever it was, told him where McNee was headed—and why. Reticent at the best of times, McNee gave no indication how he would cope. But Cameron sensed in the man a latent fury seething and pressing for release. He rode after him.

   Less than a quarter mile from White Lake, McNee rode into a gully, unforeseen because of the heavy snow. The mare's front legs plunged almost to the top of her shanks. Repeated attempts to move the horse forward were to no avail. He dismounted and, with considerable effort, turned the animal around and led her out of the culvert. He was walking the horse back along the trail, looking for another approach to Waba Cottage, when he met Cameron.

   "G'day, Dennis," Cameron said as he dismounted. McNee ignored the salutation. "What brings you to White

Lake?" McNee stared at his fellow crofter. "Are ye gonna have a talk with the Laird about the eviction?" McNee tightened his grip on his mare's halter. Cameron's gloved hand stroked his trimmed beard. He waited.

"I'm gonna shoot the son of a bitch!" McNee said. "Should uh been done long ago." Cameron took a deep breath.

"Ye'll only end up in gaol—or worse. I know how ya feel, but tis not the way to get justice. I know ye took up arms in America, but this is not America. We have the rule of law and we can go to—"

"Aye, ye has laws, and what good are they? The settlers has—"

"Tis because you're selling timber to the Buchanans. The Laird—"

"Tis legal! I has a patent!"

"Aye! And tis why ye should take the matter to the court! Ye are in the right!" Thick snowflakes began to fall.

"And wasn't John Drummond in the right? McNab made him an outlaw; forced him off his lot; forced him out of the township. What fucking good were *his* rights?" McNee hawked and sent a stream of yellow saliva into the snow. "Duncan says McNab never forgets a slight. Duncan says the bastard's vindictive. It don't matter how long . . . how many years . . . he must have his pound of flesh."

"John's situation was not the same. McNab swears the government gave him timber rights to the land. Tis true, we have never seen the proof, but . . . if ye do violence to the Laird, the law will be on us; not just on you—on all of us! Nay, we have persevered without violence. Ye will put us all in jeopardy if ye do violence to the Laird." Cameron saw the frustration in McNee's eyes. "Let's go home, Dennis." The men held one another's gaze. Cameron stroked his beard and waited. Finally, McNee's shoulders dropped. He yellowed the snow at his feet with another stream of saliva.

Then he mounted his horse and the animal plodded back through the virgin snow. Cameron followed a few yards behind.

***

TIS NOT THE life I envisioned when I accompanied the McNab from Perthshire. When I look back, I dinna think I gave much thought to what sort of life twould be. The McNab said we would be welcomed as royalty—and treated thus. Aye, he was right! On our arrival. But there be no aristocrats, no royals in McNab Township—nor in any township. Nay, what patricians we have are in the Family Compact—the government in Toronto.

I am a Piper. Tis my only craft. Tis true, I am housed and Lipsey tends to my small garden. Our cottages being in close proximity, on many occasions I sup with the Laird and his children, partaking of Miss Hunt's delectable *cuisine*. But except for a *ceilidh* at a settler's shanty, and those occasions when the McNab entertains at his Kinnell estate—rare since our settling in White Lake—there be no call for my services.

But "time marches on," as tis said, and so I will bring ye up to date on what has transpired. It saddens me to tell ye, but . . . I no longer feel close to my Chief. Aye, I see the Laird most every day, but I find our encounters most disheartening. The McNab has a pinched, desperate look, the visage of an obstinate man. Tis no wonder! His position is precarious. Most precarious. He has at last been successful with litigation against Dennis McNee. The Magistrate ruled the exchange of lots between Mr. McNee and Mr. Watt illegal because they did not obtain new location tickets from the Laird *before* the exchange took place. Pooh! What nit-picking! Alas, it seems not to matter. Lipsey delivered the judgment to Mr. McNee, but the crofter has not vacated his land, and the McNab dare not send Sheriff Lyle to enforce the order: to do so would further provoke those in Toronto who wish to see him relieved of the township. Perhaps tis just as well. I heard on good authority that Mr. McNee threatened violence to the Laird. Not only threatened it, but would have carried it out had Donald Cameron not intervened. Tis, for certain, a ticklish situation. There is no danger of Mr. Watt being evicted. He and the McNab have become . . . what is the cant saying?—ah, *oui*, "bosom buddies."

"At least the rascal has no ready market for my timber," the Laird told me with much glee. That's because the Buchanans' business has failed, an unfortunate occurrence complicated by the sudden and tragic death of Andrew from an unknown illness.

If only matters between the McNab and his *other* settlers were improving! But, nay, they have deteriorated even further! There be no peace, no sign of respite from the endless feud between the Flat Rapids crofters—they now call themselves farmers—and the Chief. Tis most regrettable. And now London has sent word that the Honourable Charles Edward Poulett Thomson is coming out as our new Governor General. This news has only added to the McNab's woes.

"He is known to be a radical," the Laird informed me over tea and Miss Hunt's tasty butter tarts. "Aye! *More* radical than Durham! Ah, but at least Lord Russell . . . we must be grateful for the wisdom of our new Colonial Secretary; at least he has the common sense to counsel Thomson *not* to entertain Durham's harebrained scheme, what he calls 'responsible government.' Tis obvious to men of learning that Her Majesty's representative canna be responsible to the Home Office *and* heed the capricious, self-serving whims of the colonials. These are foolish times we live in, MacGregor, foolish indeed."

The McNab fears Mr. Thomson will strike the final blow and take away his township, leaving him destitute. He sent a hasty post to the Attorney-General, his friend Kit Hagerman. He offered to withdraw all legal claims against his settlers and, for nine thousand pounds, surrender his claim to the five thousand acres allotted to him by Sir Peregrine when that honourable gentleman placed the township in the Chief's hands. Ah, but Sir George thought the claim extravagant: he proposed to the Executive Council a sum of two thousand pounds. Fortunately—fortunate for the McNab—Bishop Strachan, although no longer on the Executive, the good Anglican cleric still wields considerable influence. We are told that after much bickering, he convinced Council to award the Laird four thousand pounds, one thousand of which was dispatched immediately to Waba Cottage.

"Tis a bleak day, a bleak day indeed," the McNab said on the afternoon we received the news. Then, with his very next breath, his buoyant spirit rebounded. "But I am still in charge of my township, MacGregor!" I could think of nothing to say; I acknowledged his anxiety with a nod. Tis true, however, the McNab *will* retain control over his township. But he is to desist from collecting the quit-rents that are his due and . . . here is a fine example of . . . twas clear from the government order that the Laird was to cut timber *only* on his own 850 acres. But he still claims a right under the patent issued by Sir Francis. He has given Mr. Roddie a license to cut on the lots of Hugh Alexander and Colin Carmichael. Why my Chief persists . . . no doubt he will be back in the dock at the next Quarter Session. I am tired and disillusioned by all this strife. I have my pipes for solace. And for that I am grateful. But what is to happen to him? What is to happen to us? Nay, I do not know. I no longer feel close to my Chief, but tradition, ah, yes, tradition binds us. He is still Patriarch of Clan McNab.

Perhaps . . . nay, if I am to be honest with ye, there be a more *bona fide* reason for my despondent mood: my Colleen and I have once again had a falling out. This time tis

not an indiscretion. She has spurned my invitations to move
to White Lake. Since receiving the gift of a mare, she rides
over to visit on occasion, but most often it is I who journey
to Pakenham. I canna get a reason—at least none
satisfactory—for her unwillingness to share my humble
dwelling, my stone cottage. Tis more sturdy, more spacious,
more comfortable than her log shanty. New Irish—even
some Scots!—are settling in Pakenham Township. A few
bring capital with them, and I know, because Magistrate
Richey told me, she could fetch a pretty pence for her land.
Every time I mention this, she says she will mull it over. I
think tis more to change the subject. I reminded her of the
Highland custom of handfasting; I feared the raucous howl
she let loose would bring the whole settlement on the run. I
should have known, the girl doesn't give a whit for the
disapproving . . . the pinched lips and furrowed brows of
dreary Puritans. Tis, I think, why I am so fond of her.

The other day we had a row when I arrived sodden,
having been caught in a brief spring downpour only a
quarter mile from her shanty. She laughed at the sight of me,
but when twas apparent I was in no mood to be cheered, she
teased me by slowly peeling off my wet garments and
matching the removal of each piece of apparel by discarding
one of her own. When we were starkers, she wrapped us in
a quilt of soft wool. Aye! My mood improved considerably!
Afterwards, lying on the quilt, satiated, I thought it
propitious to ask if she had considered my request. She
pushed me off the bed with both feet, my heavy frame
landing with a thump on the rough timbers. Then she
jumped up, wrapped herself in the quilt and berated me
while pacing in a circle around her constrained quarters.

"Why do ye keep on about White Lake? I am content
here. Tis better to have distance between us. If we be always
together . . . we'd go stale. Aye! Stale! Stale! Stale! I would
tire . . . we would tire . . ." While she was ranting, I fell over

trying to get a leg into my still damp trews. She quit pacing, stared at my near-naked figure prone on the floor and let out a roar before the vexed look in her eyes returned.

"Colleen," I said, struggling to my feet. "I have . . . we have been courting some . . . I canna remember how . . . if ye go back to Perthshire . . . it's been several . . . tis time . . . tis customary to wed or—"

"Nay, Malcolm. I like ye; aye, I love ye, but I will nae marry ye! I see the wives . . . good women, hard-working, but old, worn down caring for husbands an children, with precious little time for theyselves. Tis worthy what they do, but tis nae the life for me." I didn't know what to say. I finished dressing and my Colleen did likewise. Then she said, "They are my own here. Tis true, some look down their noses, but these are my people. I would be surrounded by Scots at White Lake. Presbyterians! Ugh." This last did not have the ring of truth. She had lived among Scots—Presbyterians—in Perthshire for many years. And she had many friends, the less judgmental, those accepting of contrariety. I should have let the matter drop, but, nay, I pressed on.

"I dinna believe we can go on . . . I mean tis not practical to . . ." I didn't know what I was trying to say, but her look . . . I knew I should say no more.

"Out with ye."

"Colleen."

"Out with ye!" She pushed me towards the door, opened it, pushed me again and I stumbled out. She threw my cloak after me and closed the door with a violent thud. I was about to re-enter when Nellie whinnied and I looked over at my faithful mare: she was shaking her head from side to side. I thought her a Sibyl, and so I mounted and started for home. About a half mile from White Lake, I was caught in another downpour, drenched through to the skin for the second time that day.

✻✻✻

"I SAY WE has suffered enough; the government is not gonna to listen to our grievances; tis time we took the law into our own hands; tis what our forefathers did when the clan was set upon; tis what they do in America. Petition! Petition! Petition! And what's they got us? Nothin! We is still treated like peasants, no better than they was in France; the people rose up and rid theyselves of the despot; tis time we do the same. I say we brings the tyrant before the people—we brings him before this meeting—we tries him and shoots him; there is nothin more we can—"

"Ah, Duncan, listen to yourself, lad!" Donald Cameron interrupted McDonald's rant to the men of the township who had gathered in Angus McLaren's spacious new barn on a sunny June morning. "Tis true, McNab has treated us like peasants. But this is not France! We are not Frenchmen! And we are not Americans! Scots, aye, we are Scots! Proud Highlanders! But we are not rogues! We are simple crofters; farmers. We have the right to seek redress in the courts, and we have a new Governor General. I am told Thomson is a man of honour, a man who will listen to our grievances."

"Ye be a good soul, Donald," McDonald said. "An we is grateful for what ye has tried to do for us, for all of us. But ye is bein . . . what's that word?—naive. We has appealed an appealed, and what has it got us? Nothin."

"We understands your anger, Duncan," Lorn McCaul said. "McNab has caused me much hardship, too, but think about it, lad; if we shoot him the law will be on us. We will be no better than outlaws. In France . . . twas altogether diffrent. And the French is hot-blooded!"

"I agrees with Donald," McLaren said. "When the sheriff raided me farm, I wanted to shoot McNab. But I has thought about it; we must try all means legal to free us from the tyrant. Duncan, ye say the people in France rose up. Aye, that they did! They rose up in Lower Canada, too! Blood spilled everywhere! Is that what ye want?"

"Men, we is all of the same mind," Iain Storie said. "We all feel Duncan's anger. But Donald and Angus is right. Me thinks we should use more paper and draw up a new petition. Would ye take it to Thomson for us, Donald? It means a trip to Toronto, but it should nae be an unpleasant journey, it's been a warm summer."

"Aye, I'll take a petition to Toronto—if the majority wishes?" There was a moment's silence before an "aye" from near the back of the gathering prompted the others to voice their support for yet another petition. Cameron nodded acknowledgment and gazed at the earthen floor while stroking his neatly trimmed beard.

"What is it?" Hugh Alexander asked.

"I have another idea." The men waited. "Have ye heard of a Mr. Francis Hincks? He's the editor of *The Examiner* in Toronto."

"Aye, I've heard the name," Storie said.

"He's an Irish, a Reformer. He supports Durham's idea of responsible government. Tis why he founded his paper some two years ago. Since I'll be in Toronto, why don't I take him a list of our grievances? Tis no way of knowing, but he might publish them. Ye can be certain everyone in the government reads his paper." This suggestion was greeted with another chorus of "ayes." "Good. That's settled. Now, about the statute-labour." Mention of this subject evoked heated grumbling. Despite the arguments of the pathmasters, the Laird and Magistrate Richey had ordered the year's statute-labour to be worked on two roads some eight miles distant from the settlers' homes.

"Since Perth be on your way to Toronto," Hugh Alexander said, "ye could come with me an Colin to the Quarter Session; the court be hearing our suits against Roddie for the timber." And so Cameron agreed to present yet another petition to the magistrates sitting on the Queen's Bench in Perth.

- - -

The Grand Jurors of our Lady the Queen on their oaths present. That having fully investigated the complaints of the inhabitants of the Township of McNab, they on their oaths say, that Archibald McNab of McNab and Andrew Richey of Pakenham, Esq., have not apportioned the statute-labour of the Township of McNab for the present year equitably or according to justice; that the said Archibald McNab has acted tyrannically and oppressively, and is a nuisance to the public at large, and especially to the people of McNab; and they recommend that the statute-labour be laid out according to the wishes of the settlers of McNab, as represented by the Pathmasters of the said Township.

Donald Cameron stifled a smile when the Clerk of the Peace read the Grand Jury's findings to the Bench of the Quarter Session. A few hours earlier, the chairman had rejected the farmers' petition requesting equitable apportionment of the statute-labour. Now Cameron noticed a spasm in the old man's jowls as his brittle voice ordered the clerk to file away the presentment and take no action on it. The settlers had gained another small victory, especially having the Laird described as "a public nuisance."

Next on the order paper were the *suits* brought by Colin Carmichael and Hugh Alexander against William Roddie. The farmers cited the government's Order-in-Council instructing McNab to restrict the cutting of timber to his own acreage. Roddie produced the licence given him by McNab and swore under oath that the Laird had indemnified him against the farmers. But the magistrates were not about to defy their superiors in the Family Compact: they quickly rendered verdicts for the plaintiffs. This, too, buoyed Cameron's spirits. He spent a few minutes congratulating Carmichael and Alexander before boarding a coach to continue his journey to the provincial capital.

In Toronto, Cameron met briefly with William H. Lee, Thomson's secretary, who assured him he would "lay the petition before His Excellency, the Governor General." He then walked to the office of *The Examiner*. Mr. Hincks was not in. He left the information with a clerk who promised to bring it to his editor's attention.

On the long, bumpy coach ride home, Cameron's thoughts turned to the hardship imposed upon the farmers because of the apportionment of the year's statute-labour. He could think of no way around it until he remembered that the legislature had recently added another layer of bureaucracy with the appointment of wardens in the townships. Their duties included the power to commute each ratepayer's statute-labour. He recommended this procedure to the McNab wardens who, sympathetic to the settlers' predicament, agreed to commute the statute-labour for four years, thus enabling the men to work on their own concessions and side roads.

This act of insubordination infuriated Chief McNab and the magistrates in Perth. They complained to the Attorney-General, who informed them that the wardens had acted within the law: the commutation of the statute-labour would stand.

ON THE AFTERNOON of July 13, 1840, when Francis Allan, Crown Lands Agent for Bathurst District, returned to his office in Perth following a dental appointment, he found a single sheet of paper shoved under his door. The post bore the wax seal of the Governor General of British North America. Nursing the ache in his jaw caused by the dentist's packing of an abscessed tooth, Allan sat down at his mahogany desk and read the letter.

Toronto, 8ᵗʰ July, 1840

Sir, — I am directed by His Excellency, the Governor General-in-Council, to inform you that His Excellency has appointed you a Special Commissioner to investigate the complaints of the settlers in the Township of McNab in your District, and you will report directly to His Excellency-in-Council. You will proceed, immediately on the receipt of this communication, to the work of investigation, taking the petition of Donald Cameron and others as your basis. You will be minute and particular in your examinations, and will visit every lot, value the same, and if possible see every settler personally, and ascertain from him the truth or falsity of the complaints made to the Government.

I have the honour to be, &c.,

W.H. Lee, Secretary to
His Excellency the Governor General,
British North America

***

ALAS, I BELIEVE tis over. The McNab is acting like a man possessed—possessed with malice towards *any* who question his absolute authority. And his authority *is* being questioned. At the highest level of government. Tis true, he escaped prosecution for illegally cutting timber on the lots of Mr. Carmichael and Mr. Alexander. They brought *suits* against Mr. Roddie instead—and won! But last summer, Thomson . . . in August, London bestowed upon him a peerage; he now proudly bears the title, "Lord Sydenham." But in July, the Governor General appointed Mr. Francis

Allan—the Crown Lands Agent for the District of Bathurst—he appointed him a Special Commissioner to investigate the settlers' complaints and report his findings directly to him—*not* to the Assembly, nor the Executive Council. Tis indicative of the man's concern. And tis not as if he has idle hands. Only two weeks after appointing Mr. Allan, Lord Russell introduced his *Union Act* in the British Parliament, and the honourable members passed it. Tis now Lord Sydenham's unenviable task to bring it to fruition: to unite the two Canadas. A most unenviable task indeed. I know Mr. Allan was thorough with his queries. He travelled the township and consulted many, if not all the settlers. Now we shall see what comes to pass.

Ye would think hanging on tenterhooks awaiting yet another report would suffice, but, nay, three weeks ago . . . ah, it causes me distress even to think about it. Three weeks ago we returned from the fall Quarter Session, where my Chief embarrassed me—utterly disgraced the good name of Clan McNab—with a vindictive charge against fifty of his settlers. The charge? Conspiracy! I could nae believe my ears when the Clerk of the Peace read the charge. I canna imagine what the McNab was thinking. The Grand Jury dismissed the charge as frivolous; dismissed it out of hand; the Clerk of the Peace barely containing a snicker when announcing the Jury's findings. Twas one more of the Chief's ill-fated and foolish schemes to punish his settlers for some perceived wrongdoing. Conspiracy! Lowly crofters who toil on their land from morning till night! Tis pathetic! Laughable and pathetic!

And now there be another attack upon my Chief. Four days ago, while in Toronto, the McNab received a great shock when he picked up a copy of *The Examiner*. Tis a Toronto newspaper sympathetic to the Reformers. Unbeknownst to him, the settlers had sent their grievances to its editor, Mr. Hincks. His front-page article . . . tis most upsetting . . . it presents a history of the township and attempts to discredit the Chief's hard work; aye, to make my Chief appear a most despicable villain. Tis a scandalous diatribe. The McNab, as was his entitlement, made haste in responding to the libellous publication. Upon his return, he gave a copy of his dispatch to Mr. McRae and to myself.

Toronto, 12 Nov. 1840
To Mr. Hincks
Editor of the Examiner

Sir: — I have observed with great surprise in your paper of the 11th instant, an article containing the most grave and extraordinary charges against me - charges as untrue as they are unfounded, and as they are calculated to bring me into public odium with my own people and the world, and also as they reflect seriously upon my honesty and good faith toward my countrymen who came out under certain arrangements entered into between themselves and my agents in Scotland, I shall take such steps against you for the protection of my name and character as I may be advised. I request that you will publish this letter in your next paper. I am, Sir, your obedient servant.

Archibald McNab

The Laird has ordered Mr. McRae to serve an action for libel against Mr. Hincks. He is seeking damages of one thousand pounds. We await the editor's response; perhaps in this week's *Examiner*.

- - -

AH, THE POWER of the press! The McNab's libel suit has not deterred Mr. Hincks. There be no apology. Nay, he attacks the good name of the Laird almost weekly. He has posed several questions from the report of Lord Durham's commission. The McNab told me he will not take the bait and respond: he says he will set the record straight in court. The trial is scheduled for the fall Assize in Toronto. Mr. Hincks seems confident in winning. He has stated quite boldly—to quote from a recent article in *The Examiner*— "We can assure Mr. McNab that we are quite ready to meet him before a jury of our countrymen, and we incline to believe that if he persist in his prosecution, he will have cause to lament before its termination that he is not able to go into court with hands as clean as our own." Tis not only brazen in tone, tis disrespectful. The proper address be "Chief McNab" or "McNab of McNab"; tis nae "Mr."

No doubt the good citizens of Toronto are reading these calumnious editorials. Word has come to us that *all* members of the Assembly—even those on the Executive Council—have been shaken by Mr. Hincks's accusations and flustered and humiliated in scrambling to mount a credible defence. Alas, I fear my Chief may be spurned as a political liability. Tis what one would expect from the spurious loyalty of politicians.

Ah, but at least I am no longer spurned by my Colleen. Months ago I ceased with my entreaties that she share my humble abode at White Lake. We have continued as always, the ride to Pakenham so routine, Nellie hardly needs my hand on the reins. Tis true, we have not had a row for sometime, and our love-making is most satisfying, but . . . it saddens me . . . the feelings I had in Perthshire have returned. Tis not that I don't like . . . love her, tis just that . . . I want something more. Ah, but what? I do not know. At times I think tis simply that the purpose for my life has fallen away; I fear tis simply boredom.

One day not long ago in Arnprior, I met Colin Carmichael. We talked about his successful *suit* against William Roddie: he and Hugh Alexander have collected the fine, and I know Mr. Roddie, who paid the Chief the duties on the cut timber, has asked to be reimbursed. Whether the McNab has done so or not, I do not know. Then we chatted about goings-on in the township and he asked what I did to keep busy. I felt embarrassed and ashamed in my feeble attempt to put on a good face. But Colin, while lacking in schooling, is a perceptive man and I believe he sensed my lack of purpose. He asked why don't I ask the Laird to give me a separate croft to farm? Tis an understandable suggestion, Colin, I said, but if ye could see me with a hoe . . . with a plough, my furrows would travel as straight as a garter snake, or worse, resemble one of our ill-kept roads. Nay, tis not a practical option.

I still practise my pipes daily and I am forever trying my hand at a new *piobaireachd*. Young Allan has shown an interest, and only yesterday the Laird asked me to give his son lessons. I said I would be delighted to share the faculty handed down through generations of MacGregors. I will instruct him on the practice chanter. If he shows promise, the Laird said he would order a stand of pipes from MacDonald in Edinburgh.

I must resolve my misgivings about my Colleen. Except that I don't know what I am to resolve. Tis trying, but perhaps if I am patient my emotions will sort themselves out. Perhaps tis just the turmoil . . . the uncertainty of the McNab's future. And mine! Perhaps tis the two combined, plus my indolence from lack of a *raison d'être*. Perhaps . . . whatever the cause, I canna go on like this.

***

DENNIS MCNEE WAS still on his lot almost two years after receiving McNab's notice to vacate. Following his confrontation with Donald Cameron at White Lake, the truculent farmer stood watch for the anticipated arrival of the sheriff. In daylight hours, he stood watch at the window in his shed, the flintlock loaded and in hand. After sunset, he sat well into the night by the window of his shanty, the rifle resting on a stool beside him. Flora's timid pleas that he relinquish his surveillance went unheeded.

A week passed and then a month and another month, but neither the sheriff nor McNab made an appearance. His fear of imminent confrontation gradually dissipated, only to be replaced by gnawing uncertainty: What was going to happen? When was it going to happen? His anxiety caused him sleepless nights and his neglect of the farm resulted in disrepair. When stress finally got the upper hand, he rode over to talk to Donald Cameron, only to learn that McNab—fearful of arousing animosity among the assembly—had brought the notice of eviction before the Quarter Session to reinforce his position, to ensure he was completely within his rights. Since McNee failed to appear—not that unusual, because many settlers found travelling to Perth both time consuming and time wasted—the court issued a *writ* of possession. But Cameron told him McNab had greater concerns than taking possession of an additional one hundred acres, and that was likely the reason the Chief hadn't asked Sheriff Lyle to enforce the eviction.

Rather than ease his mind, his conversation with Cameron only served to increase his apprehension. He even contemplated deserting the property and moving to another township. Many immigrants had done just that to escape the Laird's persecution. But McNee quickly dismissed the notion. He had run from Perthshire. He had run from Albany County. He would not run from McNab Township. He began work each day just after sunrise. He instructed his middle boy to stand watch, and he kept his flintlock nearby. When the Buchanans' business failed, McNee allowed himself to hope that since his timber patent was now worthless—there being no other sawmill in the township—the Laird might decide not to evict, especially if, as Cameron said, he had more pressing concerns.

As the months wore on, he wearied of the constant surveillance. It wasn't that he made a conscious decision to abandon the watch: work on his farm simply pushed it from his mind and the family's life carried on in the same manner as that of the other farmers. He no longer had income from the timber, but his acreage—a tract of arable land just outside the rocky terrain of Flat Rapids—yielded an abundant harvest. Come fall, he sold his produce in the expanding community of Bytown, skirting around White Lake on his journey there and back.

FOR THE ORIGINAL settlers, their recurring hope of escaping the bondage of feudalism had peaked and plummeted in an erratic rhythm over the past fifteen years. Now, in the fall of 1840, once again they were riding a crest of unfolding events that seemed to promise a final resolution—a final victory. As had been true since the settlers' arrival—true, in fact, since humans began chronicling their lives—those whose nature it was to be positive were optimistic; those whose nature it was to be negative were pessimistic. After fifteen years of ongoing disappointment, it was difficult to argue with the naysayers. But thanks to the unassuming leadership of Donald Cameron, who always listened attentively to the cynics and then somehow mustered an argument that persuaded them to keep trying, despair had slowly given way to a rising sanguinity. Except for McNee's failed attempt, the farmers had not resorted to violence. They had persevered through the courts, through a justice system flagged with political patronage and vitiated with judgments that favoured the obsequious henchmen of the Family Compact. *Ceilidhs* had become more frequent, but the fanciful stories and traditional songs shared evenings with talk of the McNab/Hincks libel trial, now only a few weeks away.

***

TIS A MILD winter's day, a perfect day for a stroll in the crisp, clean air. Nay, I can only sit in my cottage and wonder: how has it come to this? The McNab is the laughing stock of the township. Aye, the whole province! Even in the state of New York! His relentless, pig-headed . . . It has been almost two weeks since the trial in Toronto, his libel action against the editor of *The Examiner*. He won. And by winning, the Jury placed a value on his reputation—on his character: five pounds! The Laird of McNab, 13th Chief of the proud and illustrious Clan McNab . . . I have before me a copy of *The Albion* of New York. Here is how the paper reported the outcome of the trial: "Small Potatoes – The McNab of McNab, a *quasi* Canadian nobleman and Highland Chieftain, obtained from a Toronto jury the sum of £5 for the loss of his character"

I believe if the Judge, Mr. Justice Jonas Jones, hadn't charged the Jury as he did, the twelve good men would have rendered a verdict for Mr. Hincks. Of course my Chief had as Counsel experienced practitioners of the utmost competence, men of the highest rank: Attorney-General William Henry Draper and Solicitor-General Henry Sherwood, who were ably assisted by Mr. John Willoughby Crawford, the latter's law partner.

Mr. Sherwood opened the case for the McNab. He read into the public record the text under dispute and then, in a tone I thought rather flowery and contemptuous, argued it was self-evident that any right-thinking man would find the passages clearly libellous.

Ah, but Mr. Hincks had not engaged greenhorns for his defence. He, too, was ably represented by Mr. Adam

Wilson, the Honourable William Hume Blake and the leader of the Reform members in the Assembly, the Honourable Robert Baldwin. Mr. Baldwin . . . aye, this gentleman will have a distinguished political career! Tis true, he is not a natural orator and, a tall man, he has a pronounced stoop and a pallid complexion not countermanded by his flat, vacant eyes. But he has a quality even more important, a quality that shames the pretentious, obsequious manner of most lawyers and politicians: he is passionate in his beliefs. In a speech of some two hours, not only did he methodically and precisely present the settlers' grievances, he forcefully and elegantly defended the constitutional right of freedom of the press against the tyranny . . . what he called the tyranny of the Family Compact.

Mr. Baldwin and his colleagues then introduced into evidence a number of documents, some dating back to 1823. Most telling . . . most disturbing was a communiqué dated July 20, 1838, from Mr. John Radenhurst, our province's Acting Surveyor-General. He was replying to a recommendation from the Executive Council that the Chief be awarded a patent-deed for five thousand acres, free of expense. Donald Cameron told me at the time, but I did not . . . nay, I could not . . . the memorandum says the lots the McNab selected for his patent-deed are the lots upon which he has placed his settlers, and tis why Mr. Radenhurst did not concur with Council's recommendation to grant the patent. Mr. Radenhurst swore the oath and testified to the veracity of the document. I was sitting in the public gallery directly behind my Chief, who sat erect, his bearing regal, as usual, in full Highland dress. Twas difficult to tell—my view obscured by his high collar—but when Mr. Radenhurst was giving testimony, it appeared the nape of my Chief's neck turned the crimson of his tunic. Ah, but twas not the most damaging evidence. Mr. Baldwin then produced a map of the township he had obtained from Mr. Radenhurst's office.

Had I not seen it with my own eyes . . . the settlers' names had been crossed out and in their place . . . the Laird's name inserted! There is no doubt who wrote . . . after thirty-two years, I know my Chief's hand.

Mr. Baldwin called many of the settlers as witnesses. In turn—twas like a litany—each testified that the McNab demanded payment of quit-rent. Some had paid according to their means; others—those in Flat Rapids—said the land did not yield adequate crop. Some had stopped paying when they suspected twas not legal. Listening to their grievances . . . twas as if . . . I was familiar with most, aye, perhaps all of their accounts. But hearing them all at once . . . tis what the experience of the converted must be like. I was struck with an awakening—an epiphany. I believe I have known for some time, but could not bring myself to accept . . .

And then there was His Lordship's charge to the Jury! Tis shameful, most appalling, the way men twist the truth to justify the ends. When Mr. Draper . . . one can easily see why his elegance in the courtroom has gained him the *sobriquet*, "Sweet William." When our renowned Attorney-General finished his address to the Jury—twas simply a fluent and forceful argument that the settlers had signed bonds and knew their financial and legal responsibilities to the Laird. When Mr. Draper sat down, his Lordship pulled his robes around his shoulders, scowled, as he always does—a grave expression in conflict with his wavy mane of silver hair—he told the court, to my utmost amazement—to the utmost amazement of near everyone present in the courtroom—he told us that Mr. Hincks's Counsel had not justified publication of the articles in question. Mr. Jones said the settlers knew from the agreements they signed with the McNab that their deeds were to come from the government, so twas not possible for them to *believe* the McNab owned the township. Tis typical of how lawyers manipulate the law to suit their purposes. Everyone in the township—aye, even in neighbouring townships—believed the Laird *owned* the township. He told me as much on many occasions. I heard him tell it to others. He passed it off as his own private property. And yet, in charging the Jury, Mr. Jones told them—I remember his exact words—he told them "it was impossible that the witnesses could have believed anything of the kind." I am sure he sensed the utter astonishment in the courtroom, because he went on to tell the Jury that it was quite common for an agent of the Crown delegated with responsibility for settling a township "to speak of it as his own." Tis nothing but a contemptible distortion of the facts! Ah, but His Lordship ranks high in the Family Compact. He be a staunch defender of this oligarchic regime; my Chief, a minion, it saddens me to say. Except for Donald Cameron, and one or two others, the settlers are not men of schooling. They are loyal clansmen: crofters raised from boyhood to trust the word of their Chief. Aye, they believed twas *his township*! Even Mr. Cameron! Twas his sworn testimony and that of the others. Even under cross-examination by Mr. Sherwood.

Twas not the only casuistry by His Lordship. Mr. Jones advised the Jury that the McNab's petition for a patent-deed on the lots of his settlers was, in his words, "justifiable and deserves no reprehension." Eh! I thought I misheard but, nay, I did not. With those words I am certain David Hume, our renowned Scottish moralist, turned in his grave. I did not know . . . I thought my Chief was acting in the best interests of his clansmen. Such is the duty of a noble Highland Chief. But Mr. Radenhurst's testimony and the map . . .

After hearing His Lordship's reasoning on these points of law, twas no surprise when he dismissed—casually dismissed—the settlers' claims of false imprisonment. "The imprisonments were legal," the Judge said. True. By the letter of the law they were legal. But when loyal clansmen—crofters with no desire other than to provide for their families and pay homage to their Chief—when such men are required to sign bonds they canna read nor whose meaning fully comprehend . . . the law, whose adherents are forever espousing its logic, need be tempered by reason.

His Lordship did concur with one charge published in *The Examiner*. Twas by a writer unidentified. The article said the McNab's liaison with Miss Agnes Hunt is—to use the words in the accusation—"a demoralizing and baneful influence on the rising generation in this section of the country." I learned later, to Mr. Hincks's credit, he had instructed Counsel not to pursue this point vigorously. Ah, but that did not keep a few witnesses—the virtuous Presbyterians—from gleefully testifying as to its accuracy. Tis the way the morally superior cast damnation on those who fail to share their righteous outrage at being human. Alas, I only wish my Chief's conduct with Miss Hunt *were* the most shocking of his actions. Tis his actions towards his settlers—actions sanctioned by the government—that be truly demoralizing to the rising generation. The McNab and Miss Hunt have raised two lovely children. Aye, they will have to contend with the sneers of the upstanding citizens of the township. But they are of strong character; I believe they will overcome and prosper.

Of course, tis not possible to see into the minds of the twelve jurors. From my vantage point, the men appeared to listen attentively to the evidence presented by opposing Counsel. It seems, as Mr. Hincks wrote in last week's *Examiner*, the Jury rendered its verdict in favour of the McNab because Mr. Hincks's Counsel failed to prove one single point—a point, as Mr. Hincks says, that be of no consequence whatsoever as regards the real merits of my Chief's conduct towards his settlers. The point being whether or not the McNab was declared a "public nuisance" by a Grand Jury at the Quarter Session in Perth. Twould be the sitting this past summer.

Twas Donald Cameron's testimony that when the
Quarter Session Magistrates refused his petition to change
apportionment of the statute-labour, he took it before a
Grand Jury already assembled in the courthouse. He said
the Jury deliberated a short time and then returned a
presentment in which not only did they recommend the
statute-labour be laid out according to the settlers' wishes,
but they said the McNab had acted in a tyrannical and
oppressive manner and was a nuisance to the public. Donald
testified that the paper was read in court by the Clerk of the
Peace, Mr. Berford, whose Christian name escapes me at the
moment.

Ah, but Mr. Berford testified . . . most reluctantly, but he
testified he could not recollect reading such a paper. After a
meticulous and vigorous examination by Mr. Baldwin, he
did acknowledge something of the kind was brought in by
the Jury. Documents of this nature are kept in Mr. Berford's
office, but the witness said he was unable to locate any such
document. Of course Mr. Berford is an employee of the
government, his amnesia on this point most convenient to
the Family Compact whose oppressive rule . . . the trial has
opened my eyes to their tyranny.

Mr. Hincks says, in hindsight, he wishes he had called
more witnesses to prove the authenticity of the Jury's
presentment. Perhaps he means Mr. John King, who was
foreman of the Grand Jury. But he says, quite
understandably, tis a tremendous expense to bring persons
from the Bathurst District to Toronto; and the defendant
acknowledges that failure to do so was the principal cause of
his weakness on this point, and clearly the sole cause of the
verdict in favour of the McNab. But the renowned
newspaper editor—himself the member for Oxford in the
Assembly—says in his paper that the public will judge the
verdict on the evidence. He makes no apology for his
publications and says he glories in his conduct with regard

to his dealings with the settlers. Despite the verdict going against him, as directed by Judge Jones, he says he feels triumphant.

Alas, that is not the way my Chief sees it. When the Jury foreman read the verdict, the McNab appeared to hear only "verdict for the plaintiff;" placing the value of his character at five pounds did not seem to register, for he jumped up from the table and grasped Mr. Draper's hand and then the hands of Mr. Sherwood and Mr. Crawford.

"A *soiree*, MacGregor! As soon as we are home I will summon my loyal clansmen and we will celebrate our glorious victory," the McNab said on the coach ride home. "I trust your pipes will be well tuned." I said "aye" in response but without enthusiasm. I tried in vain to distract my thoughts by gazing at the passing snow-covered landscape. Tis the first time in memory . . . the first time ever my heart did not swell at the prospect of performing the glorious music of my beloved Scotland.

The *soiree* at Waba Cottage did not have *la vie* of old. The McNab has alienated most everyone in the township. Only a few remain loyal: ingratiating settlers, toadies who have shunned the community, have spied on their neighbours and reported to the Laird, who has rewarded them with generous perquisite. I, it shames me to tell ye, must count myself among them. Nay, twas never my intent but . . . I canna believe how naive . . . Tis true, I have friends—good friends—among the settlers. But I canna imagine life without my Chief. Tis my calling, as twas the calling of my father and my grandfather and my great-grandfather. Tis not easy to break a tradition, a proud and noble tradition.

At the celebration of his *victory*, the clowning of a court jester would pale next to that of the McNab's raucous behaviour. His bluster, his swagger, his backslapping had a bogus ring, visibly more pronounced than usual; shored up with generous consumption of spirits. Brandy in hand, he told William Roddie, Alex Yulle, and the others that he would regain control of his township and punish those responsible for instigating the disloyalty and rebellion against him. I fear my Chief suffers from delusions. Twas the festival of Hogmanay—the eve of the New Year; a celebration historians say we Scots inherited from the Vikings. Tradition has it that on Hogmanay animals are slaughtered for a mid-winter feast. Tis the idea of slaughter . . . I sense in my bones tis portentous. I know not what lies ahead.

PART EIGHT

We are united!

Lord Sydenham's astute political gamesmanship has appeased the constitutionalists of the Family Compact, the radicals of the Reformers and the French of Lower Canada. I would not have believed such diplomatic juggling possible! Tis a most superior demonstration of political skill. The McNab received dispatches almost daily from his friends on the Council. Twas how we learned that Mr. Thomson— Lord Sydenham—was ably assisted by Sir George Arthur in winning over the anti-union opposition among the Assembly. The *Union Bill* makes promises to all sides: we shall see if they come to fruition.

Ah, but it saddens me to tell ye, the spirit of goodwill voiced in the union of the Canadas has *not* united the Laird with his settlers. Strife is as rampant as ever. If the Hincks trial was not embarrassing enough—exposing my Chief to public odium—I fear the document that arrived with yesterday's post will seal his fate. I had just finished lunch when McDermid knocked on my door to inform me the McNab requested my presence. I was well bundled and I don't think twas only the cutting northeast wind that caused the chill I felt while making my way through the heavy snow. Nay, my intuitive nature told me the Chief had at last received the commissioner's report. I hesitated at the door of Waba Cottage before lifting the brass knocker—a distinctive ornament in the shape of an Egyptian Pharaoh's head that has always intrigued me. Miss Hunt opened the door and acknowledged my entry with a stiff bow. I sensed the Laird's companion was more overwrought than usual. I attempted levity, inquired about Allan and Kitty, and was informed they were at the Miller's for their daily tutoring with Helen. The Laird was seated in his cushioned chair beside the hearth. He was drawing heavily on his meerschaum pipe, his full attention given to the papers in hand.

"Ah, MacGregor, there you are," he said, as I approached the armchair opposite his. "I have abominable news, *most* abominable; they are determined to take away my township. Sixteen years! . . . sixteen years I have devoted to helping these . . . these Jonahs—and it comes to this!" The McNab waved the papers before me. "I am being accused of every imaginable slight." He pulled a handkerchief from his tunic and wiped perspiration from his brow. "I will fight it; I will fight it as I fought Hincks; I will fight as the Chiefs of Clan McNab have always fought. Tis a proud tradition and I will not allow these . . ." He picked up the loose papers on the table beside him. "I have obtained three copies of this vile publication. McDermid has delivered one to Mr. McRae; here is your copy. Tis comforting to know I can count on your loyal support."

I took the document from his outstretched hand. I had not yet taken my seat, intent as I was on listening to my Chief go on about how indignant and misunderstood he was. I was about to sit down when I decided I would be more comfortable reading Mr. Allan's report in the privacy of my own cottage. I was about to say so when Miss Hunt appeared in the doorway and announced the arrival of Mr. McRae. Twas more incentive for my departure; the unctuous comportment of the Laird's solicitor . . . tis most distasteful.

"Ah, Wilfred, tis a sad day, a sad day indeed," the McNab said, rising to greet his lawyer.

"Do not trouble yourself, Archibald," Mr. McRae said. He unbuttoned and pushed back his suede overcoat, freeing his considerable girth to strain against his waistcoat. "Nay, do not trouble yourself. I went over the report this morning. The indictment is nothing new; tis an old tune; we will reply; we will set the record straight."

"Chief," I said, pausing to regain his attention, "since I have not had the opportunity, I would ask leave that I may fully ingest the report in my own quarters."

"Aye, aye, MacGregor, whatever ye wish," the Laird said with a gesture of dismissal. It is obvious that on this matter the McNab places more weight on the opinion of his legal adviser than that of his Piper—a view with which I wholeheartedly agree. Clutching the document, I bowed, and made a hasty exit.

**

"HAS YE SEEN it?" Iain Storie asked Donald Cameron the moment he opened the door to his shanty. It was mid-morning and Storie had tramped through a heavy snowfall to talk about the report that had the community in a buzz.

"Come in, Iain. Nay, I haven't," Cameron said.

"G'day, Elizabeth," Storie said as he removed his hat. The Cameron children were outside building a snowman.

"G'day, Iain," Elizabeth said. She was placing loaves of bread in the new stone oven Donald had constructed at the side of their fireplace. "How are Margaret and the children this wintry day?"

"They's fine, thanks."

Donald pulled a third wooden chair near the hearthstone and motioned to their visitor to sit down.

"Would ye care for a cup of tea?" Elizabeth asked.

"Aye, a cup of tea would warm me innards," Storie said.

"I am told Sydenham's time is taken with uniting the Canadas," Cameron said.

"Aye, tis understandable. He will have much to see about," Storie said. "McDermid says the Laird has a copy of the report and is preparin a response. He says it condemns McNab."

"I hear that as well," Cameron said.

"I was talking to Helen Miller," Elizabeth said. "She says Agnes told her the Chief is beside himself. She says Mr. Allan be a conservative and the Chief was certain the report would favour him. Agnes says the Laird is most distressed; he canna believe Mr. Allan would say such things."

"Such things?" Storie said. "Until we see a copy . . . Do ye think Thomas could get us a copy? From his brother? Until we see the report we winna know—"

"I can ask," Cameron said. "When I spoke to Mr. Allan last summer I thought he was sceptical of our grievances. But Walter told me by the time he spoke to him the commissioner was seeing things differently."

"Aye, Walter told me that as well," Storie said. "Tis nae surprising; Mr. Allan is said to be honest and plain-spoken."

"If that's true, the report could embarrass the government," Cameron said. "These being politicians, they will take no action unless forced to."

"That's for sure, and ye is right, Sydenham is gonna be busy," Storie said. While Elizabeth served tea, the farmers gazed into the fire, shadows flickering across their pensive faces; the flames crackled and winked at them. Had they achieved victory, only to have it shelved?

***

AYE, TIS OVER. The McNab canna wriggle out of this dilemma. I have read Mr. Allan's findings—twice. The government agent has been thorough—thorough indeed. He accuses the Laird of apportioning the statute-labour solely for his own gain. I canna deny he is right. It's been some sixteen years and the roads be . . . here is how Mr. Allan describes two of them: "The two roads of approach on the southeast side of the township are most wretched—one of them all but impassable; a horse going to the belly every few rods." Tis true! My own Nellie has gone to the belly . . . ah, my apologies to Duncan Ban Macintyre. I am nae a poet.

Mr. Allan does not use the word "liar" to describe my Chief. Perhaps he believes, as I now do, the man be . . . tis apparent he be suffering from delusions. The agent says even though the McNab told him he had conveyed provisions for his settlers from Bolton's Mills in Beckwith Township, "that one pound of provisions was never conveyed from hence, or anywhere else, at his expense for the benefit of the settlers." I canna be certain the Laird provided *no provisions*, but, tis true, in the early years many settlers solicited victuals on credit from the good-hearted and generous people of Beckwith and Fitzroy. Mr. Allan says the settlers told him that had it not been for the generosity of people in neighbouring townships, "they possibly might have perished." I remember the McNab telling me twas all a misunderstanding, that he promised provisions to only a few of the men.

Ah, but . . . I canna believe . . . Mr. Allan says the McNab "wrote to one or more of the inhabitants of Beckwith cautioning them against trusting or crediting his settlers." Had I not heard the testimony at the trial of Mr. Hincks, I would not believe . . . tis most reprehensible that my Chief would act with such malice towards members of his clan.

The agent says he was unable to place a value on the Laird's income from timber duties, but he says it must be "immense" because the Chief has been collecting duties for years on timber cut on the lots of his settlers. He even accuses the McNab of "locating lots in names of persons apparently for no other purpose than to obtain the timber." If that were not appalling enough, he says the Laird "has passed great quantities of timber as having been cut in McNab Township taken from adjoining townships." Tis most distressing. *Most distressing*! I have always thought my Chief a man of high moral principles. But these accusations . . .

Of course, Mr. Allan addresses the never-ending squabble over quit-rent. He asserts that the McNab has collected rents illegally, a charge testified to at Mr. Hincks's trial. The agent accuses the Laird of speculating on lots on which he was supposed to locate his settlers. I have no head for business; I canna verify the truth of this charge. But, tis true, there is much gossip among the settlers that the Laird and some members of his Cabinet-Council have made scandalous profits buying and selling lots. Ah, that sort of thing . . . tis the purview of lawyers.

Mr. Allan cites a number of other instances where he alleges the Chief has dishonoured the name "McNab." And his observation in the penultimate paragraph is most upsetting. He says the McNab has conducted the township's affairs "in the worst possible manner for the interests of the settlers or the country." And then the agent concludes with a statement which canna be disputed: "The devotion of Scotch Highlanders to the Chief is too well known to permit it to be believed that an alienation such as has taken place between McNab and his people could have happened unless their feelings were most grossly outraged." Tis *the* most telling comment of all! Nothing more need be said. We Scots hold our clan Chief in awe. Disloyalty to a Chief is tantamount to disloyalty to one's heritage. It is to dishonour one's ancestors. Tis near unheard of. But in defence of my Laird: the power of a clan Chief lies in the land. The McNab was compelled to forfeit his land at home. Tis most humiliating—*the* most humiliating blow to a Chief. The McNab puts on a brave front. His is a magnanimous spirit: outgoing, free-handed in his generosity; some would say prodigal with his hospitality and promises. Aye, but he is also a man of great pride. I don't think he has ever let me see his pain—the pain of being forced to flee his beloved Highlands like a common criminal; forced to shoulder the burden of others' sins; cast as a fugitive, though it be no fault of his. Tis why I believe he has governed the township thus: the fear of losing the land—*his land*—is ever present. And now . . . I dare not think—will it come to pass?

I FEEL I am living in a state of suspended animation. I wake in the morning from a restless sleep and tax my brain for a reason to rise. The McNab's time is taken in forming a reply to Mr. Allan's censure. I am avoiding him; not that he would notice. I am grateful he is distracted and does not require my presence—as Piper or companion. When my stomach will no longer be silent, I prepare simple meals in my cottage. I did not believe the day would ever dawn when I had no appetite. My Colleen . . . we have had a wet spring; the roads, as Mr. Allan says, near impassable. I didn't want my Nellie going to the belly. I am enamoured with the agent's clever phrase; more enamoured, it seems, than with my Colleen. Our abominable roads have served as a fine pretext for not journeying to Pakenham. She has not ventured to McNab. I suspect for the same reason. The roads that is. I canna get a grip on what is causing my despondency. There be no incident, nothing I can point to and say, tis the cause. Ah, but we are creatures of habit, of that there be no doubt; and so each morning I take up my pipes, but the notes sound flat and sour, as if my beloved instrument senses my distress.

A few days ago—I don't remember the exact day—the heavens, needing time to replenish the clouds with moisture, allowed the sun to dry the earth, and so, after much dawdling, I roused my fortitude and ventured into Flat Rapids. I have never seen so little activity. Tis as if everyone is awaiting the government's response to Mr. Allan's findings. At Donald Cameron's, I spoke with him and Lorn McCaul and Angus McLaren. They said the wet weather was making it near impossible to work the land. Then, with their next breath, they inquired as to what the McNab was doing about Mr. Allan's report. I could only tell them what they already knew: the Laird and his solicitor are preparing a response. And then I added: how they propose to defend the indefensible, I do not know. This comment raised the eyebrows of all three farmers. They said nothing. Perhaps they were as surprised at hearing it from me as I was at saying it aloud. Donald said he asked Mr. Radenhurst to get him a copy, but it had not arrived. He did not ask to borrow mine. He knows twould not be proper for me . . . Donald is too principled a gentleman to make such a request.

Elizabeth Cameron served tea sweetened with fresh maple sugar. To be hospitable, I sipped a cup before bidding the settlers *adieu*. But I was hardly mounted on Nellie for the ride home when my thoughts were again consumed with my Colleen. I rode Nellie hard. I am tormented with a fierce anger; I believe tis because of a nagging feeling she is again unfaithful. Ah, but tis only a feeling. I am like the Magistrates in Perth: finding guilt without reliable evidence. Her independent nature . . . tis something I like and admire; but tis also a clash with my upbringing; I am *au fait* with a girl's place in the Scottish clan. But she is nae a Scot. The Irish, unless they be Papists, are more free-spirited than we Scots. Tis simply their way. When I reached the road into White Lake, I resolved that I would ride to Pakenham and confront her; as soon as the weather . . . ah, I am doing it again; I have made such a resolution before. But this time I am determined—as soon as I know what I am confronting her about.

THE MCNAB HAS shown me his reply to Mr. Allan's audacious and disrespectful report. Most amusing, most amusing indeed. My Chief canna rival Sir Walter Scott, but he certainly—and most eloquently—indulged his imagination. I was grateful to read the missive in the privacy of my own cottage; it evoked many a sad chuckle.

The Laird says he granted Peter Fisher his lot to build a carpenter's shop. Nay, Peter is a fine tailor, but I would have no confidence in his proficiency with a hammer and saw. Duncan McDonald's lot was deeded so the crofter could build a schoolhouse. Ah, poor Duncan, a hard-working soul, but the man can hardly write his own name or add a simple sum; and he is known to have a grand fondness for a toddy. Twould be a horror, indeed, should the settlers entrust him with the schooling of their children. Tis true, as the Laird states, Charlie McNican in Canaan was granted his lot for a blacksmith's shop, but tis not, as he says, for "public benefit." Nay, I know, because Charlie told me the McNab collects a tithe on every horse the farrier shods. Tis an establishment more for the benefit of Charlie and the McNab. Apparently there be both a phantom sawmill and gristmill in the township. If that be true, the Chief has kept them well under wraps. He says they have been operating in Arnprior for ten years. Tis what is called "stretching the truth." The Buchanans built and operated a sawmill for three years, until the unfortunate demise of their business five years ago. As for the nearest gristmill, tis in Pakenham; I pass by it each time I visit my Colleen. Tis a long journey for the settlers—some travel by foot—but tis the only means they have of grinding their grain into flour. I have heard gossip that a new man, recently arrived from Ramsay Township, is considering erecting a gristmill on nearby Waba Creek. Twould be a blessing indeed. Ah, but not only are there phantom mills; apparently, there's a phantom ferry as well. And in Flat Rapids! At least that is why the McNab says he deeded a lot on the Madawaska in his own name. And it came as a complete surprise to learn the township contains slate quarries. They, too, the McNab has kept well hidden these many years.

The rejoinder continues in this manner. The McNab attempts to alleviate some of Mr. Allan's charges; others he simply ignores, such as lots given *gratis* to members of his Cabinet-Council and other colleagues. Then, just before his summation, the Laird says he granted his Piper a lot and the deed to go with it. My humble dwelling is located on his *own* acreage! Not more than a hundred yards from Waba

Cottage! And he says I have "a large family of sons!" Ah, I am a rogue, a real rascal!

Alas, I fear the Laird is no match for Lord Sydenham. I shudder to think of the consequences when the Viscount reads my Chief's fictitious reply.

❋❋❋

DONALD CAMERON CALLED a township meeting as soon as the courier delivered the message sent by Thomas Radenhurst from Perth. The lawyer had received a dispatch from his brother, John, in Toronto. The Executive Council of the new government of the united Province of Canada had adopted the report of Crown Lands Agent Francis Allan.

"Is it true, Donald?" Iain Storie asked, being the first to arrive at Cameron's barn.

"Aye, Iain, tis. Tis not all we had hoped for but—"

"Eh! What do ya mean not all we had hoped—"

"There are some conditions, but they will not—" Several horses pulled up outside the barn door, which Cameron had opened wide on this hot and windy August afternoon. The riders strode into the barn, a few sporting expansive grins, others, expressions of doubt.

"Is it true, Donald?" Angus McLaren asked.

"Aye, lads, tis . . . tis indeed."

"Ye don't seem too sure," Robert Miller said.

"Tis jus more of the Laird's dirty work," Duncan McDonald said. "I'll believe me land is free an clear when I has the deed in me hands. Even then I dinna—"

"Ye's a Doubting Thomas, Duncan," Lorn McCaul said.

"Ye's right, Lorn. Sixteen years! Sixteen years, Lorn! I has a right to be a Doubting Thomas. Aye, a Doubting Duncan too." Several men chuckled. "I dinna trust the new government any more than the old. Tis the same bunch a—"

"Ah, Duncan, let up, laddie!" Hugh Alexander said. "Let's hear what Donald has to say."

"We don't have all the details yet." Cameron unfolded two sheets of paper and the men crowded around him.

"What's it say?" Colin Carmichael asked.

"It says the government is giving us nine years to pay for our land an—"

"What?" McLaren said. "I has already paid for me land! I've been workin it sixteen years! Twas supposed to be a free grant!"

"I told ye!" McDonald said. "I told ye! The scoundrel be in cahoots with the new government! The Laird gets more money and we canna—"

"Nay nay, Duncan, tis not so!" Cameron said. He read from the note. "It says we pay the Crown Lands Agent four times a year, and for many there will be no payments cause they are subtracting rents already paid. Angus, the land was not a free grant, and the government says we knew that. It says our lots will be assessed at their value *before* we made improvements; when they were, as Thomas puts it, 'in a state of nature.' And that's not all!" Cameron paused, savouring the next piece of news. "It says McNab has to give up the patents he's holding on our land, and on our timber. And . . . he can no longer collect quit-rents!"

"Is ye sure of that?" Alexander asked.

"Tis what it says right here." Cameron pointed to words near the bottom of the second page. "McNab has no right to collect quit-rents. Tis illegal." The men wanted to believe what Cameron was telling them. But after sixteen years of disappointments . . . Then Walter Ross, who had been listening attentively, spoke up.

"Ye know, I's thinkin, maybe cause . . . I's thinkin cause it come from Thomas—"

"Aye, I was thinking the same thing," Miller said. "Thomas's brother is in the government. And he's always been honest with us. But after sixteen years, tis still hard to believe."

"We won, men," Cameron said. "We won!" The men looked expectantly at McDonald.

"Aye, Thomas has nae let us down," McDonald said. He turned towards Cameron. "Ye's a good man, Donald . . . if what ye say be true." His weather-beaten face broke into a grin. "I think a wee celebration—" The others voiced agreement. Carmichael rubbed his palms together and watched McDonald pull a hip flask from his coveralls. The celebration, however, was about to be cut short.

FLORA McNEE WAS spilling the chicken's entrails onto the thick pine slab that served as a cutting board when she heard hoofbeats outside her shanty. Dennis had ridden off a short time earlier. He hadn't said where he was going; she thought perhaps to Arnprior for supplies. Flora assumed he'd forgotten something and returned. She had just placed the fowl in a pail of cold water when the door opened and three men entered: the Laird, Lipsey and Deputy Francis Maule.

"Good afternoon, Mrs. McNee," Maule said, tipping his hat. "Is Mr. McNee here?"

"Nay, he's gone; I dinna know where; me thinks to Arnprior," she said, as she wiped chicken fat from her hands onto her apron.

"I have a *writ* of possession," Maule said. "The law requires me to order you to leave the shanty." Stunned, the woman stared at the men. Four of her children had taken their slingshots and gone to the nearby woods. The remaining seven, the youngest ones, were sitting in a circle in a corner. They had been playing catch, and the nine-year-old was about to toss the small rubber ball to his six-year-old sister when his hand halted above his head; he joined his siblings in gawking at the intruders. "Gather what you can carry and leave the shanty."

"Dennis ain't here," she repeated. "Wait till he be back."

"Nay, I shan't," the Laird said. "Ye were ordered to leave more than two years ago. This is my property; I will wait no longer. Lipsey, take the furniture out and pile it at the side of the road." The hunched minion picked up a small table in the middle of the room. McNab and Maule stepped aside so he could carry it through the door. Mrs. McNee and the children hadn't moved. Lipsey returned and McNab pointed to other pieces of furniture, which the servant then lugged out of the shanty.

"Ye should wait till Dennis be back," Mrs. McNee said again. "If he be in Arnprior, he shan't be long." McNab emitted a loud snort. Maule walked over to the woman and held out the *writ*, which was rolled and tied with a string. "I canna read." Maule unrolled the paper and read the court document. "I dinna know what ye's sayin; tis fancy lawyer words, but I's nae leavin me home. Wait till Dennis be back." Maule looked at McNab.

"Mrs. McNee," the Laird paused while Lipsey hauled the remaining two wooden chairs through the door. "Gather the young lads an lassies and leave this instant. Ye are occupying my property. The law says . . ."

"I dinna care what the law says. Wait till Dennis be back." Maule had retied the *writ* and placed it on the table next to the cutting board. "I's nae leavin me home."

"Tis nae your home," the Laird said. "I have a registered patent for this lot. Ye are trespassing. Now gather the young uns and be gone." When the woman didn't move, McNab walked over, grabbed her by the arm and pulled her across the floor. Her children got up and followed them through the door.

"I'll be leavin now, Chief," Maule said. "The *writ* has been served."

"Aye, thank you, Francis," McNab said. They watched the deputy mount his horse and ride off. "I dinna want these disgraceful shacks on my property. Burn them down." Lipsey gathered some kindling and lit it.

- - -

AT DONALD CAMERON'S, the farmers were about to toast their liberation from the Laird when a strong gust of wind from the southwest carried a whiff of smoke into the barn.

"Do ye smell it?" Miller asked, but the others were already scurrying towards the open door.

"'Tis Dennis McNee's place!" McCaul said. The men rushed to their mounts and rode off towards McNee's lot. They covered the short distance in minutes. Flora McNee and her children were clinging to one another by their household possessions, which were in a heap at the side of the road. The shanty and outhouse were burnt almost to the ground. The cattle had rambled off into the pasture.

"We can save the barn!" Storie said. A new structure, the fire's tentacles moved slowly over the green pine. The men drew upon their experience and quickly formed a bucket brigade from the well. Intent upon their task, no one noticed Mrs. McNee scampering towards the barn until she reached the open door.

"Tom! Kitty!" she shouted.

"Flora!" Cameron shouted. The woman looked around. Then she dashed passed the flames into the barn. "Flora!" Cameron followed her into the burning structure. Crouched in a corner were four-year-old Tom and three-year-old Kitty. Mrs. McNee scooped Kitty into her arms; Cameron did the same with Tom. Flames caught dry straw in the horse's stall and began snaking towards the entrance. Cameron and Mrs. McNee rushed the frightened children outside. A short time later the bucket brigade extinguished the flames. The charred barn, still standing, smouldered.

"'Twas . . . twas the Laird," Flora McNee said as the men gathered around the family.

"Eh! What is ye saying?" Iain Storie asked. The men attempted to calm the children. The older ones had returned from the woods when they saw the flames; the young ones were sobbing and clinging to one another. Mrs. McNee struggled to regain her composure. The men waited for her explanation.

"What do you mean, Flora?" Cameron asked. Through choking sobs, she told the men what had happened. When the family left the shanty, she hadn't notice Tom and Kitty run into the barn. She said as soon as Maule was out of sight, McNab ordered Lipsey to set fire to their log home and the outhouse; the Laird set fire to the barn. Then the two men mounted their horses and rode away.

"Where is Dennis?" Cameron asked when Mrs. McNee finished her story.

"I dinna know," she said. "Maybe in Arnprior. I dinna know. We needs supplies."

Only the presence of the hysterical woman and her children kept the men from stinging the air with curses. While Cameron and Storie rode off to get buckboards, the others did their best to console the family. They arranged to take them into their shanties and assured them they would have a new log home, larger than the one destroyed.

SEETHING RAGE COURSED through Dennis McNee with an intensity far greater than the heat given off by his still smouldering homestead. Lorn McCaul, who had been designated to wait for his return, quickly allayed McNee's worst fear by assuring him that his wife and children were safe. Then he related Flora's story as to the cause of the fire. The farmer said nothing. His heart hammering, he stared at the charred ruins—the destruction of his livelihood. McCaul explained that Cameron, Storie and McLaren intended to lay criminal charges against McNab. A sneer was the only hint McCaul had that what he said had registered.

***

I AM HUMILIATED. I am ashamed. The McNab was arrested and . . . Mr. Cameron, Mr. Storie and Mr. McLaren sought out the residence of the nearest Magistrate, Mr. Alexander McVicar, and when told of my Chief's *malfaisance* the officer of the court had *no* choice but to issue a warrant for his arrest. The Assize in Perth still some time away, the Laird was brought before a Tribunal in Pakenham Village. I accompanied my Chief at his request—and because tis my duty.

"We will hear from the wit—" Mr. McVicar began, but was interrupted by Magistrate Andrew Richey.

"Nay, we shan't," Mr. Richey said. "Tis a matter for the Crown; the Quarter Session court will hear the case . . . if there be a case."

"If there be a case!" Mr. McVicar said, his incredulity at Mr. Richey's comment quite apparent. "Mr. McNee's homestead was burned to the ground, and most of his tools destroyed. Two of his young uns—"

"Tis Chief McNab's property," Mr. Richey said. "He had a *writ* of possession. A man has the right to do what he wishes with his own property. Tis a dispute for the Crown . . . for the Quarter Session."

"Mr. Richey, the Quarter Session . . . tis several weeks before the court—" Mr. McVicar said before being interrupted by Magistrate Scott.

"I agree with Magistrate Richey," Mr. Scott said. "Tis a serious criminal charge against an upstanding member of the community; and tis too grave . . . tis clearly a matter for the Crown."

"Gentlemen," Mr. McVicar said. "Need I remind officers of the court of well-established British law. To no one will we sell, to no one will we deny or delay right or justice. All the witnesses are here present. We should hear their evidence and then rule—"

"Nay, Mr. McVicar," Mr. Richey said. "Ye may quote the *Magna Carta* if ye wish, but it does not apply here."

"Not apply, Mr. Richey?" Mr. McVicar said. "Was it not feudalism that brought about—"

"I agree with Magistrate Richey," Mr. Scott said, cutting short Mr. McVicar's argument. "Such a charge . . . such a *serious* charge against a Scottish nobleman . . . twould be wasting our time; the Attorney-General would overrule our decision. Chief McNab is a man of principle; he has a fine reputation as a high-minded gentleman; he will argue his case before the Quarter Session"

"And what of Mr. McNee?" Mr. McVicar said. "And *Messieurs* Cameron, Storie and McLaren? They are the aggrieved parties; at least Mr. McNee is. To take the matter to Perth is costly. Does Mr. McNee have the means to take his case before the Quarter Session?"

"I don't know," Mr. Scott said. "But whether he has the means or not . . . tis no concern of ours."

"I vote to refer the matter to the Crown," Mr. Richey said.

"Aye, I concur," Mr. Scott said. I could see the frustration on Magistrate McVicar's face. He appeared to tax his brain for further argument, but he was unable to summon a rebuttal. His colleagues had out-voted him. I tell ye, twas most embarrassing to witness the haughty, presumptuous attitude of Magistrates Richey and Scott—the Laird's good friends.

Alas, it may not have mattered. Twas all hearsay. Dennis McNee and the others were not present when the incident took place. After dismissal of the proceedings, a tearful Flora McNee told again what happened, and Deputy Maule verified as to having served the *writ* and carrying out the eviction. But the officer of the law said he was not present when the alleged fire was set. *Alleged*? Aye, I too would have thought Mrs. McNee suffering from hallucinations, but the charred ruins of the shanty are testimony to the truth: the woman did *not* burn down her own shanty! If the injustice of the Laird's despicable act were not enough . . . I know he had a legal *writ* of possession; but it does not sanction an act . . . I canna believe . . . an act of barbarism! My Chief was near responsible for the deaths of a wee lad and lassie! Tis inexcusable.

While I know Mr. McNee be a hard-working man—his farm has been most productive—I, like Mr. McVicar, suspect he has not the means to proceed with expensive litigation. I fear this injustice . . . this vile, outrageous act will go unpunished. Of course, the McNees are being looked after. Their neighbours rallied round, as they always do—have always done. They built the family a new home on a nearby vacant lot: one, Donald Cameron says, on which the Laird holds no patent. Tis a more spacious shanty than the one destroyed, with two more rooms. The men say the barn can be moved to the new land. They have already moved the farmer's shed, which was not put to the torch.

There is talk of lynching the McNab. And tis not just idle talk. Not just Duncan McDonald's wild bluster. I hear tis supported by respectable members of the community. Even Francis MacAulay! Colin Carmichael told me the pious Elder said he longed to bring back the old days when a bullet would find him for the deed.

Mr. McNee is sullen and much aloof. He said not a word in Pakenham, but I fear . . . I sense a concealed violence in the man. Donald Cameron . . . aye, Donald be a steadying force; he will do his best to bring the men to their senses. I dinna think any harm will come to the Laird. But then . . . when I see the charred ruins of the McNee's home, I canna help but think what the McNab . . . Tis no use; I can no longer defend my Chief; I can no longer respect him. Tis a sad day, the saddest day of my life. I canna even take solace in my pipes—nor my Colleen. This morning I began to play my new *piobaireachd*. It had no vigour, the notes flat and bitter, without spirit. I put my pipes away and contemplated my future with the McNab. I dinna know if there be a future with Colleen. Tis a most difficult . . . Alas, I dinna even know what I am deciding. I feel at home in the township. And yet, Scotland beckons, the Highlands, Perthshire beckons. I dinna see how the McNab can continue to live in the township—*his* township. And what am I to do about my Colleen?

**

DONALD CAMERON KNEW what Dennis McNee's reaction would be. It was, in fact, his own reaction—feelings that rarely surfaced in this benevolent gentleman. The morning after their brief appearance in court, he rode over to the new shanty where he found his neighbour in his shed. When Cameron entered, McNee glanced up from under his broad-brimmed hat, said nothing, and returned to the task at hand. He was standing at his forge, heating lead in a ladle and pouring the molten liquid into a small, round mould. The results of his labour were evident: a number of .75-calibre balls were strewn over his workbench; his Brown Bess leaned against the wall. Cameron began with small talk: What did he think of the new shanty? Did Flora find it more convenient? Did the young uns like the extra space? McNee ignored him. Finally, Cameron stroked his trimmed whiskers and asked the question he really wanted answered.

"What are you going to do, Dennis?" Cameron moved closer to the forge. McNee poured lead into the mould. Cameron stepped forward and gently gripped the farmer's left forearm. McNee's head jerked up, his smoke-grey eyes seething, sweat trickling across the creases in his forehead.

"I'm gonna shoot the fucker! This time ye winna stop me!" Cameron released his grip. "Tom an Kitty . . . they wake in the night screaming; they think they's in the fire. The other young uns is havin bad dreams, too. And Flora . . . her nerves . . . she keeps sayin McNab is comin back; she be ever at the watch. Ye saw what happened in Pakenham. Tis the same bunch in the government. Tis the same as at home; the same as in America. There be no law for the likes of McNab; those bastards who suck the asses of the politicians. Ye has been tryin for what . . . fifteen years? sixteen years? McNab destroys me land, nearly kills two of me young uns—they near *burned* to death!—and his friends say take it to Perth. Nay, I will not take it to Perth. I will shoot the fucker! The son of a bitch! I will put an end to him for all of us!" Cameron held McNee's gaze.

"I understand your anger, Dennis. Tis also how I feel." Cameron paused. "But tis not the same as before. Don't you see? The Laird is desperate. Aye, he still has a few toadies around here . . . and there are still a few in Toronto who'll listen to him. But Thomas Radenhurst says McNab has lost the confidence of the government. Burning your shanty was the act of a desperate man. He's finished. We have won. If ye had come to the township meeting you'd know: the government has approved Mr. Allan's report; his recommendations; we are free of the feudal tyrant."

"I dinna believe—"

"Thomas says Mr. Hincks . . . ye know, the newspaper man, the man McNab sued; he's a member of the assembly, a Reformer. Thomas says Hincks will speak out in the assembly; he'll force the government to take action on the report. Hincks is a good man. We can trust him. When the report is published, the government will have to act. Twould be too embarrassing to do otherwise." Cameron paused, tugged at his whiskers and watched as the hard lines in McNee's face dissolved. "We're neighbours, Dennis," Cameron continued in a softer tone. "Nay, we're not all of the same clan; but we are a Highland community in this foreign land. Tis not so different as our ancestors. Ye know yourself, twas when the ancient clans united . . . tis how we have today's clans. We are Scots, and so we are clansmen. We are The Friendly Society of McNab. And we have won without violence. McNab has no more power over us. We are free."

In the glow of the forge's embers, the men held each other's gaze.

***

AFTER THE HEARING in Pakenham, I saw little of the McNab. I avoided Waba Cottage, and I was summoned only once. Twas not only . . . the government adopted Mr. Allan's report. The McNab lost his township. When I saw Sheriff Lyle's horse tethered at Waba Cottage . . . McDermid told me the officer delivered an Order-in-Council instructing the Chief to surrender his patent for timber rights and his undelivered patents on lots. He said the Laird's compensation for settlement was reduced from four thousand pounds to twenty-five hundred; one thousand of which he had already received. I didn't know . . . I don't know what to say to my Chief. McDermid says he is bearing up, his manner cheerful. But the secretary says he detects a melancholy beneath the brave facade. Twould be inhuman if it were otherwise.

Near the end of a wet summer, the weather finally cleared, stealing away my bogus excuse for avoiding my Colleen. But it shames me . . . I made a few half-hearted stabs at practising jigs and reels requested at a *ceilidh*, puttered around my cottage, puttered in my garden—Lipsey is laid up with a sore back—rode into Arnprior and visited the McNab's tenants at Kinnell; whiled away the hours and breathed a grateful sigh when darkness fell. Then last week the Laird asked me to take a letter to Mr. Richey.

"Tis nae among your duties, MacGregor," he said, "but with Lipsey ailing . . . and I have need of McDermid; if ye would be a good lad." Of course I agreed; what excuse could I conjure? Twas just after the noon hour when I delivered the Laird's missive to the Pakenham magistrate. Since I was there, I might as well, as the saying goes, "face the music," and so I made my way to my Colleen's, wondering all the while what I would say to her. When I rode up, she and an Irish lad I did not recognize were harvesting barley on a tract near the side of her shanty.

"Well, well, well, will ye look who's here!" she said. "Unless it be an apparition, Michael." They watched me dismount and walk the short distance into the field. Tis the longest walk I have ever taken; conscious of my every step.

"How are ye, Colleen?" I said, my voice cracking with forced gaiety. She didn't reply, just looked at me as if I was someone she should know, but could not remember from where or when. "How have ye been? Tis a bountiful crop ye have. The weather's been dreadful, until the last few weeks; the fields in McNab so soggy the crofters—farmers—complain bitterly—"

"Michael, if ye don't mind finishing the quarter, this gentleman and I have some unfinished business," she said, flashing him a generous smile, like a promise of favours to come. The Irish nodded acknowledgment and Colleen started towards her shanty. I trailed close behind, relief and agitation wrestling in my stomach, and surges of heat gushing through my veins. She closed the door after me, stood with arms akimbo and looked at me again, as if trying to place me. "It's been a long time, Malcolm; I thought perhaps you and the Laird had returned to Perthshire." Her countenance went stony and twas evident she was controlling a latent rage.

"Nay," I said, "we . . ." Why, I do not know, but in that instant I found my courage. I removed my bonnet and placed it on the table. I pulled away two cushioned chairs and beckoned her to sit down. She did not move, so I sat down. I could see she was confused, baffled at the change in my deportment. Then she took the chair opposite. "Colleen." My voice was now strong and clear. "I have been tormented for many months thinking ye have been unfaithful again. I dinna have any proof . . . nay, not even any evidence. Tis simply intuition. Perhaps I am mistaken. But I canna escape this feeling. My heart . . . I am most distressed at the McNab's predicament. I need ye . . ." I looked down at the floor. I had no idea what I was saying . . . or trying to say. Then I said, "If ye are not willing to come to White Lake . . . tis beautiful this time of year, but if ye are not willing—"

"Ye need me, Malcolm," she said. Twas almost a whisper. I raised my head and looked into her glistening blue eyes. "Ye just said ye need me. Tis the first time." I was about to say, aye, I need ye when she said, "Why did ye leave me in Perthshire?" The question . . . I am sure I had a startled look. I didn't know what to reply. "I would have settled down with ye in Perthshire, or come with ye to the colony. But ye left with McNab and . . . ye abandoned me . . . why, Malcolm, what happened?" Twas like the light from the tallow flooding the darkness in my brain. "I have been burned; my heart has been burned. I am wary of giving . . . tis easier . . . safer to frolic. Ye don't get burned when ye frolic." I was stunned. I stared at my Colleen. "I remember as a young lass, my mother taught me a simple lesson: the hearth will warm ye, but don't get too close. Tis the same with the heart."

Her silent tears began to flow; my own soon followed. We sat like that for a time. I don't know how long. Then I pulled my chair closer and took her hands in mine. My breath caught the wafting scent of fresh-cut barley. I kissed her hands and now her tears flowed more freely, as did my own. We sat like that, very still, for a long time. Then I stood and pulled her to her feet. We embraced and held each other.

We were standing in each other's arms when the Irish lad opened the door, startling us.

"I finished the quarter, Colleen, is there more needs doing?" he said, before realizing the scene upon which he had intruded. My Colleen thanked him and said that was all that needed doing just now. The Irish's face reddened and he quickly closed the door. My Colleen and I renewed our embrace. We stood like that, holding one another in silence, for a very long time.

EPILOGUE
May 1853

"HOLD STILL, WILL you?"

A shawl spread across his lap, Donald Cameron is sitting on a wooden chair in the kitchen of their spacious, two-storey home while his wife trims his greying beard. Elizabeth performs the tonsorial once a month. On this occasion she's taking more care than usual because tomorrow is a special day: their twenty-year-old grandson, Donald's namesake, will marry eighteen-year-old Ann Stewart, the eldest daughter of a family who emigrated from Perthshire five years ago.

While Elizabeth snips away, Donald's attention is drawn to the chirp and chatter of birds basking in the warmth of the spring sun outside the kitchen window. He thinks the pleasing brightness of their songs a good omen for tomorrow when neighbours, old and new, will gather to celebrate. The Reverend Simon Fraser will perform the ceremony in the Free Kirk Church at Burnstown. Following the nuptials, the wedding party and their guests will gather at the Stewarts' home.

Because spring planting doesn't allow the farmers much time to socialize, the wedding will enable neighbours from near and far to catch up on goings-on. Besides reminiscing with old friends, Donald is looking forward to seeing the Camerons' daughters: Janet, now thirty-seven, and Annabella, now twenty-five, who will travel with their husbands and children from their farms near Braeside.

The Stories, Alexanders, Carmichaels and McNees will be there. Three generations of them. Of course, Walter and Ann Ross will be in the wedding party: the groom is also *their* grandson. Lorn and Jane McCaul, with no children of their own, have taken in three youngsters whose parents perished in a fire. Donald remembers a previous get-together where the McCauls beamed with pride as they paraded the children around the room. He knows how much they look forward to these occasions. Angus McLaren will be there; a lonely soul since Cathrine's passing three years ago. But Angus is not a man to let melancholy get the better of him. His grown children and his grandchildren are nearby, and he keeps active in the community.

Last week, while buying an axe handle in the Arnprior General Store, Donald ran into Duncan McDonald, who assured him he'd be at the wedding. Of the original settlers, Donald is certain no one has changed more than McDonald. He and Betty Frood, who sold her lot in Canaan and moved in with McDonald, are the parents of two boys and a girl— two men and a woman—and the grandparents of eight. Fatherhood, grandparenting, and Betty's influence have undoubtedly sobered the irascible farmer.

Donald regrets that Robert and Helen Miller will not be at the wedding. They're in Toronto visiting their granddaughter, who has just given birth to their second great-grandchild.

Although the wedding will be a celebration, these occasions always stir up memories of the past. The original settlers will regale their progeny with tales of their numerous battles with the Laird of McNab and their struggle to settle the township. The older generation complain that their children do not fully appreciate that struggle.

"There," Elizabeth says. "You look like a new man!"

"Thank you, Elizabeth." Donald stands up, puts an arm around his wife and kisses her on the cheek. He picks up a mirror lying on the kitchen table and looks at himself. "The lassies will be sparkin me!"

"Oh, go on with you," Elizabeth says with a chuckle.

How the years have flown. At sixty-three, Donald Cameron feels the peace of accomplishment; the satisfaction of having seen his son's generation, and now his grandson's generation, embark on lives where the challenge is to work the land—not to fight the tyranny of a Scottish Laird.

***

TWELVE YEARS HAVE passed since the McNab lost his township. When the final blow came I watched his spirit wither, his soul shrivel; the life's work of this proud, noble Scot cancelled by a scrawled signature on a piece of paper. I tell ye, my heart went out to . . . he was so distraught, so mortified. Ah, but he bore himself erect, his manner dignified as always. But with no reason to remain in his township, he travelled. Back and forth he went, from Canada East to Canada West. I learned he sought medical treatment in Montreal for his rheumatism and visited his cousin, Sir Allan Napier McNab, in Hamilton. Twas in that city he set up house for several years. Nay, I did not accompany him. I could not. In this province, the official occasions that call for a Piper's services are rare, rare indeed. Twould be a travesty to pretend otherwise. Ah, but I am not being entirely honest with ye. Twould not have mattered if pomp and ceremony called for the pipes every day; the unease . . . aye, the distaste with which I viewed the McNab at the time would not allow . . . tis still painful, even after these many years.

Of course, I did not say this to my Chief. I did not have to. There were many good years and many good memories. Nay, I told him my Colleen and I had reconciled, which was true. She sold her property for a good pound in the spring of 1842 and moved into my humble abode at White Lake. I explained to my Chief—because I believed I owed him an explanation, and because there was no escaping it—I explained that I was settled in the township, that I had no one at home in Perthshire, that the township, White Lake, had become my home and I would spend my remaining days . . . ah, I am not *that* old! He returned on occasion to Waba Cottage to see Agnes and the children, and to collect the rent from his tenants at Kinnell. We spoke, but there was a strain; would always be a strain. Tis, I believe, the reason I never received a letter while he remained in Canada. But he wrote often to young Allan; tis how I got snippets of news about his endeavours.

Seven years ago, he sold Kinnell Lodge to a Mr. Middleton from Liverpool. Allan told me he bargained for eight hundred pounds—a very good price—and that he intended to use the money to expand his wine-importing business. Aye, he had not lost his relish for a money-making venture! I did not say so, but I thought perhaps he should become an American. Theirs be a more enterprising spirit, more for risk-taking in business than we. But then, perhaps the Laird's investments were not sound? Allan has been secretive and protective of his father. Tis understandable. But—tis conjecture on my part—I believe the McNab's finances . . . there was a rumour his creditors . . . as at home, his creditors were pressing; something to do with the failure of a bank.

Whatever his burden, Allan says the McNab found society in Hamilton most agreeable. The good people of the city embraced him, showed him the respect due a Highland Chief. Six years ago, they asked him to lead the Highland Society in the Christmas Day Parade. But then . . . I thought it odd, only a year later he put his Hamilton estate up for sale. Allan told me that before he found a buyer, he lent his house to Sir Allan's brother-in-law when the man's home was destroyed by fire. Twas good to know he had not lost his magnanimous and charitable spirit. Allan said his father went to the seaside, Robinson Crusoe's Island in New York; apparently for the salubrious benefits of the saltwater on his ailing leg. I was relieved when he reported to me some time later that his father's health was much improved.

Perhaps because we are separated by the Atlantic, and tis unlikely we will ever meet again, whatever the reason, this past December I received a letter from Scotland. The McNab has purchased the White House of Breck at Rendall. Tis on West Maitland in the Orkney Islands. Tis nae a part of the old country I ever had occasion to visit, but my Chief describes life in the Orkneys as pleasant and cheap. He says he can take a steamboat at nearby Kirkwall and be in Edinburgh in twenty-four hours, or travel to London in about the time it would take to journey from Hamilton to Quebec. He doesn't mention his leg, but he says his rheumatism has not flared since his arrival.

My heart swelled with great joy on receiving his epistle and I wrote back immediately. I told him that Agnes, Allan and Kitty are all well. Agnes, with the help of Lipsey, has spruced up Waba Cottage. Kitty is betrothed to William Yulle, son of his friend Alex. I told him I had been honoured to perform the glorious music of our beloved homeland at Allan's marriage to Rebecca Buffam, daughter of Samuel Buffam of Lanark. Last fall she gave birth to a son whom they christened Archibald, after his grandfather. Allan has built his family a fine, two-storey home in White Lake, with a southern exposure on the village's Main Street. Alas, I felt my enthusiasm dampen when I wracked my brain to think of others in the township in whose welfare the Laird would be interested. Aye, there are a few, but very few. Tis sad indeed.

Ah, but there is no denying the community has flourished since the McNab's departure. Even before! As soon as the Crown Lands Agent began enforcing the provisions of Mr. Allan's report, one could sense a rejuvenated spirit among the settlers. Twas most evident at a *ceilidh* where songs and stories once again took precedent. I take much pleasure in accompanying Arnold Miller on his fiddle at these festive gatherings. But tis disheartening, most disheartening, when the settlers' stories turn to fanciful wild tales about the hardship they suffered under the Laird. I canna help . . . I believe my heart will always carry the sorrow.

And my Colleen has become a schoolteacher! Aye, the community *has* flourished! Three schools have been built. My Colleen is the matron—she would box my ears (tis most arousing) if she heard me call her a "matron"—but she is in charge of booklearning at the school between Flat Rapids and Robertson Corners. My Colleen and I are not of a religious persuasion. She was not raised religious. Her father said, in Ireland, there is too much hatred justified in the name of God. For my part, I am just not a believer. But most settlers are. We now have churches for members of the Auld Kirk and, for five years now, the Free Kirk. And the Reverend Buchanan no longer has to journey from Beckwith. The Mission Board at home has sent out new ministers: the Reverend George Thomson for parishioners of the Auld Kirk and the Reverend Simon Fraser, pastor to those of the Free Kirk. I am told they be fiery preachers! And tis no longer only Presbyterians in the township. Those of other faiths also have their churches and their clergy to guide them.

It has been some time since the farmers had to trek to Pakenham to grind their grain. We have been blessed with a horde of enterprising new immigrants. There are now more than fifteen hundred industrious souls in the township. Some have built gristmills and sawmills and a wool carding mill; several erected on the brook at White Lake. And our roads are much improved. Twas one of . . . when the McNab no longer had authority over the statute-labour, twas *the* first consideration. We are governed by a Township Council. We have not been subject to the capricious, self-serving quirks of the Magistrates in Perth for more than three years; ever since the government passed the *Municipal Act*, known as the *Baldwin Act* in homage to the Honourable Robert Baldwin. Now *there's* an astute politician! He and the Frenchman Louis-Hippolyte Fontaine. Together, these two men of goodwill have led our united provinces on two occasions. Aye, they have shown what people of different cultures can achieve for the benefit of both when they set their minds to it. It has been a tumultuous decade with many political changes, many growing pains in the united provinces of Canada. But the days of Family Compact rule are over. Five years ago, the Reformers won a majority and the Home Office told the Governor—Lord Elgin is Her Majesty's current representative—he was told to heed the wishes of the majority in the Assembly. Tis, at last, what Lord Durham said would come to pass: responsible government; government by the will of the people. I am slowly coming around to seeing its merits. But tis a strange custom for someone raised in the old country; a difficult adjustment when one has been steeped in the heritable tradition of a Scottish clan, where the Chief's rule is sacrosanct.

When I look back, what is most remarkable . . . when I finally learned *everything* about the Laird's treatment of his settlers, what is most remarkable is that no one—except when John Drummond pulled him off his horse—no one did violence to the McNab. Aye, I know Dennis McNee *would have* had it not been for Donald Cameron. Mr. McNee, Dennis, has become much more sociable. When he had vented his anger and saw how his neighbours rallied round after the Laird burnt down his shanty . . . tis his nature to be aloof, but I think he finally understood the true spirit of a civilized community: that violence would never resolve the matter. He told me twas the years spent in America. He said twas always the first recourse to injustice. Perhaps, but I still think it astonishing—*and most commendable*—that hot-blooded Scots set upon with such malicious oppression and unrelenting persecution . . . for I see now that that is what it was . . . I do not understand how human nature did not cry out for revenge. The only explanation: twas Donald Cameron. He has been a leader in the community since . . . a voice of reason since the first settlers arrived twenty-eight years ago. He still is. Three years ago we held the first Council meeting in our new Municipality at his home. His shanty is now his workshop and he has built a spacious new home. The men of the community, myself included, had elected five Councillors just two weeks previous. Now we five voted unanimously for Donald as Reeve. Twas no surprise! Ah, but talk at the meeting was mostly of the Laird; will always be of the Laird. Some men recalled how he gave them victuals in their time of need. Some, how he took them into Kinnell when fire destroyed their shanties. Others, whom the McNab had set upon with spite, were not so kind. Donald, as always, was prudent. I thought he showed good sense when he said the McNab will always be remembered. Some will praise him, some will vilify him, but no one will ever forget him. Sadly, I believe twill be his only legacy.

Tis time I tended to my garden. I have taken over care of my garden from Lipsey. The poor mortal is getting on in years and Agnes keeps him busy with chores around Waba Cottage. I didn't think I had a green thumb, but tis surprising what one can do when one puts one's mind to it. I have rye, oats, barley, peas, and potatoes. To pretty up around our cottage, my Colleen snitched some violets and red and white trilliums from the grove in Arnprior. They are abundant and I don't think they will be missed. Tis a simple life we live. My Colleen and I don't care for the hustle and bustle of the modern society. We have each other and we are content with what we have. I believe tis the secret to happiness. If only the McNab . . . ah, tis no use thinking "if only."

Of course, I have not given up my first love: my pipes are forever ready, and tomorrow morning I have the pleasant task of playing at the wedding of Donald Cameron, son of John and Mary, nee Ross, and grandson of Donald and Elizabeth. There will be a huge gathering of the community. After the ceremony, I will accompany Arnold Miller on the double reels. Twill be a good time in the township that bears the name of my Chief; a good time indeed.

ABOUT THE AUTHOR

Photo by Gerry Koster.

David Mulholland was raised in the Ottawa Valley town of Arnprior. He now lives in Ottawa. This is his first novel.

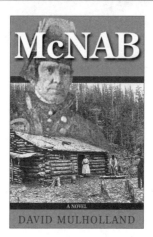